REVEALING ANNIE (POLICE AND FIRE: OPERATION ALPHA)

ON CALL BOOK 5

FREYA BARKER

Dear Readers,

Welcome to the Police and Fire: Operation Alpha Fan-Fiction world!

If you are new to this amazing world, in a nutshell the author wrote a story using one or more of my characters in it. Sometimes that character has a major role in the story, and other times they are only mentioned briefly. This is perfectly legal and allowable because they are going through Aces Press to publish the story.

This book is entirely the work of the author who wrote it. While I might have assisted with brainstorming and other ideas about which of my characters to use, I didn't have any part in the process or writing or editing the story.

I'm proud and excited that so many authors loved my characters enough that they wanted to write them into their own story. Thank you for supporting them, and me!

READ ON!
Xoxo
Susan Stoker

ACKNOWLEDGMENTS

As always my first word of thanks is to Susan Stoker who continues to be a generous and gracious host—allowing me to play in her fabulous Operation Alpha World—and is always a great source of support.

A great deal of gratitude goes out as well to Amy Hrutkay of Aces Press, who is a fount of information and a pillar of professionalism as she puts up with my frequent inquiries.

* * *

I have gathered an incredible team around me over the years I am beyond grateful for.

I would be useless without the sharp minds, keen knowledge, straight talk, clever insight, and endless patience of Joanne Thompson & Karen Hrdlicka, my unequaled editing team.

To keep me sane, hopeful, organized, informed, and on task I am entirely dependent on my phenomenal marketing team, Stephanie Phillips of SBR Media, my agent, and Debra Presley & Drue Hoffman of Buoni Amici Press, my publicists.

Thank you so much, Deb Blake & Petra Gleason, my beta readers for Absolving Blue. These women make sure the stories I give you are up to the standard you deserve.

I'm so grateful to all the unbelievable bloggers who give their time and their support generously. This industry would be hard-pressed to survive without them.

And of course to all my readers; your enthusiasm, your support, an your love for my words feeds my drive to write more!

Love you all.

Sumo

A heart attack, a broken hip, two car crashes with minor injuries, a line cook burned in a kitchen fire at a local restaurant, an accidental toe amputation, and—to round out my shift—a fifteen-year-old stabbing victim, who was barely clinging to life when we got him to Mercy Hospital.

I'm still cleaning the kid's blood from the inside of the ambulance when Cap sticks his head in.

"Heading out shortly?"

"Almost done."

"You coming for breakfast?"

It's something we try to do with our crew at least once a week after one of our shifts, but I've bailed the last few times. Mostly because it's just not the same without Blue. Ava Navarro is my partner on this ambulance, but she's been off on family leave. She and her husband, Tony—one of our boys in blue with the Durango PD—adopted a baby girl a month or so ago, and although I'm happy for her, I wish her ass was back on the rig with me.

Instead I've been stuck with Billy Bapcock, a goddamn rookie, fresh out of college. Cocky kid almost lost his damn cookies when he saw the damage the knife did to our last patient, which is why I'm cleaning the damn rig alone. He's going to have to get used to it or he'll never make it.

To top it off, I just moved from my apartment to a house I bought not too far from the station, and my living room is still full of boxes I haven't gotten around to unpacking. Add to that the sorry state of my fridge and I really don't have time to sit around the diner, shooting the shit with the boys. I need groceries, to get some work down around the house, and then hit my bed to catch up on my sleep.

"Not today, Cap," I tell Scott Beacham, captain of our crew. "Got lots of stuff to do at home."

"Happy to lend a hand, Sumo."

"Appreciate it, but it's just stuff I've been putting off."

The guys started calling me Sumo when I joined the crew years ago. Nothing to do with the fact I'm part Asian —my father is Japanese—but because my last name is Matsumoto. The nickname is kind of ironic, since I'm far from the size of a sumo wrestler. In fact, other than Blue, I'm the shortest on the team at five foot eleven.

"If you're sure," he says with an inquisitive glance.

"Yup. It's all good. Thanks, though."

He nods, rapping his knuckles on the door of the ambulance before disappearing from sight.

Cap is the only one I'll occasionally have an actual conversation with. I'm known as the crew's joker, and for the longest time that's how I viewed life, as one big laugh. That changed quite suddenly around the time Blue and

Tony hooked up. If Blue hadn't been up to her eyeballs in her own shit at the time, I'd probably have turned to her. As it happened, Cap caught me in a low moment and I laid it all out for him. He's been checking in on me since.

I gather up the dirty wipes, drop them in a garbage bag, and lock up the rig. I toss the bag in the garbage bin on the side of the station house and head over to my truck. Instead of going straight home, I'm hitting up the grocery store first. I'll be home for the next three days, so I need to stock up.

The parking lot at the City Market is relatively empty this time of the morning. I grab a cart and hit up the produce department first.

I like cooking. Love it, actually. I do a lot of the cooking back at the station house, with Cheddar—Evan Biel, one of my crewmates—coming in a close second. We're supposed to take turns but most of the guys just cook the basic stuff and Blue, the only woman on our team, isn't even allowed near the stove. She'd burn water.

Both my parents are great cooks and would often share the duty, which made the kitchen the center of the house growing up. It also made for a lot of Asian-American recipe creations, many of which I still make to this day. I save the more elaborate dishes for the station house, since it's much more gratifying cooking for the guys. At home I keep it fairly simple, unless I have someone over, but that doesn't happen that often. It's rare you'll find me calling in for pizza or picking up fast food.

The only thing I don't do is bake, despite my considerable sweet tooth, but the City Market bakery has a good selection that should get me through my long weekend.

As soon as I turn the corner, I recognize the blonde ponytail on the woman putting an order in at the bakery. I sneak up behind her and look over her shoulder at the box of pastries the girl on the other side of the counter is holding up.

"Did you leave any for me?"

I don't step back fast enough and one of Blue's sharp little elbows hits me square in the gut.

"*Jesus*, woman," I grunt.

I hear a soft chuckle I don't recognize and look up to find the bakery girl—actually more of a woman now that I have a closer look—trying to hide her smile.

"You're an ass, Sumo. You scared the crap out of me," Blue grumbles, drawing my attention.

"Losing your touch already? What are you doing here anyway? Shouldn't you be home looking after the rugrat?"

"Her name is Esme and she's not a rugrat. She can't even sit yet." She shoots me an angry look.

"Momma bear. That's a new look for you." I tug her ponytail, and as expected, she swats at my hand. "Looks good on you, though, partner." At that her looks softens a little. "When am I gonna meet the little princess?"

Because the baby had a bit of a rough start, Blue and Tony have kept visitors away so far.

"We have an appointment with the pediatrician tomorrow morning. If he clears her, maybe we can pop in this weekend?"

"Why don't you just give me a call and I'll come to you for a visit?"

"Because I'm going stir-crazy at home and besides, I haven't seen the new house yet."

She saw the exterior when I was first looking, but hasn't been inside yet.

"Fair enough. So," I change topics, as I look up at the woman on the other side of the counter. "Did she leave anything for me?"

"Oh shit," Blue jumps in. "I'm sorry, Annie. That's it for

me. By the way, this is Sumo, my partner on the ambulance and royal pain in the ass. Sumo, meet Annie, she works with me at the animal shelter."

So this is the Annie Blue has mentioned from time to time. Blue spends a few hours a week volunteering at the shelter, although these days she has a virtual shelter of her own. Her menagerie consists of three dogs and a cat, and she's been at me to take in an animal as well. When I was still living in my apartment I had an excuse—no pets allowed—but I fully expect her to get on my case again now I own a place of my own.

Annie's head is down as she tapes Blue's pastry box shut. The City Market visor she's wearing covers most of her face, and I wait until she looks up. I'm sure I must've seen her here before, but I'm ashamed to admit I can't recall. My loss, because I missed the cute nose with a slight lift at the end, the perfect Cupid's bow of her upper lip, and the incredibly long lashes behind the lenses of her bland glasses. Her hair is short—almost a boy cut—with a light wave to it. It's a nondescript brown, just like the color of her eyes.

"Nice to meet you, Annie," I finally say, reaching over the display case to offer my hand.

"You too. I've heard so much about you."

Definitely not a girl, her voice is rich with maturity, as is the small smile she rewards me with. The hand she briefly places in mine is slim, much as the rest of her.

"Nothing good I'm sure."

She snickers when I send a pointed look at Blue, who is conveniently digging through her wallet.

"Not all bad," she says, grinning at me.

Great. I don't even know the woman and already I have a bad rap.

* * *

Annie

I almost burst out laughing at the disgruntled look on his face.

Sumo.

I've seen him before, but from a safe distance. Dark, bristly hair with only a hint of silver by his ears, clean-shaven with warm brown, wide-set eyes. His surprisingly full mouth is bracketed by lines, both underlining his age and his easy smiles.

Yeah, I've noticed Sumo around town. Those broad shoulders and muscular arms on that swimmer's body are hard to miss.

If I hadn't been taking Blue's order, I would've darted into the bakery, but she would've asked questions. It's not that I'm asocial, it's just I prefer meeting people on my terms. I'm not supposed to be in the store anyway, I work in the bakery, but Jenny had to take her little one to the clinic this morning and I'm jumping in until she can get here.

I like working behind the scenes these days. Out of the spotlight, so to speak. I find it liberating. Love the feeling of dough in my hands and the smell of fresh yeast in my nose. I really lucked out with my job here. It's early mornings—I start at four—but I'm also done at noon. That gives me time to put in some hours at the shelter each day.

My other love—besides baking—is the shelter animals. I don't care what they are, dogs, cats, gerbils; I love every single one they bring in, but the dogs are my favorite. Often starved for attention, I feed off the way they can blossom with just that little bit of love. Like Blue, I'd probably have a houseful...if I had a house. My place isn't big enough and my landlord made it clear animals aren't welcome. That's one of the reasons I visit the shelter every day, to get my fix of puppy love.

I ring up Blue's order and watch as she playfully elbows Sumo again as she walks off. Then I'm left facing him.

"So what did she leave me?"

"Depends on what you're looking for."

One corner of his mouth tilts up, and I wonder what I said to make him raise one eyebrow, but it becomes clear the moment he opens his mouth.

"I have an insatiable craving for sweet things," he rumbles suggestively, and I can barely stop my eyes from rolling.

Too bad, I've encountered one too many guys like that, and I'm a little disappointed the fantasy I'd created around him in my mind is ruined.

"Well, we still have cinnamon buns and apple turnovers, but let me look in the back if we have more Danish," I offer in a friendly voice, before turning my back and heading for the bakery.

Ted, the baker whose shift overlaps mine, is just loading another tray with cherry Danish on the trolley.

"Perfect timing. We're out."

"Already?"

"Just sold the last ones."

"Any sign of Jenny yet?" he wants to know. I have a suspicion he may be sweet on her. Understandable, she's about his age—which is considerably younger than me—and cute and wholesome like the proverbial girl next door.

"I'm sure she'll be in soon."

I grab the tray off the rack and walk back out where Sumo is still waiting.

"You're in luck," I tell him, sliding the tray in the display. "Let me just grab a box."

I'm painfully aware of his scrutiny as I fold together and fill him a bakery box. I try to ignore it, but unfortunately I know exactly what he's looking at: a plain, unremarkable, middle-aged woman. Exactly the way I intended.

"Can you slice me a dark rye as well?" he asks, when I slide the box across the counter.

Again I feel his eyes on me, but when I bag the loaf and turn to the cash register, I'm relieved to see someone else is waiting for service beside him.

"See you around, Annie," he says with a wink after he pays for his purchases.

I manage a friendly smile before turning to my next customer.

Good thing I've had years of pretending under my belt.

2

Sumo

"Hey, little lady."

She stares wide-eyed at my smile, her tiny, uncoordinated hand slapping my cheek. Big eyes, pouty pink lips, and a surprising amount of dark hair standing on end.

"She likes you," Blue comments, earning her a snort from her husband.

"She doesn't know what she likes yet."

She turns her head and scowls at him. "She does. She cries when she sees her pediatrician, let alone being touched by him. Look at her, she's mesmerized."

The little peanut in my arms squirms a bit. With a sound effect too big for such a tiny person, she fills her diaper, and I can feel the vibrations in my hand covering her little behind. I chuckle at the satisfied half-smile tugging at her rosebud mouth.

"Give her to me," Blue says, reaching for her daughter.

"I've got it. You guys grab yourselves a drink and head out on the deck. Uncle Sumo will take care of Esme."

I love kids. Always have. Luckily I get my fill of them in my line of work, although not often as small and innocent as this little one.

Handing me the diaper bag, Tony grabs his wife's hand and pulls her into the kitchen, while I lay the baby down. I go through the motions of undressing her and cleaning her up, but my mind is on another child.

One I didn't even know existed until about a year ago.

Strange, I always figured there'd be plenty of time to have children of my own, even though I'm in my early forties. Finding out I already had one was far from a pleasant experience, mainly because I'd already missed out on the first thirteen years of his life.

Anger floods my blood, as it tends to do when I think of what I've missed out on. Am *still* missing out on, since I've yet to meet the boy. Oh, Chanel was quick with the excuses and good with the promises, but after she got what she wanted from me she disappeared, just like she'd done all those years ago.

All I have is a picture on my phone of a boy who looks surprisingly like me at that age. So much so, I never even questioned his parentage.

I would've liked to have known about him, been part of his life growing up in whatever way I could, but I never had that option.

Chanel and I had a brief fling back in Santa Fe. I grew up and went to college there. Even got my first job with the Rocky Mountain EMS. She used to hang out in the same bar my friends and I would frequent. It was fairly casual and lasted a couple of months, when she announced she was returning home to Minnesota. There was no contact after that, which was fine by me, it seemed whatever it was between us had run its course.

I hadn't thought of her for a long time when she called me last summer, out of the blue. This was right around the time Blue moved in with Tony; killing any secret torch I may have carried for my partner. I'd never acted on it—her friendship was too valuable to risk—but having the option taken away so permanently left me in a weird headspace for a while. I've since come to the conclusion, if I'd had any real romantic feelings toward her I wouldn't have waited around.

Chanel had caught me at a weak moment, pulling the rug out from under me with the news I have a son. I can barely remember her excuses, I was so focused on the image of him she'd messaged me. I recall her saying something about tracking me down through one of my old buddies back home, but I didn't really pay attention until she mentioned the boy being in the hospital.

A weak moment, in which I'd taken a picture—a screenshot of a hospital bill—and without asking too many questions, wired over a decent chunk of the money I'd been putting aside for the mountain home I was hoping to build. Of course there was also the promise of a visit with my son, but that never came to fruition. The moment the money was collected on the other side, Chanel disappeared, along with the boy.

"Are you okay in here?"

Tony walks back in the living room where I'm snuggling the baby on the couch, lost in thought.

"She's perfect."

I press a kiss to the top of Esme's head, handing her to her father before picking up the dirty diaper and heading to the kitchen, my heart heavy. Maybe it's time to share what I've been carrying for a year.

Dinner consists of elk burgers, topped with grilled pineapple slices and spicy peanut sauce, along with sesame and leek quinoa salad. Emboldened by a couple of cold ones, I tell them everything.

"The bitch!" Blue exclaims. Esme startles in her baby carrier, her little face twisting into a cry. "Sorry, Esme-girl," she quickly mumbles, rocking the carrier until the baby settles back down to sleep.

"Have you tried finding them?"

"I have," I tell Tony, whose investigative antennae are piqued. "Phone number was not in service, she was no longer living at the address listed on the hospital invoice, and my buddy in Santa Fe didn't know much more than what she told me."

"Give me what you know," he says, "I'll see what I can find out."

Not long after they get ready to leave, Blue still bristling when she hugs me.

"You know, she better not ever show her face or I'd be tempted to rip it off."

I chuckle, warmed by her strong arms around me and the unconditional support. Yeah, I lucked out when I got partnered with Blue.

"Easy, Momma bear, you've got a child now. Wouldn't do if her mother got herself locked up for aggravated assault."

"Don't spoil my fun," she mumbles, before letting me go.

Tony clasps my hand in his.

"Nice place you've got here. Great location."

"It's not bad," I agree.

The house is a rather standard three-bedroom, two-bath, with an open concept main floor. What makes it stand out is the large corner lot and the view of the

Animas River both from my front and back yards. It's built on the inside of a bend in the river. A lot of what I see is green, and although it's not the mountains, the view isn't shabby and I'm within easy distance to work and downtown.

"It's just a little big for you. It needs something, maybe a dog?"

Blue, like a dog with a bone herself, grins as she heads down the steps, her husband shaking his head as he follows her.

I stay on the front steps with my hands in my pockets, watching them put Esme in the back seat. Tony is the last to open his door and lifts a hand in a wave I return.

"I'll be in touch," he calls out before getting behind the wheel.

I turn to go back inside, trying not to be too hopeful at his words.

* * *

Annie

I keep my life simple and my circle small.

I interact with the people at the store, like talking with the folks at the shelter, but I rarely—if ever—socialize outside of those two places. It's not that I never go out, I go to the yoga studio three times a week and run the trails around the college on the other days, but I lead a predominantly solitary life.

My house is a rental trailer at the River View, a one-bedroom, but with a surprisingly large living space. I'm lucky it has a small carport that fits my Toyota Matrix perfectly. Off the bedroom I have a sliding door going out on a tiny deck, it just fits two chairs and a small side table, overlooking the river.

A far cry from what I'm used to but it's comfortable and I've been able to put my stamp on it. I like spending time there, reading a book on my little deck, or hanging out on my comfy old couch, watching something on TV.

Twice I've shared a meal with Edward Shelby, my elderly neighbor. He's a cantankerous old man, who doesn't have much good to say about anyone, but he adores his rotund little pug, Blossom. Some days his arthritis gets too bad for him to walk her, so I do. In return he keeps an eye on me. Not that I asked for it, but he told me in no uncertain terms a woman alone needs looking after.

Mostly his idea of protection is to sit by his front window, monitoring all the comings and goings, which is why I wave at him when I pull up to my trailer. All I see is the curtain moving, Edward never bothers waving back.

I grab my groceries from the passenger seat and unlock my front door, walking straight into the small kitchen where I dump them on the counter. I'm just shifting things around in my fridge to make room, when my phone dings with a message.

Erin: You around?

I'm not on the computer or my phone a lot these days, except to connect with my friend, Erin, via Messenger. I met her years ago in an online support group and we hit it off. She's the only real friend I have, the only person who knows everything there is to know about me. Well, just about everything. We only had opportunity to meet in person once, when I was in Texas for an interview. Erin lives in San Antonio with her husband, Conor, and their daughter.

I quickly stuff the perishables in the fridge and, leaving the rest for later, I grab my phone and plop down on the couch. It takes just a minute to sign into Messenger and call her up on video chat.

"Hey there, stranger," she says with a smile. "How's Durango?"

"Quiet."

"That's what you wanted, right? A little peace and quiet?"

It's true, even though Erin doesn't know all the details. Peace and quiet is what I was looking for and so far, so good.

"You bet," I tell her with a smile. "Although life got a little more interesting the other day."

"Oh?" she says; her eyebrows rise.

"Remember I told you about Blue? The EMT who volunteers at the shelter and just adopted a baby?"

"Yeah, I remember. Didn't you tell me the baby's name is Esme? So pretty."

"Yup. Well, she was at the bakery last week when her partner walked up."

Erin starts laughing. "The one who looks like a younger version of Russell Wong?" Okay, so I may have brought him up in conversation before. "The same guy you've been ogling from afar?"

"Yup," I confirm, popping the P.

"And?"

"He's as hot up close as he is at a distance, but I think he's a little too smooth."

"No, don't tell me that. I had hopes for you."

I snort. "Please...I'm pretty sure he's the kind of guy who would flirt with your grandmother."

"I bet if you let some of the real you shine through, you'd—"

"Erin, you know I can't be that person anymore."

"Let me talk to Conor, I told you he has friends who could help. Heck, the reason I suggested Durango is because my friend, Autumn, is married to a detective."

"Not getting anyone involved, Erin." I stop myself from blurting out that the last person who tried is currently buried at the Murietta Valley Cemetery. "Please promise me."

She scowls at me but I hold firm.

"Oh, fine, but if anything happens..."

"Nothing will happen, no one knows I'm here. No one would suspect a thing, not with the life I'm leading or the way I look now."

She rolls her eyes. "Just promise me you'll get in touch with Autumn if anything happens. You still have her number, right?"

"Yes, and I promise."

We spend ten minutes chatting, when my eye catches the bags on the kitchen counter.

"I should get back to sorting my groceries before my neighbor comes looking for the pound cake I promised him."

"All right, I'll let you go. Talk again in a few weeks?"

"For sure."

As soon as we hang up, I unpack the bags, putting aside what I picked up for Edward. By the time I step outside to drop off his groceries, he's already coming up my path, walking with difficulty. I was going to grab a yoga class, but I think I'll be giving Blossom her daily exercise instead.

"I'm sorry it took me a bit, I was on the phone."

He grumbles something I can't quite make out and holds out his hand for the bag.

"Nah," I wave him off. "I've got it. I'll walk you back. Was gonna pick up Blossom for a bit of exercise anyway, if you don't mind."

I know he has a hard time asking so I try to spare him when I notice he's having an off day. Much easier for him to accept.

"If you must."

I bite off a chuckle at his response. He'd rather cut off his tongue than say something nice, but I note he doesn't pull away when I take his arm to help him back to his trailer.

"Are you good for dinner?" I ask, as I clip the leash on Blossom's collar.

Poor dog is barely able to wag her tail she's so fat. Maybe I should take her daily whether Edward is able to or not, she clearly needs more exercise than she's getting.

"Got Salisbury steak on the menu," he shares, as he takes a seat on the small deck at his front door.

I try not to cringe, knowing he's talking about the Hungry Man frozen meals I sometimes get for him.

"I can pop it in for you when I get back with Blossom."

The old girl takes her time coming down the steps.

"I know how to operate a microwave, missy. I may be rickety but I ain't feeble-minded."

"Have it your way," I fire off over my shoulder, heading for the trail along the river.

It's pretty. So close to downtown and yet there's hardly any traffic noise. I'm glad I took Erin's advice and came here when I mentioned looking for a place to hide out. It's freezing cold in the winters and I'm not really used to the snow, but I got through my first one and now I'm enjoying the much warmer weather.

Blossom is slow as a turtle, sniffing every blade of grass. We barely make it to Oxbow Park when she plops down on her substantial ass, announcing this is as far as she'll go.

"Come on, girl. How about we try a little farther, just to that bench there," I coax, but she refuses to move. Only when I take a step in the direction of the trailer park, does she budge. As stubborn as her owner.

Heading back the going is even slower and I'm tempted to pick her up and carry her the rest of the way, but I have a sneaky suspicion that's exactly what the pooch is angling for.

The sun has sunk behind the mountains on the west side of town. It's always a surprise how quickly dusk settles here. I can see my trailer in the shadow of the trees as we slowly approach, and a sudden shiver runs down my spine.

It must've cooled down.

3

Sumo

"Back already?"

I grin at her comment as she comes walking out of the bakery in the back, carrying a tray of buns.

The past week has been busy. It usually is this time of year. Aside from our regular town population, tourism picks up in the early summer, which makes for more frequent emergency calls. Today is the start of my next couple of days off and the first chance I have to grab a few things at the store. We usually work twenty-four-hour shifts with a twenty-four-hour break, and after the third shift we get a three-day break, although during busy times, or in a year with a lot of wildfires, that schedule can change.

My initial reaction had been disappointment when I walked up to the counter to find a young girl instead of Annie. Not sure what it is, but there's something about the woman that stuck with me. Enough so, I grabbed a cart and instead of my usual path through the store, I beelined it for the bakery.

"Ran out of sweets five days ago," I admit.

"And you only show now? I applaud your restraint," she teases with an easy smile.

Yes, definitely something about her that draws me in.

"Would've come sooner but things have been busy. Tourist season," I explain.

She nods her understanding and turns to the girl who was filling a box for me.

"If you want to take the next customer, Jenny? I'll finish up with this one." She takes a look at what's already in the box before lifting her eyes to me. "What else would you like? I actually just pulled some *pastéis de nata* from the oven." At my blank look she explains, "Portuguese custard tarts. Very good, if I say so myself." Again with the easy smile and I notice how perfectly white her teeth are.

"You baked those?"

"I'm one of the bakers, yes. Only reason you caught me out here last time was because one of the girls was running late."

"I don't know what they are, but if you made them, I'll get half a dozen of those."

She shakes her head slightly before turning toward the back.

"Will that be all?" she asks when she returns and I nod. "These are still warm so as soon as you get home, let them breathe a little."

"Actually," I stop her as she moves to the cash register. "There is something else. I hoped I'd catch you here so I could ask you about a dog."

It's a blatant lie, but something compels me to keep her talking.

"You wanna ask me about a dog?"

Yeah, she doesn't sound too convinced either, but now that I've opened this door I may as well step through it.

"Blue's been on my case. I recently bought a house and she said it needed a dog. I'm guessing Tony put a stop to adding more rescues to their household, and now she's trying to fill mine." She still looks dubious, so I forge ahead, thinking on my feet. "Anyway, I'd be interested in visiting the shelter and I could probably use some advice, but I don't want to get Blue involved. She'd only get her hopes up or hound me until I give in."

"I see," she mumbles.

I'm not sure she does, so I hurry to push a little. "Look, I'd really appreciate if you could walk me through the process. I don't know when your next shift is, but I'm off for the next couple of days."

"Hmmm..." Her hum hangs in the air between us as she tilts her head and scrutinizes me like a bug under a microscope. I wait her out and eventually she seems to come to a decision. "I'm there daily from two to five, except for the weekends, those aren't set in stone."

"This afternoon then?"

I try not to examine too closely why it is I'm suddenly in a hurry to get a dog.

"Sure, if you want," she says, with a deceptively dismissive shrug of her shoulders. I'm not buying it; I didn't miss the quick smile tugging at her lips before she turns to the register.

I'm still wearing my grin when I finally leave the store, casting one last glance at the bakery. Back at home I put my stuff away, hop in the shower for a quick rinse, and dive into bed for a nap. I do make sure to set my alarm for two thirty.

* * *

I changed my mind a number of times on the way over here.

Mostly about the dog.

No one is in the small front office when I walk into the shelter. I look around for a bell or something but there isn't one. Then I spot a small window in the door to the back and peek through.

Annie is sitting cross-legged on the floor in the middle of an aisle, which runs all the way to a door in the back, with kennels on either side. She has an open book on her lap and a fierce-looking pit bull is lying beside her, his ugly head on her knee.

The dog is the first one to notice me and starts barking as he jumps to his feet. His muscular body blocks Annie, who scrambles to her feet. She holds up a finger for me to wait, and grabs the white and gray dog by the collar. She has to drag him to what I presume is his kennel and locks him inside before she walks this way.

"Hey. Sorry, the buzzer on the front entrance is broken; otherwise I would've heard you come in. Were you waiting long?"

She seems a little flustered. Without the City Market visor pulled over her eyes, I have a better view of her face. Her hair is short and messy, it looks like she does little more than occasionally run a hand through it, but it suits her face. A high forehead, full, nicely arched eyebrows, the pert nose, and that perfectly shaped mouth. The only thing out of place is those glasses, the frame much too over-whelming for her face.

"Not long."

I smile down at her, liking the way the top of her head just comes up to my nose. I'm average, not particularly tall, but Annie is a good six inches shorter. Nice.

"So, what are you looking for? In a dog, I mean," she

quickly adds, as she slips behind the reception desk, placing it conveniently between us.

"I don't really know. I've never had to pick a pet before," I admit.

"All right, let's figure this out. How many people in your household?"

I narrow my eyes on her. I'm not sure of it's an innocent question or if this is her way of finding out if I'm single. Her expression doesn't tell me much.

"Just me."

"Okay, so you'd need a dog who can handle staying alone. Might be a stretch though, with your hours, Blue says you do twenty-four-hour shifts?"

I nod my acknowledgement. I never really considered that might be a problem, but I remember now when Blue got Arthur—her first rescue—Tony helped her look after the dog.

"Shit. That's a problem, right?"

"Could be." She shrugs. "Although, I guess you could hire a dog walker."

I put my forearms on the desk and lean across, putting all the charm I can muster in the smile I flash her.

"Are you offering?"

Her bark of laughter is unexpected, but something I said is apparently funny.

"You're shameless," she chides, but she does it smiling.

* * *

Annie

He leaves without a dog, but with the promise he'll be back the day after tomorrow.

I'm not sure why—it's clear he hasn't really thought this adoption thing through—but I'm willing to indulge him. For now. Besides, it's not a hardship to have him in my space.

My first judgment of him may have been a little harsh. Sure, he's a charmer, but he seems to do it in an almost mischievous way. It seems he doesn't really expect to be taken seriously and it's just the way he communicates. At least with the opposite sex. Even of the canine persuasion.

He'd asked to meet Daisy, the pittie he caught me reading to. Actually, he asked to meet *him*, assuming the muscular dog to be male. I was a little hesitant. Daisy doesn't trust men easily, but Sumo suggested he pick up where I left off with the story. He surprised me by sitting down on the floor, reading from my book in a calm, even voice.

After her initial reluctance when I opened the gate to her kennel, Daisy slowly ventured out and sat down at a safe distance. She wouldn't let him touch her, but she didn't snarl at him, which I'd consider a win.

"Who was that?" Margaret, my boss, says when she walks in.

"Actually, that's Blue's EMT partner."

She swings around and follows his pickup truck out of the parking lot.

"Dayum. That man is fine."

I slap my hand over my mouth to keep from laughing. Margaret has at least twenty years on me, if not more, stands about five feet tall, and is the spitting image of Sophia Petrillo on *Golden Girls*. That cute grandma-look hides the mouth of a long-haul trucker and the tenacity of a terrier.

In the relatively short time I've known Margaret, she's gone through four boyfriends. Not really surprising, considering the woman has more spring than the Energizer Bunny. I have a sneaky suspicion she wears the poor guys out.

"He's not bad," I concede.

She whips her head around. "You're full of it," she accuses me, pointing her bony finger in my face. "But I'll let you off the hook for now. Did the Stephensons come pick up Max?" She ducks behind the desk and starts stabbing at the computer's keyboard with two fingers.

She makes my head spin with her abrupt change of direction. Nothing wrong with her mind yet either.

"They were here at two on the dot. I scheduled Max for neutering in two months with Doc Rivers."

"Good. Anything else I need to know about?"

"The guy from Fresh Pet Foods called again. I took a message."

"Pushy bastard," she mumbles under her breath. "Okay, it's five. Get outta here. I've gotta feed my kids."

Without waiting for my response, she pushes through the door to the kennels where she is greeted by excited barks from our residents. Everyone loves Margaret. She has a gift.

I grab my bag from behind the desk and head home.

At home I park my Matrix in the carport and head straight for Edward's trailer. He must've been on the lookout because the door opens when I walk up. He already has Blossom's leash in hand.

"Are you good for dinner?" I ask, noting he still moves tentatively.

"Got pizza coming," he grumbles, watching me clip the leash on the dog. "I could probably spare a slice."

"Save it for your lunch tomorrow. I've got leftover salad I should finish," I tell him.

"That ain't enough to fill ya."

One of the reasons I've only shared a few meals with him is because he watches me like a hawk and doesn't hesitate to comment on the quantity—or lack thereof—of food I consume.

I don't eat much. I like cooking, I love baking, but I don't eat a lot of it myself. I spent a lifetime trying to fit expectations and it's a hard habit to break, even if the people in my life now probably wouldn't care if I were ninety, or a hundred and ninety pounds. That wasn't always the case, though, and like I said; it's a hard habit to break.

It's how I met Erin. We both ended up in an online support group for people with a variety of eating disorders. She's doing much better now, more so than I am, but it's one of those things I don't think you can ever completely shake.

I force myself to smile at Edward.

"Okay, if you're sure. I'll steal a slice when I drop Blossom off."

He grunts in response before turning to his trailer, and I take off with the pooch.

4

_____

Annie

I'm worried about my neighbor.

Usually when he's not well, it's just for a day or two, but it's been over a week now. He looked almost gray when I took Blossom for her walk. I tried to get him to call his doctor, but he won't hear of it.

This afternoon Mrs. Sokoloff, who neighbors Edward on the other side, intercepted me coming back from the river. I've barely shared two words with her since I moved in, but she suddenly had a lot to say. Mostly complaints about Blossom. Apparently, in recent days, Edward resorted to simply opening the door and letting Blossom take herself out in the mornings. Which she had done—in Mrs. Sokoloff's little yard.

I was gonna talk to Edward about it, but when I got back to his trailer he was in the bedroom and called for me to shut the door on my way out. I figured that talk could wait until tomorrow, and instead, I grabbed a garbage bag from my place and went back to Mrs. Sokoloff's to clean up the dog poo.

"Relax into your pose. You seem tense tonight." The woman leading the yoga class—I think her name is Heidi— puts a hand on the small of my back. "Connect with your breath and let it center you."

I close my eyes and focus on releasing the tension with each exhale.

"Better," she says, before moving on to someone else.

I force my thoughts away from my neighbor and let my mind drift, landing squarely on Sumo. The man spent three afternoons this past week, sitting in front of Daisy's kennel, reading *Harry Potter; The Chamber of Secrets* to her. My smile is inadvertent when I recall him telling me, the second time he was there, he was surprised to be intrigued by a children's book. Clearly he'd never been exposed to the brilliance that is J.K. Rowling, but he was fast becoming a fellow fan.

Yesterday afternoon, Daisy had come far enough out of her kennel to lie down with her nose pressed against his knee. Every so often he would let go of the book and stroke her big head, which she allowed. Progress I hope will hold out until he can come back as he promised he would.

I think I've been most surprised at his patience; he hadn't seemed the type. Now I realize along with gaining Daisy's trust, he managed to gain mine, which is even more astonishing.

"Be well, and see you next time," Heidi says when I walk past her out of the studio.

I love yoga. I've been practicing it for years, mainly because even when I wasn't able to go out to a class, I could always exercise in the comfort of my own home. I've always carried tension in my body and the slow stretch and sometimes burn of yoga, the centering of my often-busy brain, helps me relax in a way little else can. Unless of course you count a good orgasm, but I haven't had one of those in quite some time.

The Yooba Yoga Studio is beside a boxing gym. As I walk across the parking lot to my car, I glance over to the gym, which always seems to be busy. Tonight a couple of motorcycles are parked in front, and when I look in through the window, I can see a stocky, gray-haired biker in discussion with the black guy I see there all the time. Behind them I make out the ring, where two men appear to be sparring.

A noise startles me and I swing my head around, only to see a stray cat scurrying into the bushes behind my car. When I get closer, I notice something on the hood.

A dead bird—its head almost severed from the lifeless body.

Gross.

I find a stick at the edge of the graveled parking lot and brush the poor carcass off the hood. My body shivers with revulsion. Damn cat.

I try to unlock the door only to find it open. In my rush to make my class, I must've forgotten to lock it in the first place. Tossing my bag in the passenger seat, I slip behind the wheel, but when I turn my key in the ignition all I hear is a click, nothing else. No engine sounds at all. That's not good.

I try again with the same result.

Damn. I know nothing about cars, other than how to drive them, but I find the lever for the hood and pop it anyway. Not that I have any idea what I'm doing.

I lean over the car, shining the flashlight on my phone on the engine, when I hear the crunch of footsteps behind me.

"Car trouble?" I almost hit my head on the hood at the sound of a deep voice.

It's the guy from the gym; the biker with the gray hair, and I almost inadvertently take a step back. The move doesn't escape him and he immediately raises both hands, palms out.

"The name's Brick. I'm a mechanic; swear to God. If it makes ya feel better, lock yourself inside while I have a look."

From the corner of my eye I see the yoga instructor lock up the studio and head this way.

"No, that's okay," I tell the man, emboldened by the sight of Heidi, but I still keep my distance as he pulls a penlight out of his pocket, shining it under the hood.

"Hey, Brick," Heidi calls out as she approaches. "Oh, hi, Annie. Didn't see you there, car trouble?"

"It won't start."

"That's a bummer. Brick'll be able to help you. He runs the auto shop up at the Arrow's Edge." I've heard the name before and have seen some of the guys in the store, wearing the emblem on the backs of their leather vests. It's a local motorcycle club. "They own the gym and the studio as well," she adds, surprising the hell out of me.

A boxing gym for sure, but a yoga studio?

"You got trouble, Annie?" The biker named Brick lifts his head up and stares at me in a way that has the hair on my neck stand up.

"Why would I have trouble?"

I watch as he holds up what looks like the cut end of an electrical wire of some sort.

"Cuz this looks like you got some. Somebody's messed with your engine."

"Oh dear," Heidi says, leaning closer to look, while I feel ice flooding my veins.

30

Brick's eyes are locked on my face from under his heavy eyebrows.

"Can't think of any," I force myself to say.

He stares at me a beat longer before he turns back to the car, dropping the wire from his hand and slamming the hood down.

"You know," Heidi volunteers, "just last week some cars in the parking lot got keyed. We figured it was bored neighborhood kids. Maybe this is too?"

Christ, I hope so. I can handle vandalizing teenage hoodlums.

"Could be," Brick mumbles before turning to me. "We should probably call the cops." Something must've shown in my reaction to that because he immediately adds, "Or maybe Heidi can drop you home, and I'll tow your car up to the shop in the morning to first have a look at the damage."

That sounds like a much better idea to me and I nod immediately. "That's fine."

Brick fishes in his breast pocket and comes up with a bent business card he hands to me.

"Gimme a call after eleven, I'll know more then."

Heidi is kind enough to give me a lift home after I retrieve my bag from my car and hand the keys over to Brick.

"How did I not know these were here?" she says, driving her car through the meandering paths between the trailer homes. The park is set back from the road and mostly hidden under mature trees by the river.

"This is me," I point at my place, wondering if I should go so far as to invite her in.

"Cute," she says. "I hope you don't mind, I'm just gonna dash."

"Not at all." I try not to sound too relieved. "Thanks so much for doing this."

She waves me off. "Oh, not a problem. Brick is a good guy. He'll sort out your car."

I watch as she drives off and walk up the path to my front door, when I hear a faint scratching noise. I stop in my tracks and listen carefully. There it is again, scratching, and then a whimper.

Sounds like it's coming from my neighbor's trailer.

* * *

Sumo

"Annie?"

The last person I expected to see opening the door to the trailer we were directed to was the slight woman in front of me.

"Edward's in the bedroom," she says, stepping out of the way and pointing to the back of the trailer.

I'm tempted to ask her what she's doing here, but it'll have to wait. Right now my job has priority.

I hurry to the old man's side. He's lying on his back in bed, his face a pallor that immediately alerts me, but his eyes are open.

"Hi there. Edward, right?" His panicked eyes focus on me. "We're gonna take good care of you, Edward. Now, can you tell me what's going on? Are you having pain?"

A grunt is my only response, increasing my sense of urgency.

"Prepare to move fast, Billy," I tell my partner over my shoulder, even as I start assessing the patient.

His heartbeat is faint and irregular, his skin is clammy

to the touch, and when I strip back the blanket covering him, I immediately notice the swelling of his ankles and feet.

Five minutes later he has nitro on board, an IV in his arm, and is on oxygen. Edward is not a small man, so it takes significant muscle power to carry him out of the small trailer, and for once I'm glad for young Billy instead of five-foot-nothing Blue by my side.

"You riding in the back?" I ask Annie, who's been standing to the side, pale-faced. I'm still not sure of her place here, but she clearly cares about the man.

An elderly woman walks up and puts a hand on Annie's shoulder.

"Go," she urges.

"But Blossom…" Annie says, looking down at the fat little dog sitting at her feet.

"I'll take care of the damn dog," the old woman says.

"But, Mrs. Sokoloff, she'll need to—"

"Oh for Pete's sake, will you hop in already? Not like she hasn't shit in my yard before."

With a firm nod, Annie takes my hand and lets me pull her up in the rig.

While Billy drives, sirens blaring, I work on Edward and am so focused on my patient; I almost forget she's there until she speaks.

"Is it his heart?"

"Looks like it," I answer honestly before asking a question of my own. "Are you related?" I cast a quick glance over my shoulder to see her shaking her head.

"Neighbor. He's alone, as far as I know."

She cares for him, though, that much is visible.

"I see. Do you know if he has a history of cardiac issues?"

"I know he has arthritis, but he never said anything

about heart problems," she admits. "Oh, wait." She suddenly starts digging through the large tote she has slung across her body. "I grabbed his wallet off the kitchen counter," she explains. "I thought you might need his information."

"Hang on to it," I suggest. "You can sort through it with the nurse when we get to Mercy."

"Okay."

The rest of the drive is quiet, the only sounds in the rig are the sirens overhead, the beep of the portable heart monitor, and the soft hiss of the oxygen. Neither of us speaks until we pull into the ambulance bay at the hospital.

"I should've known something was wrong," she softly says from behind me, her voice riddled with guilt.

"Don't," I tell her, reaching back to give her knee a squeeze. "Chances are, he may not have known himself. The early signs aren't necessarily that clear-cut."

When Billy pulls open the doors, we move fast, rushing the stretcher inside, with Annie jogging behind us. Melanie, one of the ER nurses, holds her back and I don't see her again until we walk back out the doors of the emergency room.

"You go on ahead," I tell Billy, spotting Annie sitting in the waiting area. "I'll be right out."

My partner shoots a glance at her and, with a smug grin on his face, walks outside.

"You okay?" I ask, walking up to her. I see she has her glasses pushed up on her head and is reading something on her phone.

"I'm okay. How is he?"

She drops the phone on the bag beside her and gets to her feet. It's the first time I see her without her glasses. I notice the thick fringe of eyelashes framing her large eyes first, but something looks off. I realize what when she blinks her eyes and I spot the bottom edge of a contact lens sliding back in place. Now why would someone wear contacts and glasses at the same time?

"He's in good hands and they're still conducting tests. Did you sign in with Melanie?"

"The nurse? Yes, I did, but I don't know how much they'll tell me since I'm not family."

"Why don't I drop you off at home? You can leave your number for her to call."

She shakes her head firmly. "No, I'm staying until I know he's going to be okay."

It's clear from her tone she won't budge on that. I'm two-thirds through my shift so I can't offer to stay and keep her company. I reluctantly leave her in the waiting room, have a quick word with Melanie—who promises to update Annie—and get back to my rig.

My shift moves fairly fast after that and at seven the next morning, I grab my bag and head to my truck. I'm halfway home when I change my mind and pass by my cutoff.

I find her curled up in the same chair, her head on her knees, asleep.

5

Annie

"Hey."

My head shoots up when Sumo takes a seat beside me. I need a second to get my bearings and rub at my eyes. Those damn contacts are stuck to my eyeballs.

"What are you doing here?"

My voice is sleepy and I quickly wipe at my mouth, hoping I wasn't drooling.

"I wasn't sure if you'd still be here. Why didn't you go home?"

He sounds kind and concerned, which almost makes me want to cry. I'm tired, I'm worried, and my joints are loudly protesting the hard plastic seat I spent the night on.

"They didn't tell me until around four they were moving him to the ICU. I thought I'd wait for a little to see if I'd be able to visit him. I must've fallen asleep." I try to stifle a yawn.

He puts his hand on my knee. "Why don't I go see what's going on?"

I watch as he walks over to the nurses' station for a chat. I quickly dig through my bag for a mint, hoping it'll do the trick until I can get to a toothbrush.

He doesn't have to say anything; I can already see it in his face when he approaches.

"He's still considered critical and they're waiting for some test results to come back. The cardiologist doesn't want to take any chances, but she says she passed your number on to the ICU. You'll be able to call a little later and they'll contact you if there's anything to report."

I almost automatically slip my hand in his when he reaches for me and don't object when he pulls me to my feet. I can't sit here forever.

I'm lucky it's the weekend and I'm not expected at the bakery until Monday. Plenty of time to catch up on my sleep, *after* I take Blossom for a walk.

He keeps hold of my hand as he leads me outside and helps me into his truck. We're halfway to my place, stopped at a traffic light, when I turn to him.

"You never really answered my question."

He glances over. "What question was that?" Just then the light turns green and he focuses on the road.

I'm not sure why I'm pushing, but I really want to know.

"Why did you come back to the hospital? You just got off a shift, right? Why not go home?"

A muscle ticks along his jaw, as he seems to consider his answer for a moment.

"Honestly? I have no good answer for that, but I know had I gone home without checking on you first, I wouldn't have been able to sleep."

I study his profile, a little surprised at his candor. I've

37

learned a few things about Sumo this week; there is so much more depth to him than his easy charm and good looks would suggest. Who sits on a concrete floor for an hour or so, four consecutive days, reading from a fantasy book just to win the trust of a traumatized dog? Other than me, that is.

My guess is perhaps it's easier for me to recognize his mask, because I hide behind one too. Oh, I tell myself I'm living a more honest life now than I did before, which is only true up to a point. Hiding behind a drastic change of appearance and a purchased identity is still hiding, even though my current life suits me much better.

"Where is your car?" he asks, pulling up in front of my trailer.

With concern about Edward at the forefront of my mind, I'd all but forgotten about the incident last night.

"Had to have it towed last night," I answer, rubbing at my arms when a shiver runs through me from lack of sleep and the morning chill, as I open the door.

"It broke down?"

He turns off the engine and looks at me.

"Kind of," I waffle, wondering just for a moment whether I should share. "Actually, someone messed with it."

Immediately his eyes narrow and I can feel the air go electric.

"Whatta you mean…messed with it?"

Well, shit. In for a penny, in for a pound, but I'm going to need some reinforcement before I get into last night's events.

"Look, why don't you come in? I'm happy to explain but I desperately need a coffee."

Before I finish my offer, he's already getting out of the truck. I climb down and fish my keys from my bag as he walks around to my side. His body stays close behind me as I head up the path to my front door.

"Nice," he mumbles, stepping inside. Suddenly my trailer, which always seemed roomy to me, feels a whole lot smaller.

"Coffee?"

I drop my bag on the small kitchen table and turn to grab a couple of mugs from the cupboard.

"Sure."

"Have a seat," I invite him without turning around.

I fill the Keurig with water and fish a couple of pods from the tin on the counter.

"Messed with it?" he repeats, running out of patience as I slide the first mug in the coffeemaker and hit the button.

I turn to face him, grabbing onto the edge of the counter behind my back.

"When I left the studio after my yoga class last night, my car wouldn't start. I'd just popped the hood when this biker guy walked up. He had a look and said someone had cut some engine wires."

His eyes, normally a warm brown, narrow and harden.

"Cut?"

I shrug. "That's what it looked like. Anyway, the guy is apparently a mechanic and was gonna tow it up to his shop and Heidi, my yoga instructor," I explain, "drove me home. She said they'd had some vandalism recently. Probably just a bunch of kids." The coffee stops gurgling and I turn to grab the mug. "How do you take it?"

"As it is." He takes the coffee from my hands and takes a big gulp. I'm amazed he doesn't burn his mouth. "This guy, his name Brick by chance?"

"That's him. I have his card somewhere. Do you know him? I wasn't so sure, but Heidi said I could trust him."

"You can. He's a good guy."

I have to admit, that makes me feel a little better.

"Isn't he part of that motorcycle gang? Arrow's Edge?"

To my surprise Sumo smiles, the steel gone from his eyes.

"It's a club. They own a bunch of businesses in town. Including that yoga studio you were at."

"I see." Interesting investment for a bunch of bikers. Turning around, I set to making my own cup and stare out the small window over the sink, rubbing my eyes.

"How are you gonna get around?"

I'd been wondering myself. Edward's old Buick is parked on the other side of his trailer; maybe I can use that until mine is fixed. I'll check with Mrs. Sokoloff, see what she says.

"Why do you wear glasses?"

My hands fly immediately to the top of my head and slide them down on my nose. I'd completely forgotten about them.

"Uh...distance."

"Hmm."

I freeze when I hear him get up and move up to the counter beside me, but all he does is set his empty cup in the small sink.

"Annie?"

"Yeah?" I reluctantly turn his way.

His face is much closer than I'd anticipated and I feel my cheeks flush. His eyes are intense, making me feel exposed and my gaze lowers to those full lips.

"Got a pen and paper?"

The unexpected question pulls me right out of the trance I was sliding under.

"Yes, uh, of course."

I squeeze past him and walk into the living room. I grab the pad and pencil from the small side table and hand them to him. He quickly scribbles something before ripping off the top sheet and handing it to me. There are two phone numbers and a name on the paper. Kyle Matsumoto.

"That's me," he explains unnecessarily, I'd guessed. "Top number is mine, the second one is the station in case I'm out on a call."

"Okay, but why—"

He cuts me off and what he says knocks the breath right out of me.

"Not sure what or who you're hiding from and you have no reason to trust me…yet," he adds with meaning, "which is why I'm not asking for your number, but next time someone messes with your car, or anything else happens, I want you to call me." When I don't answer right away—mostly because my mouth is hanging open—he puts his hands on my shoulders, giving me a light shake. "Annie?"

"Fine."

He cracks that gorgeous smile and leans close. For a moment I think he's going to kiss me, but instead he taps the tip of my nose with his finger.

"Get some sleep."

With that he walks out of my door, leaving me to gape after him.

It's not until later, after I've collected and walked Blossom and am getting ready for bed, when I look in the mirror and gasp.

One brown and one blue eye stare back at me.

Shit.

* * *

Sumo

. . .

It makes sense now.

The reason why those brown eyes seemed so flat against her glowing skin is because she's wearing colored contacts. Her real eye color, a gorgeous cornflower blue, suits her perfectly.

I don't think she even realized she'd displaced one, rubbing her eyes.

It had been on my lips to ask her about it, but I thought better of it. She'll find out soon enough and acknowledging it might have freaked her out. Don't get me wrong, I want to know what or who she seems to be hiding from, but I'd rather she tell me voluntarily than strong-arm it out of her.

Still, the moment I get home I call the shop up at the Arrow's Edge MC compound.

"You towed a car from the yoga studio parking lot last night?" I ask when Brick answers the phone.

"I did. She someone you know?"

"Yeah. Did you have a chance to look at it? She says her wires were tampered with."

"About to, and for the record, those wires were cut. Not someone with a lot of knowledge, 'cause he cut whatever he could get his hands on when only one would'a done to disable the car."

"Disable? You're sure about that?"

"Why else cut wires? If you just wanna mess with someone, you slice tires or throw a brick through a window."

He makes a good point, one that makes me more uneasy than I already was.

"Fuck."

"Whoever did it, didn't stay around to see what happened. Few of the boys and I had a look around after the yoga chick took her home."

"Do me a favor, call me if you find anything else?"

"She mean something to you?"

I barely know her, but fuck if I wouldn't like to. Especially after I've seen how she cares about an elderly neighbor. Whatever is going on in her life, my gut tells me she's worth getting to know.

"A friend," I finally decide on.

It can't have been too convincing since it makes Brick chuckle.

"Right. I'll give you a ring," he says, ending the call.

It's eight forty-five, normally after a shift, I'll come home, shower, have an hour nap or so, and then pretend it's a normal day so I can sleep at night. This morning I'm too restless knowing Brick might call back. I put on a pot of coffee and head upstairs to take a quick shower while it brews.

Five minutes later, in my gray sweats and old Santa Fe College T-shirt, I sit down on the couch with my coffee in hand, and prop my bare feet on the table. I flick the TV on to watch some sports reruns.

Some time later, I wake up when I hear my phone ring. I check the display but don't recognize the number. My first thought is it's Annie.

"Hello?"

"Kyle? It's Chanel."

I get to my feet and shake my head to clear it. I'm still half drowsy and I could swear she said Chanel.

"Who is this?"

"Chanel. Look, I need your help."

My head is crystal clear now and all the anger I've pushed down since she scammed me last year surges back to the surface.

"You have got to be kidding me," I grind out between clenched teeth.

"Please, hear me out," she pleads, but I can't hold back on my anger.

"Why the fuck would I listen to you? You fucking scammed me out of fifty grand. Caught me off guard once, Chanel, but it won't happen again. I'm not gonna listen to your goddamn lies again."

I'm about to hang up when I hear her say, "Bryce has nowhere else to go."

That gives me pause and I sit back down on the couch, the phone still to my ear.

Sonofabitch.

6

Annie

"Let's go, Blossom. That's enough of a rest."

The pug lifts her head, and looks at me with clear disdain, before she hoists her ample backside up and slowly follows me back to the trailer.

I finally coaxed her to the bench tonight, but after our short break in the riverside park, she isn't eager to get back on her feet.

It's been two days since Edward was taken to the hospital. He's doing much better after they managed to place a stent, improving the blood flow to his heart. They're keeping him a few more days to make sure his new medications are balanced right before they send him home. After that it'll be up to him, making sure he keeps track of his medication and eating better, which is something Mrs. Sokoloff and I have already talked about. No more Hungry-Man Salisbury Steak or pizza for Edward.

The hospital stay hasn't exactly improved his mood, as

I've discovered on my visits. Especially when I told him this afternoon we'd cleared his fridge and freezer of the things he shouldn't be eating anymore and filled it with healthier options. He didn't like that much. Luckily he didn't seem to mind I'd borrowed his wheels, since my car won't be ready for another few days. Good thing too, because I'm working tomorrow. Mrs. Sokoloff volunteered to keep Blossom at her house, as long as I'd take her for walks and clean her poop from the yard.

"Come on, girl," I coax the dog, who slows down even further the closer we get to home. "Hurry it up, your bed is waiting for you."

It's already after eight when I walk into my place after dropping Blossom off. With my alarm going off at three, it's almost bedtime for me too. I lock the door, drop my keys on the counter, and put on the kettle for some tea before I turn in. It's this Sleepytime tea I've been drinking for years now to help me settle for the night. Not sure if it's the tea, but the routine of my nightly cuppa does help me fall asleep. That, and an episode of *The Crown* on Netflix on my laptop.

While I wait for the water to boil, I tidy up my dinner dishes and wipe the counter, bumping into the piece of paper with Sumo's phone number. I brush a finger over his scribbled name—Kyle Matsumoto—and briefly consider calling him. I've been struggling whether I should explain my colored contacts, but I'm holding on to the slim hope he somehow missed it.

Oh, who am I kidding, he even asked about my glasses.

I get the feeling who I am would mean little to him, but I'm still hesitant to share, and I definitely shouldn't do that over the phone. Besides, he left me his phone number in case anything happened and nothing has.

Part of me wishes I'd given him my number as well, but

I'd thought of that after he'd already left yesterday morning. With a bit of luck, he'll show up at the shelter tomorrow.

I take the paper and stick it behind a magnet on the fridge. Just in case.

When my tea is ready, I walk into the living room to shut off lights and get my laptop, which I'd left charging this morning. But when I go to grab it from the TV stand, it's not there. I was sure I'd plugged it in this morning. Or maybe it was yesterday? Could be.

I take my cup into the bedroom and sure enough, the laptop is sitting on top of my covers.

I must've forgotten this morning.

* * *

"Morning."

I look up to find Ted smiling from the doorway into the bakery.

"Morning to you too. Had a good weekend?"

He walks in and grabs his apron from the hook, slipping it over his head.

"I did. How about you?"

"Eventful," I answer honestly, and when he asks why, I tell him what happened to Edward.

He makes the appropriate sympathetic noises as he fills the large mixer with flour.

Ted does cakes and most of the dough for the breads. He fits the loaves into molds to rise and those go in the cooler overnight, so I can start baking when I come in at four. I'm responsible for the pastries. It wasn't like that when I first started working here last year, all I did was follow my manager's instructions, but then he retired and Ted was hired on. It had been his idea to split the responsibilities. That's when I started introducing things like my Portuguese custard tarts and Canadian butter tarts that have become big hits.

Today I'm doing the butter tarts and I've been peeking into the store to see if Sumo happens to come by to resupply his stock of sweets, but I haven't seen him. By the time I refill the display case with the last tray, I'm pretty sure he's not gonna show, so I keep six of them aside and box them up.

"Who are those for?" Jenny wants to know.

"I'm bringing those to the shelter."

It's not a lie. I will probably bring them to the shelter in case Sumo shows up there. She seems to accept that, which is good, because I don't want her to make any more of it than I'm willing to admit to myself. It's bad enough I lay awake too long last night, resisting the urge to call his number.

At noon I grab my bag, the box I set aside, and say my goodbyes.

Blossom's walk is a short one, since I want to stop by Edward's for a quick visit before I start my shift at the shelter. He's in a surprisingly good mood, having been told he'll probably get to go home tomorrow.

"I'll be able to pick you up after my shift," I assure him. It'll be tight, getting him home and still making it to the shelter for two, but I'm sure Mrs. S. will help me get him settled in. The two of them are much alike, both with a bark worse than their bite.

"I can take a cab," he mutters, but I can tell his heart isn't in it.

"I'm sure you can, but there's no need. I'll be here," I state firmly, making it clear that there'll be no argument and he concedes with an unintelligible grumble.

I'm just getting back in the car when my phone rings in my pocket.

"Hello?"

"Annie? This is Brick. I'll have your car ready later this afternoon."

"That's great, but I won't be done until five." In my mind I'm already going over all the things I'd hoped to accomplish after work in preparation of Edward coming home tomorrow.

"Someone'll be here," he says, promptly ending the call.

Only then do I realize I have no idea where to go.

* * *

Sumo

"Chief, got a minute?"

I catch him alone in his office at the end of the shift. I already spoke with Cap earlier, but any time off needs to be cleared through our battalion chief, Steven Aimes.

"Yeah, sure. Come in." I shut the door behind me and take one of the chairs in front of his desk. "What's up?"

Jesus, I don't even know where to start.

"I may need some time off in the near future."

Might as well get right to the point.

"Okay," Steven says, leaning back in his chair and folding his hands over his gut. "Last I checked it's been a while since you've taken any time."

"Two years ago," I remind him. It had been an extended visit to my parents in Santa Fe when my dad was in the hospital after a stroke. Luckily, he came through with only a slight weakening of his left side. Other than a couple of

49

days during the holidays for a visit home, I haven't taken any vacation.

"Vacation?"

"Of sorts. It's not set in stone yet...*shit*," I mumble, seeing the confusion on his face. Better come clean. "Turns out I may have a son."

That has him sitting up in his chair.

"Wow, are congratulations in order?"

"Don't know about that. Let's wait for the paternity test first."

I may not have been too smart last year when Chanel called, so this time I was going to make sure I wasn't being conned. I told her on the phone the only way I'd agree to take the boy for a couple of weeks, while she got her shit sorted, was after we'd done testing to confirm Bryce is mine. I found a lab here with a location in Boise, Idaho, where she'd somehow ended up. Not surprising Tony wasn't able to get a bead on her after she told me she'd been traveling around with the boy.

I made a few calls and yesterday I had my blood taken, while she took the boy to the lab there. I confirmed this morning she'd done as promised, and was told it would take between three to five days before I could pick up the results.

"Paternity?"

"He's fourteen years old and I didn't know about his existence until last year. I've never even met the kid. Long story for another time," I cut him off when I see him gear up for an opinion. I'm on edge as it is. "Short version is, his mother is heading into rehab, she's got no one who can look after the kid, so he's going into the system unless I take him."

"Jesus...I had no idea," Steven mutters.

"Anyway, it'll take a couple of days for results to come

back, but if he's mine, I'm not gonna turn him away. I'll need some time to get to know him, figure out how the hell I'm gonna make this work."

The chief holds up his hand.

"Say no more. I'll see what we can do with the schedule. As for the rest, we'll play it by ear and, Sumo? I've got kids, you know Cap's got a couple of them, you may be going into this blind, but we can help you figure this parenting thing."

The tight knot I've had in my gut—costing me a couple of nights' worth of sleep—loosens a fraction. I stand up and hold out my hand. "Appreciate it, Chief."

"You know the guys are gonna roast you over this, don't ya?" he calls after me when I walk out of his office.

Shit. Don't I know it.

"Yeah, yeah."

I hear his chuckle as I walk out of the station.

I guess it would serve me right after mercilessly teasing any of them getting hitched and becoming parents. Fuck, Blue warned me, just last year, it would come back to bite me one day. Instant fatherhood would do it, and if they ever got wind of my interest in Annie, they'd show no mercy.

Annie.

I'd briefly thought of stopping by her place yesterday but didn't. I'm not sure if this is a good time to start anything, especially with someone who clearly has issues of her own she's dealing with.

* * *

It's two thirty when I pull up to the shelter.

So much for this not being a good idea. Guess I'm a sucker for punishment.

No one is in the front office but when I peek through the small window in the door to the back, I see her sitting in the same spot I found her in the first time. Daisy sees me, but instead of jumping up and barking like the first time, she just lifts her head and I can see her tail start thumping against the concrete floor.

"You came," Annie says, smiling, when I push open the door.

The dog gets up and I stop a few feet away, showing her the back of my hand. With hesitating steps she comes closer and sniffs me. Then she takes another step and pushes her big head against my leg. I look over at Annie, whose smile is beaming, and I carefully scratch Daisy behind the ears.

"Looks like you've been adopted," she says.

I look down at Daisy's face. She'd make a great dog for a boy. My mouth moves before I can check the words.

"I may be able to take her."

Annie's eyes go big. "For real?"

I can hear the excitement in her voice. Oh yeah, I'm gonna be the butt of many jokes.

"I'll know for sure in a couple of days."

"That's fine, and I can help you figure out what you need for her." She seems to catch herself and quickly gets to her feet, as she adds, "I mean, if you'd like."

I take her in, the brown contacts back in place and the glasses perched on her nose. However, now that I've seen what she's supposed to look like, I can't unsee it.

"Sure," I find myself agreeing.

She hands me the thick book. "Here, why don't you finish the chapter with her? Gives me a chance to get the paperwork ready. Just in case," she adds with a wink, before she turns toward the door, leaving me with Daisy.

I'm not sure how long I sit there, but when Annie

walks back in a few chapters later, the dog has her head on my lap. I stand up, stretching my muscles as she puts Daisy back in her kennel. Then I follow Annie to the front office.

"I have everything here," she says, pointing at a file folder. "All you'd have to do is sign, and there's a small adoption fee. It's got contact info for the vet, all her vaccines—they're up to date—her reports, how she does with other animals, and—"

"Annie," I interrupt her rambling, curving my hand around the side of her neck as I lean in.

I pause for a second; giving her a chance to stop me, but nothing in her face tells me this is unwelcome so I brush my lips against hers. I do it again, feeling her breath against my mouth as she sighs.

The front door swings open, and Annie jumps back, as the older woman I now know as Margaret, walks in.

"Never mind me, kids," she says, flapping her hand in our direction. "I've gotta feed my babies so you can just carry on."

I chuckle, noting the deep blush creeping up Annie's cheeks. She avoids my eyes, even after Margaret disappears into the back.

"Annie," I try to get her to look at me, which she finally does. "I'm gonna need your phone number."

"Why?"

"Because I plan to call you tomorrow to ask you over for dinner on Wednesday when I'm off."

"I don't think…"

She startles when I stroke the back of my fingers over her cheek. She never finishes her objection.

"I'd like to take you up on that offer to help me with Daisy."

It's a lie. I don't really need help. I grew up with a dog

and remember they're basically happy as long as they're walked, fed, and have a comfy place to sleep.

But if the excuse makes accepting easier for Annie... She tilts her head and narrows her eyes at me.

"Are you trying to manipulate me into having dinner with you?"

I bite off a grin.

"Is it working?"

She shakes her head and ducks behind the desk to grab her purse. She pulls open the door to the back and yells, "Margaret! We're out of here!"

"Don't do anything I wouldn't do!" the older woman yells back, followed by a loud cackle.

"Come on," Annie says, motioning for me to follow her outside. "I've got something for you, I almost forgot about it."

She leads the way to an old Buick that probably should've been scrapped fifteen years ago. She opens the back door with a loud squeal and grabs a bakery box from the back seat.

"Butter tarts," she says, handing the box to me. "But I have a favor to ask."

I peek inside and sniff. Shoving a hand in the box, I pull out a pastry and take a huge bite. Goddamn, that's good.

"Shoot."

"Do you think you could drop me off at the garage? Brick has my car ready and I don't know where it is or how I'm gonna get there. We'd have to drop Edward's car off first."

This is not news to me, since I talked to Brick this morning after he called her. I was already going to offer driving her, but this works better. It gives me some leverage.

"I can, on one condition."

"Wait, but I already got you butter tarts."

"And they're very good," I tell her, popping the rest of the half-eaten one in my mouth. "But there's something I want more."

"What?" She tries to sound annoyed, but the corner of her mouth is twitching.

I lean close, my mouth by her ear.

"Have dinner with me Wednesday night."

7

Annie

"My car is more comfortable."

I glance over at Edward, who's been complaining since I picked him up from the hospital. Yesterday's relatively good mood has been replaced by the more familiar grumpy old man.

"Like I explained, I came straight from work. Once I drop you off and take Blossom for a quick walk, I have to hustle to get to the shelter on time."

His response is an unhappy grunt.

I have a sneaky suspicion his mood has more to do with fatigue and perhaps a bit of vulnerability than actual displeasure, so I let it slide. Can't be easy to find out you've been walking around like a ticking time bomb without knowing it.

By the time we get home, he's looking a little gray, and he leans heavily on my arm when I walk him to his front door.

"Want to catch your breath here while I go get Blossom from your neighbor's?" I ask, stopping at the chair outside his door.

"Fine." He tries for disgruntled, but I can hear he's out of breath.

He sinks down wearily and leans back in the chair, closing his eyes.

"Won't be a minute. I'm sure Blossom will want to say hello first," I tell him, giving his shoulder a squeeze before jogging over to Mrs. Sokoloff's place.

She's already waiting by the door, a basket hanging off one hand and the dog's leash in the other.

"He looks like crap," she announces, having clearly observed our slow progress from the car.

"You know how it is; you can feel like a million bucks lying in bed, but two minutes on your feet wears you out." I point at the basket. "What's that?"

"He likes my meat pie," she says, daring me with her eyes to say anything. "And before you tell me it's not good for him, I made it with ground turkey and hid a bunch of vegetables in there. He won't know the difference."

I try to hide my smile under her sharp scrutiny. These two are made for each other, both bristly as all get out on the surface, hiding good people inside.

"I'm sure he'll love it," I assure her, taking Blossom's leash from her. "Come on, girl. He'll want to see you before I take you for a walk."

Edward is still sitting with his eyes closed, but his color is a little better when we walk up. Blossom waddles up to him, her back end swaying from side to side with excitement. When she reaches him, she shoves her snout against his leg and Edward's hand immediately reaches down to scratch her head.

"Still here, old girl. Still here," he mumbles.

"Barely," Mrs. S. scoffs behind me, making no effort to hush her voice.

"Come to finish me off?" he snaps, his eyes now opened to slits.

"Much more fun to see you suffer slowly," the old woman fires back, pushing past me and into the house.

I might've reconsidered leaving these two alone if not for the faint smile on Edward's face. He's enjoying this.

"I'm just gonna take her for a quick pee and then I'm off. Mrs. S. has my number if you need me."

His eyes are closed again as he shoos me away with his hands.

* * *

It's getting close to the end of my shift when Sumo calls.

I'd be lying if I said I hadn't been waiting for it and was starting to wonder if he'd had second thoughts.

He ended up driving me up the mountain to get my car. I'm not sure what I'd been expecting, but I was surprised at how well-tended the club grounds looked. Sure, we had to pass through a chain-link fence, which was a little strange, but the buildings looked well kept, and I certainly wasn't expecting window boxes and barrels with annuals. Not at all what I'd have thought an MC compound would look like.

What was even more surprising were the kids. A bunch of them were eating at one of the picnic tables, while a group of men were congregated around a smoking grill. I recognized one or two faces from the store.

My car had been waiting outside the double bays of a garage, and less than ten minutes later I drove it down the mountain, Sumo's truck behind me. Last I saw of him was when I turned left to go home and he kept going straight.

"Hey."

"Annie. Six thirty okay for you tomorrow? Or is that too late?"

That would give me an hour and a half to get home, walk Blossom, and grab a quick shower. In my previous life, getting ready for a dinner date would've taken me hours, but life is much simpler now. Although I'm not sure this qualifies as a date, at least that's what I tell myself.

"Nope, that's plenty of time. Can I bring anything?" I mean in addition to the éclairs I plan to make tomorrow morning, but let that be a surprise.

"No. Just yourself. Anything in particular you like to drink?"

"Water from the tap is fine. I don't really drink that often."

"Cheap date," he jokes, chuckling. "I'll make sure I have some wine and beer just in case."

Okay, so it's clearly a date.

Nerves suddenly clog my throat, making my voice sound hoarse.

"Sounds good. I'll see you then."

I'm about to hang up when I hear him say, "Annie?"

"Yeah?"

"Do you know where to find me?"

Shit.

"Uh, no I don't." I feel like an absolute idiot.

"Why don't I text you the address. I'm just on the other side of the river from you."

"Oh, okay. Sounds good."

I slap the heel of my hand to my forehead. Clearly I'm out of practice, I have zero game.

"Annie?"

I can hear the amusement in his voice.

"Yeah?"

59

"Relax."

* * *

Relax, he said.

I feel like I'm on caffeine overload, even though I only had my regular two cups this morning. My first batch of éclairs came out of the oven too dark, so I had to whip up a second batch. I almost bit off Ted's head when he asked what was wrong with the tray I'd shoved aside, and he wisely retreated to his corner of the bakery.

The whole day went like that, slightly off balance, and I never quite got it back.

I snapped at Edward for complaining about Mrs. S. and instantly felt guilty, then I got mad at Blossom who decided halfway home from her walk she was done and sat her ass down. I tried to put on some mascara, but the only tube I could find was so old I couldn't even get the wand out.

Then, to top it all off, I realize standing in front of my tiny closet; I have nothing that would qualify as date-worthy to wear. Frustrated, I grab the one shirt I'd bought in a melancholy mood a few of months ago, when I saw it in a store window along Main Street. The color had jumped out at me, reminding me of my eyes I so carefully hide behind the bland brown contacts. It's nothing special, three-quarter sleeves with a bit of a flare and a relaxed scoop neck, but the high-quality fine knit feels luxurious against my skin.

I match it with a clean pair of functional jeans and my plain white Keds before taking a quick glance in the mirror. It doesn't look right and I think I know why.

Taking in a deep breath for courage, I make a quick

stop in the bathroom before grabbing the box of éclairs, my purse and keys, and head out.

I'd added his number and address when he sent it over and followed my phone's GPS instructions to get there. A regular house, but in a great location. I pull into the driveway beside his truck and sit for a minute to calm my racing heart.

Out the passenger side window I can see the park where I take Blossom for her walks on the other side of the river. So close and yet separated by the deep, churning body of water. The symbolism gives me pause. Perhaps this wasn't a good idea.

Before I can change my mind and back away from his house, my phone dings with an incoming text.

Sumo: Are you gonna sit out there all night?

* * *

Sumo

She looks different. More vulnerable, somehow.

I quickly open the door before she has a chance to ring the bell. When her eyes come up to mine, I take in a deep breath.

Those eyes. The same color as the shirt she's wearing. Beautiful, although I can see the apprehension lurking in their depths. She's exposing herself to me, and I'll be damned if that doesn't make me feel great.

"There you are."

She gives me a little smile in response and I quickly step aside, inviting her in.

"I brought dessert." She hands me the familiar bakery box. "I know you said not to, but I couldn't show up empty-handed."

"You keep this up and I'm gonna have to double my workouts before I double in size."

I catch her quickly checking me out before her gaze meets mine.

"Doubt there's much of a chance of that happening."

I shrug with a smile, and with the box in one hand, I place the other in the small of her back and guide her through to the kitchen.

"Have a seat."

I point at the stools on the other side of the counter, separating the kitchen from the dining room, but she walks right by them, heading for the wok on the stove.

"That smells amazing." She lifts the lid I covered it with to keep it warm and peeks inside. "What is it?"

"Just a chicken stir-fry in some coconut cashew sauce."

"And here I thought we'd be having burgers or steak, or something you can toss on a grill."

"If you'd prefer that, it's not too late to make it happen."

Wide-eyed, she shakes her head vehemently. "Don't you dare. I can't wait to taste it."

I admit, feels good to have her excited to try my food. Hope it lives up to expectations.

"I just need to steam the rice, but why don't I grab us something to drink and we can sit outside?"

"Okay. I'd love some water."

"As long as you don't mind if I grab myself a beer."

"Not at all."

I watch as she opens the sliding door and heads outside. I quickly hit the on button on the steamer, fill a glass with ice and water, and grab myself a beer from the fridge, before joining her.

"Are you gonna take off if I ask why you hide those stunning eyes behind plain brown contacts?" I ask gently, watching for her reaction.

She tenses slightly, but seems to square her shoulders before facing me.

"Because they're easy to recognize."

That's for damn sure, the unusual blue color would be hard to miss. Her answer also confirms that she is hiding from something, or someone.

"And you don't want that," I prompt.

"I don't want that," she repeats. "Let's just say, I've come to love my quiet life here in Durango. I don't have to be anything other than who I am. Unfortunately for me, that's only possible if I'm not recognized."

I'm about to question her on why she feels she needs to be anyone else, but at the last second I realize how hypocritical that would be. We all have our masks—I do as well —each for our own reasons.

"Makes me feel twice as fortunate you're willing to show me."

She tilts her head at my words, studying me closely.

"You don't recognize me, do you?"

"Should I?" I counter right away and she smiles.

"No. I guess not. I'm glad you don't, actually."

I could ask her what she means, but I'm content letting her decide what and when she wants to share.

We sit quietly for a few minutes before she breaks the silence.

"You know, I grew up in a house much like this. Same layout, also on a corner lot, but we didn't have quite this view."

Her comment leads to a sharing of backgrounds over dinner. I learn she grew up in the Midwest and was the only child of older parents, who had given up hope of ever having children. A good childhood, from what she tells me, but she lost her parents when she was only in her twenties.

I give her an overview of my background, including a description of our family dog, Kiko, who was the bane of my mother's existence, but my father's shadow.

"You gave me the impression you didn't know much about dogs," she says, an accusation in her voice, but humor in her eyes.

"I never claimed that. You offered to help with Daisy and I couldn't let the opportunity slide."

Her eyebrows lift high. "Opportunity?"

"To invite you over for dinner."

"And a lovely dinner it was," she says, pushing back from the table. "But I should really get going. I have to get up early."

"Leave those," I tell her when she gets up and starts collecting dishes. "I'll grab them later."

She sets them down on the counter and turns to me, a tight smile on her face.

"I mean it, dinner was amazing, thank you so much," she says, looking a little unsure.

"Dessert was better." That earns me a more genuine smile and I grab for her hand. "I'll walk you out."

I lead her all the way to her car, where I swing her around and cage her in with my arms on either side. Her hands come up and land flat on my chest.

"I want to do this again," I confess. "Maybe on a night when neither of us have to get out of bed early."

The flash in her eyes tells me she didn't miss my implication. Good. I want her knowing where I'd like to take this. From the way her fingers curl in my shirt, she's not averse to the idea.

"That would be...nice."

I lean my body into her, pressing her into the side of

the car, while I lower my head. With my lips a fraction from hers, I wait until she lifts up to close the distance. This time I don't hesitate, I sweep my tongue along the seam of her lips and she immediately responds, granting me access to the sweet flavor of her mouth. I taste a hint of chocolate and cream, and groan when her tongue slides against mine.

Her body feels small, and I have an overwhelming need to wrap myself around her and protect her from the world. I'm sure she can feel my erection pressing in her stomach, but it doesn't seem to scare her.

Her arms slide up and hook around my neck, while I bring up a hand to cup the back of her head, deepening the kiss. Instinctively my hips move, seeking traction, and I hear her groan in my mouth.

Jesus, I'm dry-humping her in my driveway. If I don't stop, I'll have her naked, up on her hood. I'm not usually that much of a Neanderthal but there's something about her.

"*Wow*," she mouths when I reluctantly lift my head.

Those blue eyes are shiny with heat and her lips swollen and wet. I have to take a step back before I go at her again.

"You can say that again." I barely recognize my own voice. "Best get in the car, Annie," I warn her.

When she is behind the wheel, I bend down and stick my head through the open window, giving her a hard, close-mouthed kiss.

"I'll call you tomorrow."

She nods in response and, still looking a little dazed, starts her car and backs out of the driveway. I watch until I can't see her anymore. As I walk into the house, my phone starts ringing.

8

Sumo

He's a skinny kid. The baseball cap and longish hair he tries to hide behind only enhances the scowl on his face.

Bryce.

I still can't quite wrap my head around it.

When Chanel called Wednesday night to let me know the results had come in by email, I rushed upstairs to check my inbox. I must've sat there for an hour, just staring at the confirmation I am the new father of a fourteen-year-old boy. When it started to sink in, I went down to the kitchen and dug out the bottle of Jack I knew I still had somewhere.

It didn't really help; the next morning I woke up with a hangover, which didn't make processing my situation any easier.

Then I called my parents.

Dad was quiet, but Mom more than made up for it with her screaming. That didn't do my throbbing head any

favors either. She's always wanted grandkids, although she's never been one to rub it in my face constantly. She'd been ready to drop everything, get in the car, and drive up here to welcome the boy to the family when he arrived today. That's when Dad calmly spoke up and suggested maybe to give the boy some time to adjust before descending on him.

They're driving up next weekend, giving us a week to get used to each other. Looking at him, I'm not sure that'll be enough.

I spent Thursday making arrangements with my chief for two weeks off to start, stocking up with groceries, and getting one of the spare bedrooms ready for him. That night Steven had dropped off an old bike that used to belong to one of his kids, so the boy would have a way to get around. He stayed for a beer and some quick pointers on how to deal with teenage boys.

Heck, I'd been one myself and it scares the fuck out of me to think of the trouble I used to get into.

Now it's Friday, and barely forty hours after getting the news, I'm standing at a gate at the Denver airport, waiting for my son to look up and see me.

"Bryce?"

He stops in his tracks, letting other travelers pass him by as his eyes slowly come up to meet mine. We have the same eyes, his filled with as much trepidation as I imagine mine are. He looks like he might turn and run back on the plane, and frankly, I don't blame him. I'm fighting the same urge, but I remind myself I'm the adult here.

I square my shoulders and walk up to him, holding out my hand. Reluctantly he reaches for it.

"My name is Kyle," I settle for.

"I know."

His mumbled voice is deeper than I expected.

I motion to the backpack he has hanging off one shoulder. "That's not all you have is it?"

"Got a suitcase."

"Okay, let's go find that before we grab some lunch. Our flight to Durango doesn't leave until three, so we've got time."

I'd ended up paying for the flights—given Chanel didn't have any money—but I wasn't entirely sure he'd show until I saw him coming off the flight from Boise. She's supposed to be checking into a rehab facility this afternoon. She promised she'd only be a couple of weeks and would contact me as soon as she got out. I don't know what to believe, but it doesn't really matter; the kid is mine and there's no way I'd let him get swallowed up by the system.

He walks half a step behind me but I can feel his scrutiny. If I'm freaked out, I can only imagine how he feels. I have no idea what his life has been like. That's what has me most on edge, not knowing what I'm wading into, so I'm trying to play it easy. Relaxed.

His suitcase is old and far too small to hold a fourteen-year-old's belongings. He's determined to carry it himself and I don't argue. I get it.

"Burgers okay?" I ask when we get to the food court.

He shrugs, but I catch him checking out the different vendors and start walking to the one he looks at most longingly. I order a meal for myself and step aside so he can order for himself, which he does only after I prompt him.

Lunch is mostly silent, the kid is clearly hungry, wolfing down his cheeseburger and fries before I'm even halfway through. Then he starts watching me while I eat and I'm about to ask him what's up when he starts to talk.

"Mom says you're a firefighter." It comes out more like

an unhappy statement than a question, but at least he's asking.

"No, actually. I work for the fire department but as an EMT. I drive an ambulance."

"So, like…when people get burned and stuff?"

"Also, but we get calls to all kinds of things; accidents, medical emergencies. Last year we got a call out to one of the hiking trails up in the mountains because a girl had fallen down a cliff. My partner, Blue, she had to rappel down to stabilize the patient so we could pull her up. We get all kinds of calls."

He nods, looking at me with a little more interest.

"Cool," he mumbles, and I feel like I've just been given my first father-of-the-year award. Only to have it rescinded the next moment when he adds, "Kind of a girl job, though."

The flight to Durango is blissfully short, but I panic when we get into my truck and I realize the silent, brooding teen and I have little—if anything—in common. That's probably what prompts me to pull into the left lane when I spot the shelter on the other side of the road.

"What's this?"

"There's this dog I've had my eye on," I tell him, noticing Bryce's eyes light up instantly. "She's a bit shy, though."

It occurs to me I should probably have called Annie after our dinner Wednesday as promised, but she was barely out of my driveway when my life changed on a dime. There was so much I would've had to explain, and maybe I wasn't up to that. Fuck, I'm not sure I'm up to it, but looking at the expression on the boy's face, it's too late to turn around now.

* * *

Annie

I crack a big smile when I see Sumo walk in.

I'd been waiting for the phone call he promised yesterday, and again today. I'd almost started thinking I might've imagined the heat we generated outside in his driveway Wednesday night as only on my part. That maybe it had been just me who still had weak knees the next morning.

He shoots me a smile back, but it's reserved. Behind him a skinny kid walks in, his hands in his pockets, and his ball cap pulled low over his eyes. Then he lifts his head and I suck in a sharp breath.

"Annie, this is Bryce." I turn my shocked eyes on Sumo. "My son."

I'm pretty sure I would've remembered him telling me he had a teenage son. I mean, that's pretty basic information to share you'd think.

Realizing I'm still staring with my mouth half open, I quickly recover, slap a smile on my face, and offer my hand.

"Hi, Bryce," I manage, as he gives my fingers a barely-there squeeze before dropping his hand.

"Hi," he mumbles, looking at the toes of his scuffed sneakers.

I turn to Sumo, who looks decidedly uncomfortable.

"I just picked Bryce up in Denver, he's going to be staying with me for a while."

"That's great."

Neither Sumo nor I miss the soft snort coming from the boy. Somebody is not happy to be here.

"Anyway, I'm sorry to drop in like this but I was wondering if you'd mind if I introduced Bryce to Daisy."

At the dog's name the kid's head shoots up.

"That's her name? Don't tell me she's one of those fluffy things?"

I see panic on Sumo's face and I quickly jump in, not quite knowing what I might be wading into. I'm flying blind.

"Actually, she's a gorgeous gray and white three-year-old American Pit Bull Terrier. She's a bit leery of men though, but she's already getting used to your dad."

"A pittie?" Bryce certainly looks more interested now. "Aren't those dangerous?"

"Like any other dog, they can certainly be trained to be aggressive, but most pit bulls can make great family dogs."

"Oh." He sounds unsure.

"Tell you what, she may feel a little overwhelmed if all of us show up at once, but why don't you and I go in there and I introduce you to her from outside her kennel."

I open the door to the back and wait for the kid to walk through. Then I throw a glance at Sumo who mouths, *Thank you.*

The boy stands in front of Hunter's kennel. The shepherd lab mix who was dropped off yesterday has his front paws up on the gate, trying to stick his nose through.

"He's our newest guest. A sweetheart, you can pet him if you like."

Bryce looks a little self-conscious but puts his hand out for Hunter to sniff. When the dog licks him, his mouth twists in the faintest of smiles.

"And this is Daisy." I stop in front of her kennel. "Hey, girl, you're getting to be really popular. You're getting all the visitors," I mutter my usual nonsense.

The dog wags her tail, but she nervously glances over at Bryce, who comes to stand beside me.

"She scared of me?"

"Maybe it's your ball cap," I suggest. "It casts the top half of your face in shadows. Dogs see and recognize faces, apparently, they can even read your mood. When they can't see your face, it can make them unsure."

Bryce doesn't take his eyes off the dog as he removes his cap and tucks it in his back pocket. I'm shocked at how much he looks like his father. Daisy reacts immediately, taking a few steps closer, and her tail now wags furiously.

"Are you okay if I let her out?" I ask, earning me a quick glance and a nod.

Ten minutes later Bryce is in the small fenced pen out back, throwing a ball for Daisy, and I go in search of Sumo. I find him sitting in the front office, his head back against the wall and his eyes closed.

"I'm sorry," he says the moment I sit down next to him. "I wasn't sure."

"Sure about what?"

He doesn't move, other than his eyes opening at my question.

"Him. Bryce. Swear to God, I met him for the first time this morning at the Denver airport."

I'm sure it wasn't hard to see the surprise on my face.

"What? How old is he?"

"Fourteen," he says, and starts to tell me about a phone call he received last year out of the blue.

By the time he's done talking, I'm bristling with indignant anger on his behalf.

"Unbelievable. Why? Why would she do that?"

"Ah shit," he mutters, leaning forward and rubbing a hand over his head. "I wish I fucking knew. All I know is she's heading for rehab today and the kid doesn't have anyone else."

I rub a sympathetic hand on his back.

"He does. He has you."

Sumo snorts. "Not sure how helpful that'll be since I don't have a clue what I'm doing here."

"Look. I'm sure this is a shock for both of you and there probably aren't any easy answers, but I'm positive you'll figure it out." I bump my shoulder into his, trying to lighten the mood. "He seems like a good kid. Daisy likes him, and you know how picky she is."

A corner of his mouth pulls up in a lopsided grin.

"She does, huh?"

"Go look. He's tossing a ball for her out back."

He gets up and walks to the door, but then abruptly turns back and stops in front of me. He pulls me to my feet and plants a hard kiss on my lips.

"I'm sorry I didn't call."

"You had other things on your mind."

He drops his forehead to mine, those deep brown eyes searching my face.

"Still, I could've—"

"So are you guys a thing or something?"

Both of us turn to find Bryce in the doorway, Daisy pushing her way around him to get to Sumo, who immediately goes to his knees.

"Hey, girl," he rumbles at the dog who is happy to see him.

"So are you?" Bryce repeats staring at his father, but I answer.

"We're still getting to know each other, Bryce. Kinda like you and your dad."

He seems to take that in and shrugs. "Cool." In the next breath he asks Sumo, "If we're taking the dog, can we call her Dee?"

"Dee?"

"Yeah. She's a badass dog, she needs a better name than Daisy."

9

Sumo

"Cool."

That seems to be the word of choice for Bryce, although it comes out with a little more enthusiasm this time.

It's what he said when he saw the river, and again when we walked into the front door of the house. The hint of excitement is in response to the PlayStation 4 I point out underneath my big screen TV.

"Do you play?"

He shrugs. "Sometimes, at a friend's house."

I take that to mean he doesn't own a system, and I promise myself the kid won't leave here without a system of his own. In the meantime, I may move this one down to the rec room where I have my old couch and a second TV set up along with a home gym. It'll give him a space to hang out and will save me from listening to gaming all day. A person can only take so much of that.

He follows me through the house to the kitchen, taking everything in with curiosity. I realize I have no idea where he's lived or what he's used to, but I have a sneaky suspicion if his mom was hooked on drugs, it can't have been much.

I dive in the fridge and come up with a beer for me.

"Not sure what you like to drink, so I ended up getting a selection. Pick your own."

I give him an encouraging nod when he hesitates a moment, but when I keep the fridge door open for him, he sticks his head in and comes up with a Diet Coke.

"I like this," he mumbles, cracking the tab on the can.

"Perfect. Anything in the fridge or the pantry," I point at the door, "is fair game. You eat or drink the last of something, you mark it on here."

I show him the whiteboard I hung on the side of the fridge. It's the same system we use at the station house; that way the list is there for whomever is going for groceries. Works there, so I figured it would work here too.

He doesn't talk much, but I figure his head is probably spinning worse than mine. Can't be easy to be sent off to a father you've never met before. He probably didn't have a clue what to expect, and I don't blame him for being wary of me. I'm hoping bringing Daisy home tomorrow will help him settle in.

"Are you okay if I throw some chicken on the grill?"

"I don't mind chicken."

"Good. Why don't you go check out your room upstairs? It's the second door on the left. I emptied the closet so you can put your stuff away. Tomorrow you can help me cook."

I swallow a chuckle when I see the shock on his face when I add that in. I'm guessing he doesn't have a lot of experience in the kitchen, but my parents would disown me if I didn't continue the culinary family tradition. We have a lot of time to make up for, by the time I was twelve I could hold my own in the kitchen.

He puts his can down and beelines it for the stairs, grabbing his bags from the hall.

I'm grilling the skewered chicken when he ventures outside, his face pensive.

"Do you have an old blanket?"

His question surprises me. "Why? You don't like the comforter?" I stopped in at Walmart and picked up new bedding for him, hoping the simple plaid set was acceptable for a teenager.

"It's fine. The blanket is for Dee. She's gonna need a bed."

"Right. There should be pen and paper in the drawer beside the fridge. Why don't you grab those and make a list of things you think she might need. I was hoping to go pick up some stuff tomorrow morning anyway."

I watch as he ducks inside, noting he ditched the ball cap somewhere along the way. He could do with a haircut but I know better than to suggest one.

Over a dinner he wolfs down, we compile a list. Mostly dog stuff, but I also ask him to add things he may need. I've noticed his shoes are pretty worn and the clothes he wears aren't new, and a little too big. Still, when he shoves the pad to the middle of the table I can see he's only added two things at the bottom, deodorant and underwear.

Shit.

"Okay." I shove my plate to the side and lean my elbows on the table, time to tackle some tough stuff. "I'm not sure what your mother told you, but here's what I know. I met her fifteen years ago when I was working in Santa Fe, where I lived at the time. She was vacationing there. We spent some time together and after a couple of weeks she returned home to Minnesota. I never heard from her again until last year. That was the first time I learned about you."

I can see that surprises him.

"Last year?"

"Yes, you had surgery for a burst appendix."

He nods, and I'm glad to see at least that had been the truth.

"But why..." His voice trails off as his mind is processing that information. "She called you for money," he suggests, a scowl on his face.

I nod.

"I couldn't get ahold of her after that. You guys disappeared."

His scowl deepens.

"We moved to Idaho. She had a friend who offered to drive us. She said we'd have a better life there after Grandma died."

That's the one bit of information Tony had been able to provide me with, the death of Chanel's mother.

"Did you?"

He looks at me like I'm the biggest idiot.

"Whatta you think?"

Right. Stupid question. I try a different one.

"So when did you find out about me?"

"Last week. Always told me she didn't know who my father was."

Oh, he's pissed and I get it. From what I can glean, his life hasn't exactly been easy. He probably grew up thinking that was the hand he was dealt. Now he finds out things could've been different. I imagine he's always been protective of his mom and finding out he's been lied to all his life must sting.

"I'm sorry, Bryce. I wish there was a way to go back and

change things, but there isn't. All we can do is move forward." I run a hand over my head, trying to pick my words carefully. "I'll be honest with you, I'm flying by the seat of my pants as much as you are, but maybe there's a way we can try and figure out what comes next together?"

He doesn't say anything, and appears to be focused on ripping strips off the paper napkin, but I get the sense he's heard me.

"All right. Enough heavy stuff for one day," I announce, getting up to clear the dishes, when he gets up as well.

"I'm tired. Gonna go to bed."

He doesn't wait for a response and heads for the stairs.

"Bryce?" I call after him. He stops and turns to look at me. "Night, kid."

* * *

Annie

"I can't believe you did that."

I lean back in my chair and prop my feet up on the deck railing. From here I can take in the river while keeping an eye on Edward's place next door.

My neighbor was in fine form this morning when I went to pick up Blossom for her walk. I get he's frustrated but there's no need to take it out on the hands that feed him. Quite literally, since I caught Mrs. S. storming out of there as I walked up, and he didn't have a nice thing to say to me. I guess we're both letting him stew for a while.

"I know," I tell Erin.

I called her after I got back from my walk, needing to connect with the one person I could talk to about anything. Well, almost anything.

"And he didn't recognize you?"

"Not even a twitch."

"Are you gonna tell him?"

If that isn't the million-dollar question I've been struggling with. To tell or not to tell.

"I don't know. I probably should. He's not stupid, he's figured out I'm hiding, but I haven't exactly shared and he hasn't asked."

"Interesting," she mumbles.

"What do you mean?"

"I'm just surprised he hasn't tried to pull it out of you, especially since something is clearly happening between you. Most guys I know would go into high protective mode."

I reach to set my coffee cup on my small side table, only to find it on the other side of my chair.

"He's had a lot going on this week," I jump to his defense, even though I don't think she meant it as criticism. "He just discovered he has a son he never knew about."

"Are you freaking kidding me? How can you not know?"

"If the mother lives in a different state and doesn't tell you for fourteen years. That's how." That seems to silence her, but now I'm on a rant. "Who would do that? And get this; she put the kid on a plane to stay with him while she goes into rehab. Can you believe it? She's pawning off her son on a guy she knew fifteen years ago for a vacation fling! For all she knows, he could've ended up a horrible person, a molester, even a serial killer. What kind of mother does that?"

While I catch my breath I hear Erin's soft chuckle in my ear.

"Feel better?" she asks sardonically.

"I held back," I admit, and that makes her laugh even harder.

"I think I got the picture, though, and I have to admit it sounds like he has a lot on his plate."

"Yeah." I'm losing a bit of my steam. "Which is why I needed to talk to you. What am I doing? One minute I'm living a nice, quiet, predictable existence—just what I was looking for—and the next I find myself hit by all these curveballs."

"Sounds like life to me," Erin points out calmly. "Messy and real. You have to know that predictable existence you mentioned wasn't really living, right? Life is by definition not predictable, or perfect, for that matter. You know as well as I do recovering from an eating disorder, control is an illusion."

She's right. I know she is, but it's hard to let that compulsion to control go.

"Annie, I realize it's not easy. I'm aware that whole situation back home messed with your head, but you got away from that. You've gotta live a little, girlfriend. You can't hide out forever."

I try to ignore the little pang of unease when she reminds me, but it keeps popping up. Long after the call ended and I made my way to the shelter.

The truth is; there have been a few times I've wondered if perhaps I wasn't as well-hidden as I thought.

* * *

My heart warms when the kid stops in front of Hunter's kennel, giving him a little rub before he moves on to Daisy's.

"Do they get along?" he asks.

"Hunter and Daisy? Yeah, they do, that's why they're side by side."

"Don't get any ideas, kid," Sumo grumbles behind me, and I turn around grinning.

"Not to worry," I reassure him. "Hunter belongs to a very nice older lady, who unfortunately fell and broke her hip. She didn't have anywhere else for him to go, so we're just looking after him until she comes home from the hospital."

Bryce may have looked a little disappointed until I open the gate to Daisy's kennel.

"Hey, Dee," he says gently, and immediately the dog's tail starts wagging. "You wanna come home with us? We got you a nice big bed."

I catch Sumo watching his son with a faint smile on his lips.

"You've got supplies then?" I ask him, and he turns that smile on me.

"Went shopping this morning. Not something I plan to repeat anytime soon, so we got everything we could think of. Bed, bowls, toys, leash, bones; the works."

"Food?"

His hand reaches out and tugs at the short hair by my ear.

"Yes, and food. Smart-ass. Same brand you told us to get."

In the meantime, Bryce has successfully coaxed Daisy out of the kennel and she seems happy enough when he ruffles her ears before clipping a leash on her.

"I'm gonna miss her," I admit, bending down to give her some loving.

"You can come visit," Bryce blurts out, his face immediately flushing as he peeks at his father. "I mean, if that's okay."

"More than okay." Sumo winks at him before turning to me. "In fact, why don't you come for dinner after your shift?"

The little bubble of excitement in my chest almost immediately deflates.

"I can't," I say, disappointed. "I promised Mrs. S. we'd have dinner with Edward tonight. A bit of an intervention, since he's been an absolute bear the last few days."

"Then how about tomorrow? We'll be able to report on Daisy's first night."

"Dee," Bryce corrects his father. "We really need to lose that flower name."

"Daisy's actually growing on me," Sumo teases with a grin.

"And I'm wondering if I should be upset, because my last name is Flowers," I add. Poor Bryce looks mortified until I start laughing. "Just giving you a hard time. Dee is a fine name for her, and yes…" I turn to Sumo, "…tomorrow night is great."

I walk them out to the truck and make sure Daisy's okay being lifted in the back seat. She looks around a little nervously and I can't resist giving her another snuggle.

"You're going to have a nice big yard to run around in, lucky girl. And I'll come visit you tomorrow."

Bryce surprises me when he climbs in the back with the dog.

"In case she gets nervous," he explains, looking a little sheepish.

"I think that's a great idea."

I close the door and turn, almost bumping into Sumo, who puts a hand on my hip and raises the other to lift my chin. Then his lips are on mine. A sweet kiss with a hint of promise.

"Bryce," I mumble against his mouth and he lifts his head.

"He'll get used to it."

I read plenty into that comment and I can't hold back a smile.

"Tomorrow, what can I bring?"

"Yourself," he says, as he rounds the front of the truck.

"That's what you said last time," I call out after him.

He gets behind the wheel and lowers the passenger side window, leaning over with a big grin on his face.

"I know, and as I recall I ended up with you *and* éclairs."

10

Annie

I can hear them arguing when I walk up with one of the peach crumbles I just pulled from the oven.

"...is still my house, old woman. I'm not a child!"

"Then maybe you should stop behaving like one!"

Oh, wonderful. Sounds like Mrs. Sokoloff started the intervention without me.

Blossom is waiting by the door, her fat little body wiggling along with her tail when I enter.

"Hey, girl. I'll take you later, okay?"

"Finally," I hear Edward from the kitchen. "Annie's here."

He's sitting at the small table, glaring at the back of Mrs. S. who is pulling something from the oven.

"Sorry if I'm a little late. Dessert took a little longer than I'd anticipated." I set the pan on the counter. "That smells delicious, Mrs. S. Anything I can do?"

"Yes," she answers without hesitation. "Talk some sense

into that man, will you? And..." she quickly adds before Edward has a chance to voice his protest, "...my name is Hattie."

My neighbor looks like his head's going to explode any second. I ignore his glare and sit down in a chair across from him.

"What's going on?"

At first he doesn't say anything and tries to stare me down, before he finally turns his eyes to the older woman.

"Sick of being treated like I ain't got no sense. Been looking after myself for most of my seventy-two years. Never needed no woman to help me do that, and now I've got both of ye's in my business all the damn time. Telling me what to eat, what to do. It's enough to drive a man batty."

His voice steadily rises as he talks, but when the last word leaves his mouth, the starch seems to go out of him as well and he slumps in his chair.

"Well, maybe—" Hattie starts, but I lift my hand cutting her off. Yelling at each other isn't gonna help, especially since it's clear Edward's pride has taken a hit. She humphs and turns back to the salad she's putting together to go with the delicious-smelling lasagna sitting on the stove.

"I can see how that can happen," I sympathize in a soft voice. "I don't think any of us would enjoy feeling like our independence was taken away. Not only that, but if my body let me down to the point I'd ended up in the hospital, I know I'd be scared to boot."

He harrumphs at my mention of fear, but he doesn't rant or rave. I'm calling it an improvement.

"Me too," Hattie says quietly, in a show of support I wasn't expecting. "Scared senseless like I was eight years ago. Remember that, Edward?" She turns to me, leaning her hip against the counter. "He found me in my garden.

I'd plumb passed out while weeding my pansies. Was heat-stroke, but it knocked me on my ass for months. Times I thought I'd never get out the other side. Got so down on myself I stayed in bed days on end." She turns her gaze to Edward. "If I recall correctly, you were the one barging into my bedroom, browbeating me to get my ass out of bed or else. Remember that, Edward?"

Another harrumph from him, eyes focused on his clasped hands on the table in front of him. I cover them with one of mine, a move I'm surprised he allows.

"We help because we care, Edward. Just like you were there for Hattie and have been keeping an eye on me. Don't even try to deny it; I know you do. We're just doing what you'd do for us, no questions asked. I realize it's not fun being on the receiving end, but don't take your frustration out on us. It's simply not fair."

There's a pregnant pause and I wonder if he's getting ready to blow his top, but he surprises me by suddenly sitting up, his eyes on Hattie.

"So are we gonna eat any time soon, or are you just gonna keep yapping? I'm starving here."

Dinner is amazing, with Edward in a far better mood after our little talk. The only uncomfortable part is when Hattie keeps throwing sharp looks at my plate. Edward notices too.

"Don't bother. That one eats like a damn bird."

Hattie keeps the comments I'm sure are percolating to herself, even when I pass up on the dessert I brought.

"You guys, eat. I'm just gonna take Blossom and I'll do the dishes when I get back. No arguments," I warn them both.

I love living this close to a body of water. In the summer, no matter how stuffy the days get, the nights tend to cool off nicely with an ever-present soft breeze coming off the river. Blossom seems a little more lively than normal and actually walks out in front of me instead of lagging behind. It's no longer a struggle for her to get to the bench in Oxbow Park and tonight she's the one to pull me a little farther. Her stumpy nose is to the ground, snorting as she seems to be on the scent of something.

"What are you after, girl?"

There is plenty of small wildlife here, and mostly harmless, but occasionally you can bump into something a little more risky like a rattlesnake or even a mountain lion. I always stay aware when I go for runs, although I haven't been running lately. Haven't done much yoga either. With Edward not well and Blossom's walks, it's taken up those empty pockets of time I would fill with exercise.

Suddenly the dog stops dead in her tracks, drops her head down, and emits a low growl so uncharacteristic for her, it has my hair stand on end. I scan the trees and the brush, trying to spot whatever has her so spooked, but I see nothing.

"Let's turn around, Blossom. Come on," I prompt her, that feeling of unease creeping up my neck like cold fingers. "Let's go," I say a little more firmly, giving her leash a yank and she finally gives a little.

It takes a while before she stops turning to look behind us every few steps, but I continue to throw glances over my shoulder when we reach the edge of the trailer park.

I'm still on high alert fifteen minutes later, after having done Edward's dishes, and am on my way home.

I don't fall asleep until the faint light of dawn sneaks through my blinds.

* * *

Sumo

. . .

"Can I take her down by the river?"

Bryce, who just worked his way through a stack of pancakes that could've fed half of the guys at the station house, is standing by the door with Daisy's leash in his hand and the dog wagging at his heels.

Last night we'd walked her together after dinner, and the rest of the evening she'd spent playing in the yard with the boy. I let her do her thing in the backyard again this morning while waiting for Bryce to get up, which he finally did at eleven.

"Give me a second and I'll come with you," I tell him, wiping my hands on a towel.

It's not necessarily that I don't trust Bryce—he seems to genuinely care about the dog—but I have no idea how she will react to other people or other dogs they might encounter.

"I'm not gonna run off," Bryce says a little put out.

"Didn't think you were." I grab my sneakers and sit down on the stairs to pull them on. "But we're all still getting to know each other. If we both go, maybe she'll get used to us faster. Besides, it's been a long time since I took a dog for a walk, I've been looking forward to it."

He doesn't say anything when I open the front door, wait for him to clip the leash to Daisy's collar, and lead her outside. Not until we get to the riverside.

"You used to have a dog?" he finally asks.

"Yeah, growing up. His name was Kiko, a German shepherd mix. He lived to be almost sixteen years old; I think I have some pictures somewhere. If not, my parents probably do."

I take a few more steps before I realize Bryce stopped

walking. I look over my shoulder and see him rooted in place, shock on his face.

"Bryce?"

"Parents?"

Well, shit. I've been so focused on keeping things casual, not wanting to overwhelm him, I realize I failed to tell him he didn't just find a father; he found a set of grand-parents too.

"Yeah, my mom and dad live in New Mexico," I inform him gently. "They were as surprised as you are to find out they had more of a family than they thought. Mom was ready to get in the car when I told her about you, but I told them to hold off until next weekend. Give us a chance to get to know each other first. I hope that's okay?"

I watch him swallow hard and he seems to force his feet moving again.

"It's fine," he says, his voice sounding a little rough.

God, I feel for the kid. As much as it was a shock for me to discover I have a son, I can't even imagine what it's like for him, discovering he has a family he didn't know he had.

"My mom is bubbly, always in a good mood, always looking at the positive side of things. Dad is quiet, but don't let that fool you into thinking he's not paying atten-tion, because he is." We've fallen back into step as I fill him in. "He's got a wicked sense of humor and will say some-thing unexpected in the middle of a serious conversation that'll have everyone cracking up."

"I never had a dog. Or a grandpa," he mumbles.

"Right. You had a grandma, correct?" I prod carefully.

"Yeah, she died." He falls silent after that and I follow suit, giving him time to digest, but it's not long before he asks, "Do you have a brother or sister?"

"No. I was an only child, but the people I work with—my

crew at the fire station—they're like family to me too. Blue is my partner on the ambulance, and she's like a sister to me." At least she is now, but I don't bother mentioning that.

"Your partner's a girl?"

"Yup. She's pretty awesome too. You'll meet her and her family soon enough." I feel a little guilty for not having called her already, something I'm hoping to rectify today before Annie comes over for dinner. Heck, there's a lot Blue doesn't know yet. "Maybe one day this week we can stop in at the fire station and you can have a look around, meet the guys."

"Sure, whatever." He shrugs his shoulders in an attempt to come off indifferent, but the small smile he tries to hide betrays him.

The rest of the walk is quiet, each of us lost in thought. I'm curious to know more about what his life was like, but I don't think it's a good idea to barrage him with questions. Much like I did with Daisy, I'll just be patient until he comes to me.

* * *

"Hey, baby," Annie coos when she walks in the door, sinking right down to her knees to receive an excited greeting from the dog.

"Guess that wasn't for me?"

She looks up with a grin and I'm happy to see those gorgeous blue eyes staring up at me.

"Har-de-har-har."

The moment she gets to her feet, I hook a hand behind her head and lower my face to hers.

"Now those eyes, I *know* those are for me," I mumble a second, before covering her mouth with mine.

My play had been to ease into the physical stuff, get her

used to some casual touching, maybe steal a peck or two before shoving my tongue down her throat, but something about this woman throws me off my game. From zero to sixty in no time flat.

Her taste turns me on, but it's the way she instantly responds, molding her tight little body against me as she winds her arms around my neck, that has me fighting the urge to strip her naked where we stand. In my front hall that is, where at any time we could be interrupted by a fourteen-year-old bundle of primed hormones.

I release her lips, only to go back in for a final taste before pulling away.

"Wow," she breathes when I take a step back.

"Yeah. Sucks I can't do what comes natural right now," I admit, adjusting my rigid cock in my jeans, an action she follows with hungry eyes. *Fuck me.* Dinner with my son in attendance suddenly doesn't seem like such a good idea.

"Oh shit," she whispers, her eyes flying over my shoulder. "Forgot about Bryce."

"Babe, I about forgot my name for a second there." She flashes me a quick grin. "He's in the basement. Got him set up with a game system, a couch, and a TV. His reward for helping with dinner prep."

I take her hand and lead her through the house to the kitchen, Daisy following on our heels.

"Drink?"

"Water is good." She wanders over to the stove and lifts the lid of the pan. "What are these? Pot stickers?"

"Got it in one." I put some ice in a glass and fill it with water. "You can leave the lid off. Bryce helped me make them. We're having it with sticky ribs and coleslaw."

"Oh, my God. You put me to shame. Just so you know, I'm never cooking for you," she teases.

"Doesn't bother me," I tell her, handing her the glass

and digging a beer from the fridge for myself. "As long as you provide dessert." I look around me. "You did bring dessert, didn't you?"

She slaps a hand against her forehead.

"Yes, I did. I left it in the back seat of my car. Hang on, I'll—"

I just manage to catch her as she suddenly tries to dart past me.

"Give me your keys, I'll grab it. You keep an eye on my pot stickers."

She hands them to me and I head outside. There's a nice breeze coming off the Animas River as I unlock the car. There's a good-sized baking pan sitting on the back seat, covered in tinfoil. I take it out and can't resist lifting the foil and taking a deep whiff. Peaches. Damn.

As I turn to go back inside, I see a flash of something, or someone, ducking behind the brush on the edge of the river. I wait for a second to see if whatever it was reappears, but nothing happens.

I walk inside just as Bryce's heavy footfalls come up the basement stairs.

"Hey, Bryce," Annie greets him, startling the boy, who seems to have his head down most of the time.

"Oh, hi."

I set the pan on the counter and grin as he opens the fridge door. That didn't take long for him to get used to.

"Annie brought dessert. Peach…what is it, a crumble?" She nods in response. "Here, kid, take a whiff of this." I peel back the foil and Bryce takes a peek.

"Looks good," he mumbles, suddenly looking at Annie with a puzzled expression on his face. "Your eyes are blue."

The kid's perceptive. I notice his scrutiny seems to make Annie uncomfortable.

"Yes, they are."

Bryce looks over at me with question marks all over his face before he turns back to her.

"Mom would have a fit." Annie's face pales at his words.

"Hey, Bryce, maybe—" I try to defuse the obvious tension, but he's not done.

"She watches you all the time."

Puzzled, I turn to Annie whose eyes now look guilty.

"Wait, what? How does your mom know Annie?"

I'm not sure what the hell is going on, but whatever it is someone better tell me soon.

"Not Annie, it's Annabel Fiore," he answers.

Annie's hand comes up to the base of her throat and she looks almost scared now.

Who the fuck is Annabel Fiore?

11

Annie

Crap.

From the confused look on Sumo's face I can tell I was correct in thinking he has no clue as to my identity, but I made a huge mistake assuming his fourteen-year-old son would be equally clueless.

"Bryce is right," I finally volunteer. No way to put the genie back in the bottle. "I was born Annie Flowers, but when I was twenty-one with stars in my eyes, I changed it to Annabel Fiore."

I don't tell him I almost broke my parents' hearts when I did that. Both died not long after I left home and the guilt has eaten at me.

"Dr. Vanguard from the show Memorial Hospital," Bryce explains, but I don't think it's really helping. "Mom watches that show all the time. She was really upset when you died last year. Can't believe I didn't recognize you before."

"It's the eyes," Sumo says distractedly, his focus still very much on me.

"You don't have any idea what we're talking about, do you?" I ask him gently.

"Don't watch much TV," he says with a shrug before taking a deep swig of the beer he left on the counter. "So you're an actress. What are you doing here? Research for a new role?"

His tone is sharp and I flinch. I get why he'd be upset, though. I've discovered over the years not many regular guys are willing to put up with someone like me. At least not for the long run. A fling, maybe, something to brag to their buddies about, but that was never about me. I can already see the way Sumo looks at me changing.

It'll be a hard sell to try and convince him what he knows of me is more real than what a lot of people who have followed me for the past twenty years on daytime TV think they know, but I have to try.

"If you'll let me, I'll try to explain."

He stares at me hard before nodding firmly.

"Let's take this outside so I can finish off the ribs."

I'm a little nauseated at the prospect and not so sure I'll be able to eat anything. I'm going to need a little reinforcement.

"Do you think I could have a beer?" I ask him, and he raises an eyebrow.

"Bryce, grab Annie...I mean Annabel a beer?"

"Annie, please. That's who I am."

He doesn't seem too convinced but slides the door open for me and follows me onto the deck. Bryce, who doesn't try to hide his curiosity when he comes outside with a cold beer for me and a can of Diet Coke for himself. I'll be selective in what I share.

"Like I said, I was twenty-one and had dreams of becoming an actress…"

When I first took that bus to LA, fame and fortune were motivators. The thought of people recognizing me on the street a dream. That didn't last. Although I gained some popularity, I never became the next Meg Ryan who also had her start in a daytime soap. She'd been my idol for so many years.

As for the fortune, I was paid per episode. The first three seasons I was on the show I didn't even appear in every episode and could barely survive on what I got paid. I had to supplement with a part-time waitressing job. After that it got a little better, especially after Dr. Daphne Vanguard became a regular on the show. My per episode pay went up as well, and after twenty years I made a healthy living and I had plenty put aside.

Having people recognize me? That was the thing that got old fast. Oh, it was fun at first—exhilarating even when someone would come up to me at a restaurant or in a store —but I quickly discovered I couldn't just turn that part of it on or off at will.

"I don't mean it to sound like a complaint, because it's the life I chose." I sit back and take a sip of the second beer Bryce fetched me, while Sumo pulls the ribs off the grill. "But people have this idea of you that doesn't really match the person inside. For instance, in one episode a few years ago my character had to save the life of a murderer and for years after people would verbally attack me for that. I'd be walking down the street or stopping at a gas station and someone would get up in my face over something a character I played did. It can get scary."

I'll save how scary for another time, when there aren't young, innocent ears to overhear.

Sumo has said little while I was telling my story. Every

so often he'd look over his shoulder but most of the time I was talking to his broad back. A little unnerving, because I haven't been able to read him.

"Is that why you changed your hair and eyes? So people wouldn't recognize you?" I glance over at Bryce who asked the question. "Why you're hiding?"

"Pretty much. It got to be too much. Some fans can get…invasive."

Sumo slides the platter of ribs on the table and sits down beside Bryce, across from me. I can't help feeling a bit disappointed, especially after the welcome I received earlier. It feels like a cold shoulder.

"Let's eat," Sumo orders. The boy doesn't have to be told twice and I chuckle at the amount of food he piles up on his plate. "Leave some for Annie, will ya?"

"Sorry," he mumbles, his jaw already clamped around a rib as he shoves the plate to me.

"This is amazing, Sumo."

The meat just falls off the bone and the sweet and spicy flavor is to die for. The pot stickers are filled with finely chopped leek in a chickpea paste and the coleslaw fresh and crunchy. Everything is unbelievably delicious.

"Good."

"Why do they call you Sumo?" Bryce suddenly asks his father.

"The guys at the fire station started calling me that. Short for Matsumoto. Now everyone does."

"What do you like better, Kyle or Sumo?" I want to know.

"I'm used to it. It's just my family that still calls me Kyle."

So noted.

* * *

Sumo

"I should go."

"Stay," I find myself saying when Annie starts getting up. "I'll make us some coffee."

I wait for her to sit back down before going inside after Bryce. I'd just sent him in to put away the new clothes we bought today. He hadn't said a thing when I marched him into a store earlier and had him pick out a few things, and the bags were left sitting at the bottom of the stairs when we got home.

He still doesn't talk much. At least not to me, he doesn't seem to have a problem talking to Annie. I swear the boy's already half in love with her, especially after that dessert. He'd had two helpings of it.

Busying myself with coffee, I think about the revelations of the past hour or so. My first emotion had been anger. It felt like I'd been played for a fool—used—but then she corrected me when I tried to call her Annabel. The way she looked at me when she said Annie is who she is, something in me believed her. There is nothing about her that's ever struck me as disingenuous. There is nothing fake about the way she is with the animals at the shelter, the care she showed for her neighbor, the warm acceptance she's shown Bryce, and certainly not in the way she's responded to my kisses. No guise there, I'd bet my life on it.

Still, she may be hiding from the spotlight now, thinking she wants a simpler, more anonymous life, but how long before she misses it?

"Is everything okay?"

My head snaps around as she steps into the kitchen,

Daisy slipping in with her before she closes the sliding door.

"Why do you live in a trailer?" I hadn't realized the question was on my lips until the words formed.

She walks over to the island and pulls out a stool, sitting down as she aims her unwavering blue eyes on me.

"Because it's a good place to disappear."

"No one would expect you to live in a trailer," I conclude and she nods.

"Exactly."

"Is that also why you're working at the City Market?"

She suddenly smiles and shakes her head.

"No, that's by choice. I found an ad in the paper for help in the bakery and I jumped on it. I'd like to think if I hadn't ended up where I did, I might've been a baker."

"Let me guess, the shelter because you love dogs?"

The coffee maker gurgles and I grab a few mugs from the cupboard.

"Yes, and also for a little companionship."

My hand holding the coffeepot hovers in the air as the vulnerability seeping through those few words suddenly puts things in a clearer perspective. I may not be able to imagine what her life was like before she decided to disappear, but one thing I do know: she was lonely.

I finish pouring and set a cup and some creamer in front of her. Then I reach out and pluck the glasses off her nose.

"What are you doing?"

"You don't really need those, right?"

She blushes. "Just for driving," she admits, as I lean my elbows on the island and lean close.

"Let's agree on something. When you're here, when we're alone, you're just Annie. No hiding, no disguises, just you."

Her beautiful eyes shimmer as she tries to look everywhere but in mine. When they land on my mouth, I can't help myself. I have to kiss her.

It's a gentle slide of just lips and I can feel the brush of a shaky breath she's been holding. When I lift my mouth from her, she blinks a few times before rewarding me with a tremulous smile.

"I'd like that. It's been a while since I've been able to let down my guard."

Something about the way she says that has me on alert. It's not the first time she's alluded to being vigilant.

"Annie, are you in any danger?"

Her eyes drop to the middle of my chest.

"Like I said earlier, some fans can get carried away," she answers immediately. "Sometimes it's a single incident, and other times they can be persistent. For a while one of them took things a little too far."

"What you mean; too far?"

She lifts her head as she shrugs. "It starts innocent enough with notes and gifts. Then the notes and gifts become too personal and when they don't elicit the response expected, it turns to threats." When she catches my clenched fists on the counter she covers them with her hand and adds, "No one knows I'm here. I haven't received any gifts or notes, or threats for that matter, since I've been here."

"Jesus, Annie…"

We're interrupted by Bryce coming down the stairs and walking into the kitchen, empty shopping bags and a shoebox in his hand.

"Fit it all in the dresser?" I ask, as I straighten up and return to pouring myself a cup.

"Yeah. Where should I leave these?"

I point at the laundry room.

"There's a container hanging on the back of the door you can stuff the bags in, and just toss the empty box in the garage."

He nods and starts walking past me when suddenly he stops and turns to face Annie.

"I uh…thanks for dessert, it was good." Then his eyes come to me. "And for everything," he adds before heading out of the kitchen.

I'm still standing in the same spot when he comes back through a few moments later on his way to the basement.

"I'm gonna get out of your hair," Annie decides, sliding off the stool. When I open my mouth to protest, she gives her head a little shake. "Go spend some time with your son."

Despite her telling me it's not necessary, I walk her out to her car, stealing another kiss before I let her get behind the wheel.

"Let me know when you get home."

"I'll be fine."

"Call me anyway," I insist, standing back as she pulls out of my driveway.

When I get downstairs Daisy is on the couch beside Bryce, her head on his leg.

"Leave some room for me, girl," I grumble, wedging myself between the dog and an armrest. "Give me the second controller, kid. I feel like beating your ass in *Call of Duty*."

Bryce snorts as he hands it over.

Hearing him laugh out loud as he wipes the floor with me for the second time has the knot of tension I've felt since picking him up in Denver slowly unravel. Getting my ass handed to me twice is enough and I call it a night.

"Why don't you get ready for bed and I'll take Daisy for a walk."

"Dee…"

"Fine I'll take Dee for a walk. You can take her in the morning."

"By myself?"

"Yeah, why? You afraid you're gonna get lost?" I tease him and I grin when he rolls his eyes.

"As if," he mutters, starting up the stairs.

By the time I get back, lock the doors, and head upstairs, the house is quiet. When I crack Bryce's door and peek in he's already asleep, his gangly body starfished in the middle of the bed.

It's not until I get into my own bed I grab my phone off the nightstand and look at the message Annie sent me again.

Annie: **Safe and sound. Thank you for letting me be me.**

Then I open up the browser and google Annabel Fiore.

1 2

Annie

"Are you using that one?"

The new neighbor from across the way points at the empty washer I left my basket in front of. I rush to my feet and pull it out of the way.

"Nope. Sorry."

"No problem."

The small Laundromat at the park only holds two washers and two dryers. One of each had already been occupied when I got here. The woman who'd been here at the time left, mumbling she had to feed her kids lunch but would be back.

I go back to folding Edward's laundry while waiting for my own load to dry. From the corner of my eye, I catch the guy glancing my way every so often making me feel a little uncomfortable. We'd exchanged hellos in the past month since he moved in, but we haven't really talked.

He's mid-to-late thirties, if I had to venture a guess. I

never really looked too close at him otherwise, although I did notice him come home around the same time I get back from the shelter, just after five. I'm pretty sure he works construction, judging from the tools and junk in the bed of his pickup. As far as I know it's just him, I've never seen anyone else around. Mind you, I try to keep a low profile myself, so who knows what I may have missed.

"I apologize for staring," he finally says walking up to me, and my back stiffens as I meet his eyes. He's squinting like he's trying to place me and I feel my palms go clammy. "Have we met? I could swear we've bumped into each other before."

I clear my throat and swallow, darting a glance at the large window open to the parking lot, before answering.

"Well, we do live across from each other."

A quick grin turns his somewhat menacing face unexpectedly pleasant.

"That we do," he holds out a hand. "We just never properly introduced ourselves. I'm Will."

I look down at the proffered hand and shake it, quickly pulling back when he holds it a little too long for comfort.

"Annie. Good to meet you."

"Annie," he repeats. "I mean it, though, I swear we've met before." He snaps his fingers and points at me. "Did you go to school with my sister? Trish Parsons? She went to Animas High School? You were on the cheer team with her, weren't you?"

"I'm sorry, no. I went to school in Kansas."

He seems to be genuinely surprised.

"Could'a sworn." He rubs a hand over his short beard.

"I must have one of those faces."

"Must have," he repeats.

I smile at him and start loading up Edward's basket, even though I'm not done folding yet. I'm relieved when the loud ping announces my load is dry as well. It takes me a minute to dump it in the empty basket and carrying both baskets stacked on top of each other, I head for the door.

"Well, it was nice meeting you, Will."

"You too. Here, let me get that."

He hurries to open the door for me and I slip by him with a friendly nod. I don't relax until I close my own door behind me.

For all I know, I really do look like one his of sister's high school friends, or maybe he was simply coming on to me, but after yesterday's revelations I can't help feel a little unnerved.

I finish Edward's folding, and leaving my basket for after, I bring him his laundry. He's alone, sitting in his recliner, watching some game on TV. He barely looks up when I enter.

"Is it okay if I put your laundry in your bedroom?"

He grunts, which I take to be approval, so I walk through his kitchen to the bedroom in the back. I leave the basket on his bed; putting his own laundry away will be good exercise.

"Have you had something to eat yet?" I ask when I return to the living room.

"No."

"Did Hattie not come by?"

His head swivels around and he pins me with his glare.

"Blasted woman left in a huff."

Oh, good grief. I'm starting to feel like a monitor at school recess, telling the kids to play nice.

"Why did she leave in a huff?"

He squirms in his seat, his eyes shifting back to the flat-screen TV, but he doesn't answer. That probably means he's guilty of something. Without apologizing I step in front of him, blocking the screen.

"Hey! I was watching that."

"It can wait. What happened with Hattie this morning?"

He looks at me, a stubborn lift to his chin.

"My hands weren't working this mornin'. She said she'd help me shave."

He pauses as his gaze drifts out the window. When it looks like nothing more is forthcoming, I prompt him.

"So far that doesn't explain why she'd be upset."

"I mighta told her there weren't any way she'd fit in my bathroom. Doggone woman went and took it the wrong way. I meant the two of us together in there. Besides, I like my women with a bit of meat on 'em. No offense," he quickly adds.

I bite the inside of my cheek to stop from laughing. Neither of my neighbors are what you'd call svelte.

"None taken," I tell him, my voice sounding strangled. "But maybe you could've told her that last part."

He grunts again, but it's without a lot of conviction.

I leave him to stew in his chair and pull a few things out of his fridge to make him a quick sandwich. He should be able to manage that by himself, but he clearly doesn't, and it's too important with the medication he's taking that he eats regularly.

"She'll come around." I hand him the plate and set a glass of water on the side table where he keeps his meds. "When she does, make sure you tell her what you meant."

I leave him to it and check to see if Hattie's home— maybe I can lay a bit of groundwork for Edward—but she's not there.

Probably for the best. I have a sense theirs is a relationship I'm safer to stay out of.

Sometime late afternoon I see Hattie's little blue car driving by, and when I go to pick up Blossom for her evening walk, the two of them are playing cards at the kitchen table. I head to bed early because I'm working tomorrow, and every so often I can hear them laugh through my open window.

The next morning I step out of my door and find a decapitated bird on my step.

* * *

Sumo

"Are we bringing food for Dee?"

I turn to see Bryce coming down the stairs, who's changed into some of his new clothes. It's on my lips to make a comment about it, but at the last minute decide it's probably wiser to keep my mouth shut. Who cares if he gets them dirty? That's what I have a washer and dryer for.

Over breakfast I'd suggested to Bryce we take the dog on a hike in the mountains, an idea that went over well. While we were clearing away the dishes he was more animated than I'd seen him, asking about local wildlife. He seemed a little disappointed when I told him the chances of running into any large animals were slim in the middle of the day in summer, but he perked right up when I said we could hunt for tracks.

"I filled some water bottles and brought a few treats for her. She'll be fine," I assure him, grabbing the backpack I'd dropped by the stairs.

Bryce clips the leash on Daisy while I open the door, only to find a pissed-looking Blue standing on the doorstep. She glares at me a moment before her eyes glide to Bryce and her face crumples. The poor kid throws a panicked look my way.

"This is my partner, Blue," I explain to him. "I'm

guessing she just found out you were here. I have a feeling this is gonna get messy. You may wanna take Daisy for a walk so I can straighten this out."

He nods and slips by her, the dog barely acknowledging my partner.

"It's Dee," he calls over his shoulder, as he beelines it to the river.

Both of us watch him go, then suddenly she swings around, landing a hard fist in my gut.

"Fuck, Blue. That hurt."

She pushes her way into the house, giving me a smack to the back of my head as well.

"Hey! Knock it off."

She's standing in the middle of the living room, her hands in fists on her hips, angry tears rolling down her face.

"I had to find out from the chief? You've got your kid here..." She gestures wildly at the door I just closed. "And apparently you got a dog too? Fine partner you are, hell, fine *friend* you are. I've been on maternity leave for how long? And already I've been forgotten."

Shit. I know how important her place on the team is to her—she's fought hard for her spot as one of the guys—and I just managed to make her feel like an outsider. She's right, some friend I am.

I walk over and pull her into a hug, wrapping my arms tightly around her struggling body.

"I'm sorry." I wait for her to stop struggling before I release her. "I should've called you," I tell her, as she agitatedly wipes at her face.

"Yes, you should've."

"Look, a lot of stuff has happened in a very short time span and I've been flying by the seat of my pants. Can I make you a coffee?"

"Fine."

I head into the kitchen and hear her pull out a stool while I put on a pot. The hike will have to wait.

"She called last week. Chanel. She was heading for rehab and wanted Bryce to stay with me. I insisted on a paternity test."

Blue huffs, "One look at that kid and anyone can see he's yours. Spitting image."

"Yeah, well, I needed to be sure. I'd planned to call you but then everything went into overdrive. Got him off the airplane in Denver on Friday and since then..." I let my sentence trail off.

"I get it. Still pissed as all get out, but I understand. When we first got Esme, Christ, it was like living in a bubble. The rest of the world ceased to exist."

A bubble is a good description. Except it wasn't just the two of us, I pulled Annie into our bubble as well.

Before I have a chance to brief her on that, the front door swings open and Bryce and the dog walk in.

"It's safe to come in," I call out. "Close the door and come meet Blue properly."

He looks a little uncomfortable as he makes his way to the kitchen, an apprehensive dog at his heels.

"Hi." He lifts a hand with an awkward wave.

"Happy to meet you, Bryce. Sorry about the little melt-down earlier. I hope you know I was pissed at your dad, not at you," she clarifies, before turning to me with her tongue sticking out.

"As you can see she's real grown-up about it too," I tease, turning my back to get us coffee. Behind me I hear Blue asking about the dog's name, and by the time I get her coffee doctored the way she likes it and turn around, she's sitting on the kitchen floor coaxing the pup closer.

"She likes me."

"She likes the fact you smell like dog and baby spit," I correct her.

"Whatever," Blue mutters.

Bryce, who's leaning against the island, snickers.

"She has three mutts, a cat, and a baby," I explain before adding in a stage-whisper, "Also, she doesn't get out much these days."

"Oh, shut up. For your information, I was at the station to see what the schedule for the next week is when I discovered you were off. Chief offered to put us both back on for the week after that, but I'm seriously considering asking for a new partner."

I reach down, grab her hand, and pull her to her feet, so I can give her the coffee and pour my own.

"You'll do no such thing, otherwise I'll be stuck with Billy Bapcock forever."

"Who's Billy Bapcock?" Bryce wants to know.

"My temporary partner. He's barely out of diapers."

"He's a nice kid," Blue defends him. "I just met him today."

"Kid being the operative word."

"So when you go back to work, am I still gonna stay with you?"

The moment I hear the uncertainty in his voice I could kick myself.

"Yes," I respond firmly, even though I haven't really given it much thought. Yet. "That was on the list of things for us to work out this week."

"I don't mind being alone. Mom wasn't around much either, I'm used to it. Maybe I can get a job again."

Again? He's fourteen fucking years old. I look over at Blue and catch her blinking furiously. I walk over to my son and hook an arm around his neck. Other than that first handshake, it's the first time I've touched him. With my other hand I ruffle his hair.

"If you want to find something fun to do, that's fine by me, but you don't need to get a job. Like I said, we've got time to figure it out."

"I have an idea," Blue volunteers. "You should take him up to Arrow's Edge sometime this week. They always have kids around."

That's actually not a bad idea. I know Brick does an apprenticeship at the garage for some of the older kids. I have no idea if Bryce would be interested, but it's worth checking out.

"What's Arrow's Edge?"

I grin at the kid. I may not know him well, but I'm pretty sure he's gonna like this.

"It's a motorcycle club."

Sure enough, his eyes go wide as well as his grin.

"Cool."

13

Annie

"You've got visitors."

I look up from the cinnamon rolls I'm arranging on the baking trays to find Jenny sticking her head in the doorway.

"Me?" I ask, even though she's looking in my direction and not Ted, who's working on the other side of the large stainless steel table from me.

"Yup." Her head disappears before I can ask who.

I quickly wash my hands at the sink and wipe them on my apron as I walk out.

These past couple of days I've avoided going into the store, letting Jenny or Ted refill the display cases. Bryce recognizing me, and my subsequent explanation to Sumo, had left me feeling unsettled. Like I'd given up some of my control. People talk and even if they don't mean to, they might let something slip. It's one of the reasons why I haven't wanted to contact Autumn, Erin's friend. I don't want to have to depend on others to keep my secrets. It's a trust issue.

Mind you, I have plenty of reason not to trust. Over the years there have been so-called friends, people I worked with, as well as people who worked for me, who didn't think twice to share or even sell personal tidbits of my life for their own gain.

Not that I think for a minute Sumo or his son would purposely sell me out, but they might accidentally. It's what's been plaguing me since this weekend. Contemplating whether or not I should get ahead of any possible complications and pack my bags to find another place I could lay low. It's why I've mostly avoided Sumo's calls and any invitations this week.

I shouldn't be surprised to find him standing at the counter, Bryce by his side.

"Hey, guys. What are you doing here?"

I glance over to find Jenny observing us closely.

"Turns out my son has the same sweet tooth I have," Sumo says deceptively casual, even though his eyes ask all the questions. I quickly look away at Bryce and smile at the kid.

"Hey, Bryce. How are things?"

"Fine." He shrugs and tries to look unaffected like teens are prone to do.

"We've come to stock up," Sumo continues. "My parents are driving up from New Mexico this weekend and Dad also likes his pastries. I was hoping we could put in an order and pick it up fresh Saturday morning, but I wanted to make sure to catch you."

"Sure." I go to grab a pen and pad lying beside the register and notice we still have Jenny's undivided attention. "Jenny, do me a favor? Could you finish that order of cinnamon buns I was working on? They have to go in the oven right away, Mrs. Franks is picking them up at noon."

As soon as she disappears to the back, I turn around to find only Sumo standing there.

"I sent Bryce to pick out some snacks," he explains. Then he leans forward on the counter and adds in a soft voice, "You've been avoiding me all week, Annie. Why is that?"

I try to think of an excuse but can't come up with anything.

"I don't know, it's—"

"If the next word out of your mouth is 'complicated'— save it," he interrupts. "Life is complicated. Fuck, I think I have complicated down pat. That doesn't mean you ignore a good thing when it happens, just because you're scared." I glance away. With a few words he hits the nail on the head. He's right; I *am* scared. "Annie," he prompts gently, "look at me." I reluctantly lift my eyes. "We need to talk."

"I know, but Bryce—"

"He won't be there. He's spent the past two afternoons up at Arrow's Edge tinkering on cars with a couple of other kids his age. He loves it. They're having some kind of cookout tonight and he was invited. He's gonna spend the night."

I curse my traitorous body for the involuntary tingle in response to those words. I'll agree to a talk—I have a feeling I don't really get a choice in the matter—but only to explain why this isn't going to work.

"I'm glad for Bryce. It'll be good for him."

"Yeah," he agrees, his eyes warming. "So what time, Annie?"

"I have to take my neighbor's dog for a walk after dinner so how about eight?"

"How about I pick us up a pizza? We can talk while walking the dog."

He raises an eyebrow, challenging me. I'm about to stand my ground when I see Bryce sauntering this way.

"Fine," I hiss. "Now what would you like to order?"

* * *

I don't know why I'm so nervous.

I also don't know why I bother rushing to get home, just so I can have a quick shower before he shows up. Not like I intend to let him get close enough to smell a shift at the hot bakery combined with odor of wet dog clinging to me.

Shit. All we did was share a few kisses, it shouldn't feel this hard nipping it in the bud. It does, though. He's a good guy. A better man than most I've met. He's also clearly not ready to walk away from me, even after I've ghosted him for days.

I should never have let it get this far. I'd already been feeling uneasy, but it was the sight of the dead bird on my doorstep Monday morning that brought it all home. Something that in and of itself probably isn't that uncommon but, with my paranoia taking a firm foothold again after being recognized, not so easily dismissed. It also got me thinking about what happened to my car at the yoga studio and the times I felt I was being watched. I'd brushed those incidents off, forcing myself not to look at everything with suspicion. I'd been told enough I was overreacting, being dramatic. Heck, it's what David told me himself the last time I saw him before his car ended up at the bottom of a ravine.

I can't take the chance. Not with Sumo, and certainly not with his son in the picture. No way. I'll end it, pack up

115

my stuff this weekend, and head out of town. I'll miss this place, the few people I know, and my dogs, but it's better to rip off the Band-Aid.

My firm belief I'm doing the right thing is only reinforced when I catch my new neighbor, Will, watching me from his drive as I pull my car under the carport.

"Hey, Annie!" he calls out when I exit the car. Instead of answering, I give him a half-hearted wave and hurry inside.

I've barely managed to dry off when I hear a loud knock on the front door. I shove my legs in a pair of yoga pants and tug a clean shirt over my wet head before I rush to the front door, checking my peephole before opening it to Sumo.

He's carrying a large pizza box and a big smile when he steps inside, once again making my house feel small. He shuts the door behind him, tosses the box on the nearest surface, and hauls me against his body.

I don't get a chance to protest before his mouth is devouring mine.

Deep sweeps of his tongue and the rumble of his satisfied groan vibrating in his chest overwhelm me and before I can help myself I'm on my toes, my arms wound around his neck, and my body pressed close.

I'm so screwed.

* * *

Sumo

"I missed this," I finally mumble against her lips when I come up for air.

I feel it the instant realization hits her. Her body goes

rigid and the hands that were curled around my neck come down and shove at my chest. I'm not surprised.

Hell, she's been avoiding me all week. I figured if I didn't step in, and do something soon, she'd disappear altogether. I hadn't planned on attacking her at the door, but when she opened it, looking fresh out of the shower—droplets of water still in her short hair and the fresh scent of soap on her skin—I acted. I'm not sorry I did, even as she's pushing me away. For the duration of the kiss she was as lost to the moment as I was. I'm not above using that fact to lord over her head when she tries to break things off with me. Because I have no doubt that's what she intends to do.

Not giving her a chance to shore up her defenses, I grab the pizza, walk into her small kitchen, and make myself at home looking for plates.

"Sumo…" she starts, looking all kinds of conflicted. Good, I want her off balance, with her shields down. It's the only way I'll be able to get through.

"Kyle. To you I'm Kyle," I correct her, and watch as her face goes slack.

I know what I said when she was over for dinner—only family uses that name—which is exactly why I'm asking her to use it now. She knows it means something.

Admittedly, I spent the first few days of her ignoring me pissed as all get out, wasting too much time obsessively reading all I could find about her online. I scrolled through countless pictures of her; the long blonde hair, flawless skin under perfect makeup, and expensive clothes, nothing like the Annie I know.

Bryce reminded me of that Annie when I took him for dinner at the Chuckwagon last night. I wanted to give him a real 'Western' experience before the place closes down after this season. Beans, beef, and cornbread slapped on a metal plate. Eating at a long wooden table next to strangers, while a band of cowboys made country sound good on the small stage.

The kid had a blast, and then he'd turned to me and said, "We should've asked Annie to come. She would've liked this." I sat there staring at him, realizing the truth of what he said. I'd wasted days letting what I know of her be muddied by sensationalized words and shiny pictures. Annie would've loved the Chuckwagon.

So after Bryce had gone to bed, I pulled up the pictures and the articles on her again. This time when I flipped through them, however, I recognized how thin the veneer had been. There are pictures where her face may have been radiant but her body was near skeletal. The most recent picture I found was one taken last year at the funeral for a contractor, killed in a tragic accident. I must've missed it on my earlier searches. The accompanying article in a gossip rag said something about rumors having been true about 'Annabel Fiore slumming with the hired help.'

It soured my stomach.

I turn to see Annie's taken a seat at the small kitchen table.

"We need to talk," she says, when I slide a plate with two slices in front of her.

"We eat first."

After I wolfed down my half of the pie and she barely managed a slice and a half, we head over to pick up Blossom. We chat with her neighbors for a few minutes before setting off toward the river. It's not until I try to take her hand in mine, she slows and turns to face me.

"We need to talk," she repeats from earlier, her eyes gaunt.

"Okay. Let's talk. I'll go first."

I figure I'd give it to her straight to spare her trying to pull the wool over my eyes.

"You're planning to blow me off and I'm not on board with that." I ignore the sharp inhale of air from beside me. "Here's what I think, and I'm sure you'll tell me if I'm wrong. You're scared. What's happening here with me is too real, too close to the truth of you. You're so used to a world of perception and deception, you don't trust easily." I glance beside me to see she has her eyes on the path in front of her, but she appears to be listening and not objecting, so I push on. "Last weekend you revealed yourself and now you feel exposed and are getting ready to bolt. Am I close?"

It takes a long time for her to answer, but while I'm waiting, I can hear the wheels grinding.

"Partly," she admits, but doesn't follow through.

I remind myself to be patient, to let her come to me, but by the time we have the trailers back in view, I push a little more.

"Who was David Finch?"

She abruptly stops and I turn to look at her. This isn't just shock plastered on her face, it's pure fear. As her eyes start darting around, I can't help but look as well. I don't have a fucking clue what it is we're supposed to be looking for, but her palpable fear is contagious.

"Annie?" I finally put my hands on her shoulders and bend down, my face inches from hers. "Baby, look at me. Whatever it is, we'll—"

"We can't talk about it here," she hisses, twisting out of my hold and rushing back to the trailer park.

All I can do is stick by her, unless I give into my baser instincts and toss her over my shoulder, but I have a hunch that may not work out too well for me. I wait in front of her neighbor's trailer for her to drop off the dog and walk her back to her place.

To my surprise she darts into the bedroom, and comes out a few seconds later with her laptop and her purse.

"Not here," she whispers. "Your place."

Mystified at her reaction, I follow her out the door and don't even question it when she climbs into her own car.

When we pull into my driveway a little later, I get out and am ready to ask what the heck is going on, but she beats me to it.

"Inside. I'll tell you everything, I'll make you understand, but not until we're inside."

14

Annie

The second I hear the door shutting I swing on him.

"What do you know about David?"

Since the moment he uttered his name down by the river, my heart has been trying to beat out of my chest. Different possibilities went through my head. Did he by some awful coincidence know David? Did someone tell him about David? I tried to concentrate on breathing while we made our way back, but walking into the trailer I realized I couldn't stay there. Something about what used to be my little safe haven suddenly spells danger.

Distractedly, I scratch Daisy behind the ear when she walks up and butts her head against my leg. My God, I'm going to miss my dogs so much.

I saw it right away as I stepped inside the trailer, my coffee tin sat open on the wrong side of the counter, the lid beside it. Next to it my Keurig pods were stacked in a careful pyramid.

I did not do that.

Suddenly a few things occur to me. Finding my laptop on my bed instead of charging in the living room. Sitting on the porch, putting down my mug to find the table was on the wrong side of my chair. Other things, little things I blamed on being distracted like; leaving the top off my toothpaste, or finding myself out of Sleepytime tea when I grabbed the box I was sure still held a few bags.

"Only what I read online."

Sumo's expression is sympathetic as he moves a step closer. I immediately take one back, but he keeps moving.

"You looked me up?"

I can hear the pitch of hysteria in my own voice but I can't help it. I can't escape the feeling that it's happening all over again. Last time it was the notes and the gifts, but at the time I was living in a gated community, in a house with state-of-the-art security. This time it's an invasion of a different kind, almost more personal.

What is the same, however, is the look on Sumo's face. I saw that pitying look on the face of the cops, on my agent's face, and finally on David's when I told him what was happening. None of them believed me. I don't know that I can handle it if he doesn't either.

I struggle against the urge to scream and instead turn my back on Sumo, trying to calm myself down and struggling for logic. I can't stop the tears that start streaming down my face. I drop my laptop and purse on the coffee table and furiously wipe at my cheeks.

"Annie…" I feel his hand on my shoulder. "Talk to me."

The thought of sharing what I've buried as deep as I possibly could is so tempting I can almost taste it. Letting go and allowing someone else to take some of the weight would be such an incredible relief.

The next moment I find myself turned around, and my face pressed into his chest.

"S-Sumo..." Deep, hysterical sobs pulled straight from my gut make it impossible to speak.

"Kyle," he counters and suddenly I'm moving. He takes us to the couch and I land on his lap. "Baby, I'm getting worried. You've gotta breathe."

I'm not sure how long he rubs his hand over my back—slow, strong strokes all the way up to the base of my neck and down again—but at some point the tears dry up and nothing is left but an occasional full-body hiccup.

Then I start to talk, right from the very first bouquet of flowers with a note that said: 'You are special to me.' I tell him how the tone of gifts and notes started changing after that one episode I told him about when my character saved the life of a bad guy. I share how I eventually felt I had to notify the police when the messages included threats, and was told they couldn't do anything time after time. When things were moved around in my dressing room, and I felt like I was being watched all the time, I was accused of paranoia not just by the cops, but by my agent as well. Then I just stopped telling them.

"Jesus, Annie," he whispers, his breath brushing my hair and the rumble of his voice against my ear.

"David was...my boyfriend, I guess. He'd done some work on my house, a good guy. We started something casual and discreet. Neither of us was looking for much more than that and certainly didn't want any of it blasted over the tabloids."

I feel the change in Sumo's body and I don't like telling him this part, but it's important he know why I have to leave.

"Then one night we decided to break protocol; instead of him visiting at my place, he convinced me to go out for an ice cream in a nearby park. Two days later I got a padded envelope at my door with pictures of him and me sitting on a park bench, kissing. It also included a note telling me my 'boyfriend' was a dead man."

"I called David right away and told him everything."

"He didn't believe you."

I lift my head and finally look into eyes that no longer just hold sympathy—they hold concern. Still, I climb off his lap and pick up my laptop before sitting back down beside him. He quietly watches me as I power it up and find the folder labeled Cookie Recipes on my desktop. Then I hand the laptop over.

"It has everything. I started taking pictures when the first nasty note arrived."

Sumo takes the computer but his eyes stay focused on me.

"Tell me what happened," he says instead.

"He was found at the bottom of a mountain road north of Glendora three days later. The news report said it looked like he lost control of the wheel, veered off the road, and his truck went through the guardrail. As soon as I found out, I tried talking to the cops, but it was written off as an unfortunate accident."

He curses under his breath, his hand landing on my knee, giving it a squeeze.

"You were at his funeral," he announces, shocking me. He reads me and quickly clarifies, "Some gossip rag managed to snap a shot of you there."

I've steered clear from going online and only communicate with Erin. I shut down all my personal social media accounts, leaving the official pages for my agent to deal with, and took off after saying my last goodbyes to David. As for the media, after I read in a newspaper my character was killed off on the show after I went missing, I stopped reading those too.

"I was there. After the cops brushed me off again I knew I had to take care of myself. I found a guy, was charged through the nose for identification with my original name, and paid cash for a secondhand car. Then I packed a couple of things in the trunk, and took off right after the funeral. That was last summer."

He surprises me when he closes my laptop without even glancing at it and setting it on the table.

"You didn't even look at it," I point out.

"I don't need to," he says, cupping my face in his hands.

"But I have proof of everything."

He shakes his head and for a second I think he's going to tell me I'm being paranoid, but instead he presses his lips to my forehead before looking deep into my eyes.

"I believe you."

* * *

Sumo

I had to put her laptop down or I would've thrown it against a wall.

Not just because of what that psycho has done to her, but all those assholes waving her off without listening. Misogynistic fuckers, preferring to dismiss the claims of a frightened woman than to pull their heads out of their collective asses and protect her.

I watch as the tears start welling in her eyes again.

"No more crying," I tell her gently.

"You don't understand," she sniffs. "The only other

person who believes me is Erin, and I haven't even told her everything."

"Who's Erin?"

I watch as something crosses her features, gone as quickly as it came.

"She's a friend I met online years ago."

Immediately a red flag goes up for me.

"Online?"

"I've met her in person since. She lives in San Antonio and is married to a game warden. She's actually the one who suggested Durango, because a friend of hers moved here and married a local detective."

That perks my interest.

"Autumn? Her friend is Autumn?" She nods, surprise plastered all over her face so I explain. "She's married to Keith Blackfoot, who's a detective with the Durango PD." I chuckle at the realization how connected we all really are. "Keith's partner is Tony Ramirez, who happens to be married to my partner, who you know is Ava Navarro, but we call her Blue."

"No shit?"

"Small world, huh?"

"Yeah, I uhh…Erin has been pushing me to get in touch with her friend, but…"

"You don't trust the cops," I conclude. "Understandable, but for what it's worth, I trust these guys with my life. Keith, Tony, even Joe, our chief of police."

She turns away, her eyes drifting out the window and I can almost hear the wheels turning. She's still struggling with something.

"I think maybe he's back." Her voice is almost a whisper when she finally says something, and it has the hair on my neck stand on end. "Some strange things have been happening."

"Your car?" I offer the first thing that comes to mind.

"That, but there's been some other stuff." She suddenly focuses on me with panic in her eyes. "I can't go back to my trailer. He's been there, moved stuff around. He was there tonight, while we were by the river."

Her words have the blood run cold through my veins. I want to ask what makes her think that, but I hold back, afraid she'd take that to mean I'm questioning her, which I'm not.

"Then you won't. You'll stay here."

It doesn't take any thought at all. In fact, I can't imagine letting her go off by herself anywhere, even if I have to keep her here, kicking and screaming.

"Kyle…" Hearing my real name coming from her lips sounds so right, it hits me in the pit of my stomach. "If I'm right, I can't stay here. Look what happened to David, I can't take that chance."

I ignore the way she wraps her arms around her body protectively, shielding herself from everything, including me. I hook her around the waist and under her knees and lift her right back onto my lap, holding on tight as I touch my nose to hers, my eyes burning into hers.

"I need you to hear me, Annie. You're not going anywhere. Tomorrow before we go pick up Bryce, we're making a stop at the police station."

She starts struggling on my lap, but I'm not letting go.

"I can't." Her voice sounds strangled.

"You not only can," I assure her. "You *will*. I promise you will be believed."

"You can't promise that, you don't know."

"Trust me. I get why that's hard for you, given what you just told me, but I need you to trust me. You're not alone in this. Not anymore. What are you gonna do? Run off and find another town to hide out in? For how long? You want that to be your life?"

I feel the fight leave her body and her fingers curl in the fabric of my shirt.

"I'm scared," she mouths, barely making a sound.

"Fuck, Annie, I know you are. Swear to God, I'll do whatever I can to make you safe. I have good people in my life who I know will help me make sure of that."

"They don't even know me," she protests, but it's lacking conviction. I'm starting to get through to her.

"Doesn't matter. If not for you, they'll do it for me."

I don't know how long we sit like that, her body slack against mine, hands still clasping my shirt, and her head tucked under my chin. In my head I'm going through everything she's told me and, although I would never admit it to her, it has me worried.

At some point I wonder if she's fallen asleep, when she suddenly speaks up.

"I don't know what to do about work. I'm supposed to start at four."

No way she's going into work.

"Call in sick. At least for tomorrow. You have weekends off so that'll give us some time to figure things out."

"I guess I could call the night manager."

Relieved she's conceding, I loosen my hold on her enough so she can fish her phone from her purse. I listen to her side of the conversation and note it wouldn't be too hard to believe she's not well. Her voice sounds rough as she explains having come down with something.

The moment she ends the call I stand up, taking her with me.

"Where are we going?"

"I'm taking you upstairs to bed. You're exhausted."

She doesn't even protest when I climb up the stairs. I

notice how light she is in my arms. Almost too skinny. Tomorrow I'll cook her a decent breakfast; make sure she eats enough.

She's quiet when I lay her down on my bed and take off her tennis shoes. I stop there out of self-preservation.

"Get comfortable. I'm just going to let the dog out back for a pee and lock up."

I hadn't bothered turning on the light, so her face is cast in shadows when I lean down and kiss her lips softly.

"I won't be long," I promise.

Downstairs I lock the front door and take the dog out back while I stand on the deck and pull my phone from my pocket. Hoping he's still up, I dial Tony's number, and in a low voice fill him in.

By the time I head back upstairs to the bedroom, Annie looks to be asleep, and after a quick shower, I pull on a pair of old flannel pants and crawl under the covers on the other side of the bed.

I settle in on my back, tucking an arm behind my head to resist the urge to pull her close, when I feel her moving. When I look over I find she's turned her head toward me on the pillow, and her blue eyes are staring back at me. She must've taken out her contacts.

"Did I wake you?"

"No. I can't sleep, my mind won't shut up."

"Turn around."

She looks at me questioningly, but eventually turns her back to me. I don't hesitate to fit myself behind her, curving an arm around her body and pulling my knee up between her bare legs. She ditched her pants too. With her ass snuggled against me, I'm sure she can feel my hard cock.

As much as I'd love to pull down my pants and slip

inside her like this, I know this isn't the right time. That doesn't mean I can't help her relax so she can sleep.

"Kiss me, Annie," I whisper against the shell of her ear, and I feel a responding shiver run through her body.

She twists her neck so I can capture her lips, tracing their seam until she lets me in. As my tongue lazily explores, I slip my hand under her shirt, stroking the soft skin of her stomach and the underside of her small breast. Sliding my hand up to cover it, I feel the peak of her hard little nipple and she moans in my mouth when I lightly roll it under my palm. So responsive.

Wedging my other arm between her body and the mattress, I tease the edge of her panties with my fingers before slipping them underneath the elastic. She's wet and the moment I slick a couple of digits along her folds, her narrow hips start rocking for friction, causing plenty of it against my cock.

"Kyle..." she pleads, pulling her mouth from mine, and I latch on to the sensitive spot behind her ear.

I almost come in my pants when I slide two fingers inside her, the tight heat clamping down on me as she moans loudly. Pressing the heel of my hand against her clit she bucks wildly in my arms, riding my hand until I feel her pussy contract around my fingers. She shoves her face in the pillow and muffles the cries of her release.

I promise myself right there and then the next time she comes it'll be around my cock and I won't let her hide.

With my hand still down her panties and the other hand cupped around her breast, I feel her body relax completely, until she finally falls asleep.

15

Annie

I wake up to a hard body and a heavy arm pinning me to the mattress. A blush heats my face when I recall how I fell asleep last night. It hadn't taken much to get me off, but in my defense, it had been a long time.

I don't really want to move, the weight against me feels too good, but my bladder is screaming for some relief. Reluctantly I ease myself away from the heat of his body, trying not to disturb him. As quietly as I can, I make my way to the bathroom, noticing the sun is only now coming up. For someone who usually gets up at three, this is sleeping in.

After doing my business, I wash my hands, steal a little toothpaste on my finger, and splash some water on my face. Sumo is rolled on his back when I walk into the bedroom. One arm tucked behind his head and the other low on his stomach. The covers are halfway down his thighs and one knee is bent to the side.

The man had his fingers inside me and yet this is the first time I see him without a shirt. I stop a few feet from the bed and unapologetically take in his sleeping form. His nicely shaped chest is surprisingly smooth with the only distraction some script tattoo on his left pec. As my eyes trail down past the hand on his stomach, I suck in an involuntary breath at the sight of his cock peeking out the top of his boxer briefs.

From what I could feel pressing in my ass last night, I already knew he was nicely endowed, but how well is evident now. Last night being a one-way event, where only I definitely reaped all the benefit, the temptation is there to return the favor.

Before I think too much, I put my knee in the mattress, climbing up from the foot end of the bed. My eyes are locked on the bulge in his shorts. Heat is starting to pool between my legs as I reach out and carefully reveal more of his rigid cock. I slide my fingers around its girth and bend down to stroke my tongue up the thick vein running from root to crown.

I know he's awake when I feel his hips buck off the mattress as he groans deeply. I trace the rim of his crown, dipping my tongue in the small crease that divides it.

"Fuck, Annie…"

His hand cups the back of my head, fingers slipping through the short strands, as I take him in my mouth, sucking him deep, until my lips touch the hand I hold fisted around his root.

"Jesus fuck, baby, please…"

I'm not normally the one to take sexual initiative; I've never felt free enough to do so as Annabel Fiore. But I'm just Annie in this bed—with this man—and *she* feels free to do what comes naturally. I'm discovering there is no bigger turn-on than having a man—*this* man—plead his need for me.

Which is why I groan my protest when he suddenly hooks me under my arms and hauls me up his body until my nose is pressed to his.

"Lose the panties and ride me, Annie. As much as I'd like to bury my face there, I need you on my cock."

Oh yeah. The idea of his mouth on me sends a charge down between my legs, but more than that I want to feel him fill me.

My panties are off in a flash and I drop my knees on either side of his hips. He reaches over to his nightstand, and pulls a condom from the drawer.

"Hurry," I mumble.

I watch as his long, slim fingers expertly roll the condom on.

"Take off your shirt, babe," he says urgently, his eyes almost black with want.

I don't hesitate, whipping it over my head and tossing it over the side of the bed. I don't have a spectacular 'rack,' at least not without a shaper bra with padding. That doesn't seem to bother Sumo, who scissors up and closes his mouth over a breast, rolling the pebbled nipple with his tongue before releasing it. Then he tips back his head and looks at me, his fingers digging in my hips.

"Fuck, you're beautiful, Annie."

I drop my head and kiss him as he lowers me on his cock. I gasp in his mouth as he stretches and fills me until he's rooted deep. Then he wraps his arms around my hips, his face between my breasts, anchoring me in place.

"Sumo…"

"Baby, Kyle, please…"

I stroke a hand over his hair and drop my cheek to the top of his head.

"Kyle, honey. I need to move."

His arms loosen as he lifts his head to look up at me, and with my hands for leverage on his shoulders, I start riding him. It doesn't take long for me get so swept up in sensations and forget my rhythm, and he loses his patience.

"Taking over," he growls, clenching his jaw.

The next instant I'm on my back, he hooks his arm behind my knee to make more room for his hips, and drives into me hard.

* * *

It's possible I'm walking a little funny.

When Sumo loses patience, he doesn't mess around and I'd be lying if I said I wasn't a little tender.

With daylight, the reality of my situation returned, my mood dropped, and my anxiety spiked right back up. Sumo tried hard to distract me with a nice breakfast and sweet touches, but the moment we stepped out the door to head to my trailer, so I could change, the nerves hit me.

Edward is sitting in the chair by his front door, glaring at me.

"Almost called the damn cops when you didn't come home," he calls out, and I immediately feel guilty.

My eyes dart across the street where I notice Will standing by the back of his truck, watching.

"You go ahead inside and pack a bag, enough for a couple of days," Sumo says behind me. "I'll talk to your neighbor and take his dog for a quick pee." With a hand in the small of my back, he gives me a little shove toward my trailer.

"Sorry, Edward," I call back, but his eyes are on Sumo, who is already making his way toward him.

I walk up to the door, unlock it and step inside. The Keurig pods are still stacked up on my counter and I try not to look at them when I dart past to my bedroom. I quickly change into jeans and a clean shirt before grabbing the duffel bag I arrived in Durango with from the bottom of the small closet. I haphazardly toss a few things in, grab my toiletries from the bathroom, and within minutes am locking the door behind me again.

There's no sign of Sumo, but Edward is watching me as I approach him.

"I'm sorry I didn't let you know," I tell him when I'm close enough. "Things have been a little crazy."

"That's one way of puttin' it," he comments dryly.

"Look, I think maybe someone was in my —"

"Your boyfriend already asked if I seen someone hangin' around," he interrupts. "I haven't, but I'll keep a closer look."

Before I can caution him Sumo returns with Blossom, who lets me know how happy she is to see me. I feel guilty.

"And you don't have to worry 'bout my Blossom either," Edward goes on to say. "I'm startin' to feel better and Hattie said she'd be willin' to walk her if I stop moaning about food."

I'm thinking that's big; both Hattie taking the dog she claims not to like, and Edward promising to stop complaining.

"No shit?" I can't help blurt out, which earns me a grunt and a glare from my neighbor.

A few minutes later, we're on our way to the police station to meet with Sumo's buddy, Tony, and Tony's partner, Keith Blackfoot, who also happens to be the husband of Erin's friend, Autumn. I know I probably should've called Erin, let her know what's going on before she hears it from someone else. I'll have to call her as soon as we're done at the station. I'm too jittery now.

Sumo reaches over and pats my knee.

"I can feel the tension coming off you. Relax."

"I can't. What if they don't believe me?"

"Stop worrying. They will."

Easier said than done. I'm ready to argue but think better of it; I'd probably be wasting my time anyway.

Better brace for what I'm sure will be a fruitless meeting.

They always are.

* * *

Sumo

"We're gonna need your keys."

Annie stares open-mouthed at Keith.

"Why?"

"Because I want to have a look around your trailer, see if there are any signs of forced entry, and try to get some fingerprints from your kitchen."

She seems to struggle with the concept people are taking her at her word, and I wonder what the hell was wrong with the people in her life who made her feel like that.

I held on to her clammy hand while she went over every detail, starting with her name. The guys barely blinked at that information—mostly because I mentioned it in my conversation with Tony last night, but also because they're probably not in the habit watching daytime TV—and merely encouraged her to talk.

Which she did. For nearly an hour and a half, with only

a few interruptions when either of them asked for clarification. I'd already heard most of the story, which is why I was able to observe the guys' reactions. Not that I had reason to think they'd be anything other than respectful and understanding, but if there'd been even a hint, I would've set them straight.

That brings us to now, and Annie still staring at Keith in shock.

"Babe, keys?" I prompt her.

She seems to snap out of it and starts rummaging through her purse, retrieving her keys, and placing them on the table.

I feel Tony's eyes on me and turn to him. He's wearing a shit-eating grin.

"What?" I sound defensive, even to my own ears, which only serves to make that grin wider.

"Never thought I'd see the day. Thought as much last night when you called. Man, Blue is gonna flip when I tell her you've come to the dark side."

Shit. I still hadn't given my partner an update on Annie.

"Lemme guess, you're not gonna give me a chance to tell her myself, are you?"

Laughing, Tony leans back in his chair and folds his arms over his chest, looking mighty pleased with himself. Asshole.

"Not a chance in hell," he confirms. "Karma is sweet."

"All right, boys," Keith takes control, but doesn't bother hiding his smirk. "Back to business here. Annie? If you leave me your number, I'll get my wife to give you a call, seeing as you two have a good friend in common. Autumn is as down-to-earth as they come, so she's not likely to fangirl on you, but she'd make a good friend. Especially since she has some experience being the subject of a stalker."

"She does?"

Keith nods.

"Erin had more than one good reason to suggest you come to Durango."

Annie is silent when we get into the truck. Our next stop is Arrow's Edge to pick up Bryce. I wonder how much of the truth I should share with him, seeing as Annie will be staying with us for the foreseeable future. At least if it's up to me. I won't lie, but I'm thinking he also doesn't need to know every detail.

"What was Tony talking about?" she suddenly asks, "when he said Karma is sweet?"

I risk a quick glance her way and find her looking back.

"It's possible I've given some of the guys a hard time. When Cheddar—he's a guy on my crew, Evan Biel—was knocked on his ass by Tahlula, now his wife, I may have provoked him a little. Same when Tony finally got his head outta his ass and made a play for Blue."

"You're *that* guy?"

"Mmm. I may have been."

"So when he talks about Karma, he means—"

I nod with a grimace.

"Yeah. They warned me it'd be my turn one day. I laughed it off." I look over and see her glancing at me. Despite the brown contacts back in her eyes and the glasses perched on her nose, it's just Annie staring back. I grab her hand off her lap and fit our palms together, lacing my fingers with hers. "Not laughing now, *Annie-chan*. I've been officially knocked on my ass."

16

Sumo

"Nice to meet you."

Annie holds out her hand tentatively to the large black biker. Trunk flashes one of his rare smiles and her small hand disappears into his much bigger one. As soon as he lets go, Annie moves to my side and I wrap my arm around her possessively.

"Shee-it, man. Brick was tellin' me you got yourself a woman. Figured he was shittin' me, but I can see I was wrong."

As menacing as he looks on the outside, the man has a big heart. He's all about his family and the boys the Arrow's Edge MC mentors. Runaways, mostly, who the club provides with food and shelter, schooling, and emotional guidance. The last is shared by Lisa—the club's den mother, so to speak—and Trunk, who holds a degree in psychology. Not exactly a career choice anyone would expect. It's no different for any of the other guys, who all have the appearance of hardened criminals—which they might've been at one point—but instead run legitimate businesses and look out for their community.

Brick is another such example; all rough edges, but here he is, working with Trunk to make sure the boys they look after learn a trade.

Aside from Bryce, there are two other kids around the same age, bent over the engine of an old Chevy Impala. The thing looks like it's been hauled from the dump, which, as Brick mentioned to me the first time I dropped Bryce off a few days ago, is precisely what happened. He has the kids take it apart first and then repair and rebuild it.

My son looks like he rolled around in engine grease and dirt, but his eyes are smiling when he glances up at us.

"Cool, right?" he says, standing proudly beside the piece of scrap metal.

"Absolutely," I lie. "Why don't you go grab your bag and say your thank-yous, so we can get going? We've got stuff to do before your grandparents get here."

"Your folks coming up?" Brick wants to know when the boy runs out of the garage.

"I'm an only child with a surprise grandkid they had long given up on. I was barely able to hold them back a week."

He snorts and his mouth is laughing but his eyes aren't. Don't know what his story is but I'm sure there is one.

"Hey, Annie," Bryce mumbles, when he gets in the back seat of the truck with his bag.

She twists in her seat and smiles at him.

"That looked like you were having a good time."

"Yeah, the kids are cool."

The two fall into an easy conversation about cars, dogs, hobbies, and motorcycle clubs, with Annie asking most of the questions, and Bryce answering more easily than he does me. I think I get why; there's no pressure when talking to Annie, since there's nothing to lose. I'm guessing since he's already been pawned off by the one parent he's known all his life, he has little reason to trust the parent he never knew he had.

Still, I'm grateful he seems to be responsive to her, it'll make telling him Annie will be staying with us for the immediate future easier.

Daisy is beside herself when we get home and follows Bryce upstairs when he goes for a shower. He looked briefly at Annie's bag I carried inside but didn't say anything. We'll tackle that when he comes down.

"You okay?" I ask, following Annie into the kitchen.

She turns and leans her hip against the counter.

"I'm fine."

Now, I've been partnered with a woman long enough to know *fine* is code for anything from *'I don't want to talk about it'* to *'I'm about to go apeshit on you.'*

Before I can figure out what end of the scale we're at, Annie sighs deeply and starts talking.

"I really can't stay here, Kyle." Her eyes plead for understanding at my responding growl. "It's not that I don't want to, but you have Bryce, and tomorrow your parents are coming. I can't make this everyone's problem."

I take two steps and pull her in my arms.

"Let's get something clear; leaving is not an option. You may not have had a choice before, but now you aren't dealing with this alone anymore. There are good men looking into this and you have to give them a chance. Annie, where would you run next?"

"A man is dead because of me, Kyle. What if—"

Her phone starts ringing and I let go of her.

"Shit," I hear her mumble when she digs it out of her purse. "Erin, I was gonna call you."

News travels fast.

I hear the water shut off upstairs and leave her to talk to her friend, while I go to have a chat with my son.

Bryce is quiet while I explain why Annie will be staying with us.

"That's messed up," is the first thing he says. "And that creep followed her here?"

"That's what it looks like."

I kept details to a minimum but it's clearly enough to trigger Bryce's immediate concern for Annie. Apparently looks aren't the only thing he and I have in common.

"Is she in danger?"

It takes a minute before I answer that. I want to say no, but the truth is she may well be. I don't want him to be afraid, but I still want him alert.

"I don't know, which is why we need to be cautious. All of us. We keep the doors locked at all times, even when we're home. We're gonna be smart about going out together, which includes walking the dog. I also think I should get you a cell phone."

His eyes light up at that. I'm guessing he's never had one before. Almost unheard of in this day and age where most kids have their own phones by the time they're ten.

"For real?"

"Not to play games on," I warn him, and from the sheepish grin on his face I can tell that's exactly where his thoughts had gone. "But for emergencies and for safety. In fact, I think I may still have my old iPhone in a drawer somewhere. I'll see if we can get a new number for it."

"Cool."

I'm starting to recognize the intricate differences in the

delivery of Bryce's standard response. I'm grinning when I follow him down the stairs.

Much later, after a dinner Bryce helped me cook, and dessert Annie whipped up, my mind drifts from the movie on TV. I barely recognize my predictable life anymore—each day seems to bring another crisis—and yet I've never felt more in balance. My son is in the basement gaming, Annie is tucked under my arm on the couch, the dog is snoring in her bed, and tomorrow my parents will be here to complete the picture.

Everyone I care about under my roof.

* * *

Annie

"I'm nervous."

I meet Bryce's eyes. He's already taller than I am so I'm forced to look up.

"Me too," I admit, slipping my arm around his waist.

We're side by side in the doorway, watching Sumo walk up to the car holding his parents that just pulled up in the driveway. His mother is surprisingly tall as she steps from the car, only to be wrapped in her son's arms, her gray hair just visible over his shoulder.

The man getting out of the driver's side briefly glances at his family before his eyes seem to seek Bryce out. Then they slide to me, and immediately his expression hardens.

I can't hear exactly what, but Sumo is saying something to him over the roof of the car. The two men end up hugging the way men are wont to do, with a healthy dose of awkwardness and bone-breaking backslaps, before the group turns this way.

"Look at you!" his mother says, even before her feet reach the steps. "You look just like your father. Such a handsome boy."

Bryce stiffens slightly and I give his waist an encouraging squeeze before letting him go. Only for the older woman to pull the poor, frozen kid in a hug.

"Mom, you're freaking the kid out. Let him up for air." Sumo walks up and calmly untangles Bryce from her hold. "Kid, in case you hadn't clued in yet," he says, putting a casual but very telling hand in the boy's neck. "This slightly excitable creature is your grandmother, Elena."

"Call me Grams," his mother says immediately, smiling broadly through her tears.

"Cool," Bryce mumbles, looking everywhere but at her.

"This is my dad, Haru."

The older man steps forward and holds out his hand.

"And you can call me anything you damn well like."

"Haru! Don't swear in front of the boy," Elena hisses.

I can barely hold the giggle that wants to escape. Especially when I hear Sumo mumble under his breath, "Jesus, spare me."

That results in a sharp glance from his mother, which he quickly dodges by inviting his parents in.

"Let's take it inside, okay? There's someone else I'd like you to meet." With his free arm he tugs me close to his side where I cling, as frozen as Bryce was. "This is Annie."

Somehow I manage to get through the introductions when Daisy starts barking outside.

"You have a dog too?" Elena says, but as she's about to head for the back door I put a careful hand on her arm.

"Daisy—I mean Dee," I correct myself quickly with a wink at Bryce, "is a little shy with new people."

"Come on, Mom, let me give you and Dad a tour of the house first." Sumo turns to Bryce, still holding on to his neck. "Son, think you can manage getting the bags from their car?"

Bryce jerks like he was struck and it takes him a second before he can answer.

"Sure."

"May wanna bring a pack mule for your grandmother's suitcase. She packed for a year with no access to stores, instead of a week within walking distance from all necessities of life," Haru announces as he hands the car keys to Bryce, who ducks his head to hide a grin.

"You exaggerate as usual, Haru," Elena counters, to which her husband rolls his eyes.

"It's hardly an overnight bag," he mumbles defiantly, as Bryce wisely slips out the front door. I wish I could go with him.

"Before you two scare everyone off, why don't we start upstairs with that tour?" Sumo says, giving my shoulder a squeeze before releasing me.

"Shall I make some coffee?" I offer.

"If you don't mind? We'll be right down," he says, bending his head to brush my lips with his.

I glance at his mother, who has her hands clamped to her chest and looks like she's about to cry. Her husband firmly grabs her elbow and steers her to the stairs. I turn to put on a pot of coffee and process.

Bryce just passed me on his way to the basement minutes ago, grumbling under his breath his grandfather wasn't kidding. I'm still grinning as I put away the last of the dishes from the dishwasher when I hear footsteps behind me.

"One of the things I've done more of than I care to admit since I had my stroke a few years ago..." I turn to find Haru leaning against the kitchen island. "...is watch daytime TV."

I press a hand to my chest where my heart takes off in a hearty gallop, as panic takes me in its grip.

"I, uh…"

"Does my son know who you are?"

"Yes," I croak.

"From a distance I thought you were the woman who gave birth to my grandson. When I got closer you looked familiar, but I was thrown off by the hair and the eyes, only for a moment. Did Kyle mention I have a knack for remembering faces?" I shake my head. "Yeah, it can be a blessing and a curse. I literally can't unsee anything." He chuckles at his own joke.

"Eidetic memory."

He looks at me with an eyebrow raised. "Most people just say photographic memory."

"Most people didn't play a doctor for almost twenty years."

That makes him chuckle again. When he smiles he has the same laugh lines his son has and I realize—but for the first impression I had of him as a stern man—like Sumo, Haru has a sense of humor.

"Touché." The smile disappears and he tilts his head. "So, the hair, the eyes, the glasses—safe to guess you didn't want to be recognized?"

"That was the idea," I admit, turning to grab a few mugs from the cupboard. "Coffee?"

"Please."

"It worked for almost a year. The first person to recognize me was actually your grandson." Haru's bushy eyebrows both shoot up. "I'm thinking the eidetic memory skipped a generation. Kyle didn't have a clue, even after Bryce told him my name." Now it's my turn to chuckle.

"That doesn't bother you?"

I get the strong sense I'm being weighed and measured,

but I can't blame the man for being suspicious. I calmly fill his mug before handing it to him.

"That he didn't know me from Adam? No, it was a relief," I tell him honestly.

"Everything okay here?" Kyle asks. His eyes are on me as he approaches through the living room.

"Your father recognized me."

"Shit. Dad, you can't—"

"Hush, Son. My lips are sealed, although I have a feeling it won't take your mother long to figure it out. She likes the gossip rags." He looks over his shoulder. "Where is she, by the way?"

"Unpacking," he says, when I hand him a cup and am rewarded with a kiss to the top of my head. "Thanks, *Annie-chan*."

"Why don't you introduce your dad to the dog, honey?" I look over at the father, but I'm talking to the son. "I have some baking to do."

When I lift my face to Sumo, I see the question in his eyes. I have to swallow hard, it's not easy for me to trust, but I don't want him to have to keep anything from his father. Besides, with the police looking into things, it's only a matter of time before word gets out.

"Maybe you should let your dad know what's going on."

"Are you sure?"

No. Far from, but Sumo already made it clear he won't let me run, and honestly, I don't really want to leave.

"Positive."

17

Annie

"What are you cooking? Can I help?"

Sumo's mom walks in as I'm crushing filberts with the bottom of a pan.

"I thought I'd get a head start on dessert," I tell her. "I'm making a hazelnut raspberry pavlova."

"Yum. Sounds delicious. You need those eggs separated?"

She points at the metal bowls and carton of eggs I have sitting on the counter. I hesitate for a fraction, because all it takes is a hint of yolk in the egg whites to ruin the meringue. Still, this is Sumo's mother in his kitchen.

"Sure."

She must've picked up on my slight hesitation and smiles as she washes her hands at the sink.

"I'm pretty good in the kitchen."

"So your son tells me."

I watch as she expertly cracks an egg in a hand, letting

the white strain through her fingers into the metal bowl, leaving the yolk intact.

"He likes you," she says without looking at me, as she slips the yolk into the second bowl before picking up the next egg.

"I know. I like him too."

We work in silence for a bit, until I hear the tap turn on and sounds of hands being washed.

"I don't mean to pry," she says, meaning to do exactly that, but I'm not upset. "But I tried getting information from my son, who was less than forthcoming. How did you two meet? How long have you been together? Your shampoo is in the master bathroom, and I don't even know your last name."

Wow. She doesn't mess around, but when I look at her I don't see judgment, only curiosity, and definitely some concern. I can't fault her for that.

It hits me that for someone who's tried so hard to hide her identity, it's becoming ridiculously easy to let my defenses down.

By the time the men come in—led by a curious Daisy—Elena and I are in the living room on the couch, talking, while we wait for the meringue in the oven. To my surprise the dog moves straight to Elena, sniffing the hand she holds out. Clearly she's regained some of her confidence this past week.

"She browbeat it out of you, didn't she?"

I tilt my head back and smile up at Sumo.

"What can I say, your parents are good."

Then the doorbell rings.

* * *

Sumo

149

. . .

Shit.

I step aside for Blue and Tony, carrying Esme in her baby seat, to come in. In the chaos of the past few days, it slipped my mind I'd invited them over when Blue barged in here last week. I'd thought they might make for a good distraction, taking the pressure off Bryce.

Off course that was before trouble found Annie who, by the way, I still haven't told my partner about.

"You forgot, didn't you?" Blue hisses in my ear when I try to hug her. "Also, good thing my husband shares."

Oh yeah, I fucked up.

"Sorry, man," Tony mumbles, as she brushes past me inside. He sets down the baby seat and lifts up a six-pack of specialty beer he has in his other hand. "Fridge?"

"Please, I'll take the baby. Safer if I walk in with protection."

The asshole chuckles as he walks into the living room, where Blue introduces him to my parents. She's met them a few times before.

I unclip Esme's harness and lift her from her seat, a wave of longing hitting me when she snuggles her little body against my chest. It's quickly replaced with a burst of rage at Chanel, for denying me the experience with my own child.

"Oh my God," Mom titters, rushing up with her hands already outstretched. "Gimme the baby."

"Wait your turn," I tell her with a wink. "Let me get my snuggles in first."

She contents herself by cooing at Esme, stroking gentle fingers over the baby's soft hair.

"She's so precious."

Another reason to be angry with Chanel.

Annie looks wide-eyed when I make it to the living room and I give her what I hope is a reassuring smile. Dad is already in the kitchen performing host duties, and Bryce, who must've just surfaced from the basement, is shaking hands with Tony.

"Meet Esme, Annie," Blue says, giving me the stink-eye, but it softens the moment her gaze lands on her baby. "Don't mind Sumo, he's a bit territorial with her."

"I can share," I protest, which goes to deaf ears.

"She's beautiful," Annie mumbles, her smile is as soft for the baby as it is for me. "But why don't you give her to your mom? I have to check the meringue."

Mom doesn't need to be told twice and is already plucking her from my arms. I barely have a chance to kiss her little head.

That leaves Blue and I, facing off.

"I know I messed up. Things have been crazy," I start.

"So I gather."

She still looks pissed, but then she suddenly snickers, shoving my shoulder.

"Ohhh, this is so much fun," she taunts. "I was gonna call you and tear you a new one yesterday, but Tony suggested I save it and mess with you a little instead. He was right. This was so much more satisfying."

I glance over her shoulder to see Tony watching from the kitchen, a big grin splitting his face as he mouths, *"Payback."*

I haven't even had a chance to take Bryce to meet my crew at the station, which was on the schedule for sometime these coming days since we never made it in the past week. I can't imagine the razzing I'll get there when they discover I not only have a son, but a woman in my life as well.

"You've got me," I grumble, but give her shoulder a squeeze as I move past her to the kitchen.

My dad is holding court at the kitchen island, his hand loosely on Bryce's shoulder as he talks to Tony. I catch my son's eye and give him a wink before catching Annie around her waist, just as she closes the oven door.

"Sorry for the invasion," I mumble in her neck. "You okay?"

She turns in my arms and pats my chest.

"I am." I wait for her to add *'fine'* but it never materializes. "But what were your plans for dinner?" she whispers.

"I'll take care of that. Will there be enough dessert?"

She chuckles and presses her face in my chest.

"Enough for dessert, yes, but there won't be enough left for you to have for breakfast at the crack of dawn."

She's referring to the leftovers of last night's chocolate mousse she caught me wolfing down at five this morning. I'd forgotten she's used to getting up early herself. The chocolate mousse led to another kind of breakfast with me on my knees, and Annie hoisted up on the edge of the kitchen counter, her legs over my shoulders.

"Hmmm," I growl softly, tightening my arms around her. "I think I may have discovered a taste I crave more, as of this morning."

Her blush is cute as her eyes dart over my shoulder.

"Not with your parents here," she hisses.

"I don't think your mother's gonna give me back my baby," Blue says, walking into the kitchen.

It's the same as it was growing up, didn't matter who'd be over visiting, we all inevitably would end up in the kitchen.

In the end it's Dad and me together who get dinner going. Mom is too preoccupied with both the baby and her newfound grandson, who she manages to pin down outside on the deck. Luckily Annie is out there with Blue to provide a bit of a buffer. I glance out the window to see Blue hand the baby to Annie to burp.

A house full of family.

Bryce seems to feel comfortable in the presence of my father and Tony, sitting on a stool next to Tony, and although he's not saying much, he's observing.

"You may be getting out of cooking duty tonight, kid," I tell him with a grin. "But I'm counting on you to set the table outside."

"Cool," he mumbles, getting up to grab plates from the cupboard.

"See if the ladies need refills?" Dad asks. "We're about ready to put these babies on the grill."

We're putting the finishing touches on the tray stacked with skewers of meat and vegetables. Dad threw together a Thai quinoa salad and I pulled a jar of kimchi out of the pantry to round off the meal.

As soon as Bryce is out of earshot, Tony turns to me.

"You lucked out, my friend. He's a good kid."

"Yeah, from what I can tell, we may have his grand-mother to thank for that. She was apparently a constant in his life before Chanel moved them to Boise."

"Any word from her?"

"Not even a call. She told Bryce she'd be a couple of weeks at most, but if she seriously went into rehab like she said, I doubt she'd be out that soon."

"Does he talk about her?" Dad wants to know.

"Not really. I have a feeling he's been covering for her for a long time and doesn't want me to get mad. He seems more open with Annie, but he still looks at me like I'm gonna send him packing any minute."

"Poor kid," Tony mutters.

Dad bumps me out of the way to get to the sink.

"I'll grill," he announces. "You clean up, and after dinner I'm gonna take my grandson to walk the dog."

I look at my father, who may be a couple of inches shorter but is infinitely wiser.

"Thanks, Dad."

* * *

Annie

"I really think maybe I should sleep in the basement."

His body starts shaking behind me.

I'd argued all the way as he led me up the stairs earlier. He wasn't listening then either.

After Blue and Tony left—taking that adorable little nugget with them—his parents followed Bryce to bed, reminding us they'd had a long day. Kyle and I finished cleaning up the kitchen and debriefing the day. It felt ridiculously domestic. I've been here only two days and already it feels like home.

Don't get me wrong; I love my little sanctuary, except it doesn't feel that safe anymore. Tony took me aside at some point to hand me back my keys, and let me know they'd gone through the trailer and collected what evidence they could. He didn't specify what that might've been and I didn't ask. It wasn't the time or place.

For now, I'm just going to pretend this is my new normal. Except maybe sleeping in the same bed with Kyle when his parents are just steps down the hall.

"Are you laughing at me?"

I try to roll over but his hold on me tightens as he buries his face in the crook of my neck.

"You're not sleeping in the basement," he finally says,

trying to hide the amusement in his voice, and failing miserably.

"It's not right. It's bad enough you convinced me to sleep in here last night with an impressionable boy a few doors down, but with your parents here?"

His grip on me loosens, but before I can move of my own accord he has me rolled on my back, his face hovering over me.

"First of all, that boy is fourteen and I don't wanna freak you out, but that's no longer a boy, that's a teenager. He's probably more enlightened than either of us wanna think about."

"Ewww."

I make a face that has him grinning, enhancing those lines in his face I love so much.

"And second, my parents find out you slept in the basement, they'd not only insist on staying at a hotel, they'd disown me in the process."

I bite my bottom lip and his eyes drop down to my mouth, as he lifts his hand to my face. With the pad of his thumb he rubs my bottom lip.

"Kyle," I warn, as he lowers his face a fraction.

"Just a kiss, babe."

"We can't. Kissing leads to other things."

The white of his teeth flash a smile.

"Are you saying I'm irresistible, *Annie-chan?*"

"You're incorrigible," I correct him, but I'm smiling as I say it.

"Then roll over, let me hold you, and go to sleep."

I lift my head and brush a light kiss on his lips before rolling back on my side. Immediately his arm snakes around and pulls me so my back is flush against his front.

"Kyle?"

"Right here."

"Why do you call me *Annie-chan?*"

He's silent for a moment as he brushes his lips along my neck slowly.

"It's an endearment. An expression of affection."

My heart warms as I snuggle against him, and in minutes I drift off.

18

Sumo

"We need to talk."

I close the front door and turn to Annie.

We've just waved off my parents, who stayed a few days longer than they'd initially planned. Bryce said his good-byes earlier before I dropped him off at the Arrow's Edge. He'd stayed home yesterday but I could tell he was eager to get back to his new friends. When I offered to drive him this morning, he'd jumped at the chance.

Annie hasn't been back to work, or the shelter, which is something I know is bothering her.

"Sure." I walk past her, tagging her hand and pulling her with me to the couch.

I'd been pleased, although, not surprised, she got along with my parents so well. Mom had her moments—especially when Annie came downstairs on Sunday, her beautiful blue eyes on display—where she could barely contain her giddiness, but as always, Dad was right there to moderate her excitement.

We've been living in a bubble, though, barely leaving the house—Annie not at all—and I know that's not sustainable. I suspect Annie knows that as well.

"I have to go back to work. I can't just disappear."

I stop myself from pointing out it's no different than what she's done for the past year. The truth is, I'm pleased as fuck her life here clearly means a lot to her.

"Okay."

She looks at me surprised.

"That's it? Okay?"

"It's not my decision to make. I can't stop you if that's what you think you need to do."

She tilts her head and narrows her eyes at me, ready for battle.

"But?"

"But…maybe you should consider giving Tony and Keith a couple of days more to see what they can come up with. I have the remainder of this week off to decide how I'm going to make things work with Bryce when I go back to work. You could take the rest of this week with me, maybe we can figure out how to move forward from here together."

Her face softens and she lets herself sink against me. My arm closes around her.

"Your mother says you like me," she mumbles with her face pressed against my shoulder.

I chuckle. "I'd say that's pretty obvious."

"I told her I like you too."

"Good to know," I mutter softly in her hair.

We sit like that for a while, her head on my shoulder and my cheek to her hair.

"I should probably make some calls," she finally says,

straightening up. "See how Edward is doing, call Margaret at the shelter, and get in touch with my manager at the City Market and make up an excuse to take the rest of the week off."

"You could just mention you have some personal issues you need to deal with this week," I suggest, sensing it's lying she may have an issue with. "Same with the shelter. They don't need to know any more."

She turns a grateful smile on me and I feel like I've just successfully traversed a minefield.

"True."

"Go make your calls. I'm taking Daisy for a quick walk."

She leans in and I meet her lips for a kiss before she gets up to find her phone. I turn to the dog, asleep in her bed.

"Come, girl, wanna go for a quickie?"

Her head lifts up, one ear perked, and the moment I get to my feet she is too. She's proving to be a great dog. I've only had her for a little over a week and already I can't remember what life was like before her. Or maybe that's because during that same time I gained a son, and a woman, both of whom I'd do anything to keep.

There's a bit of a breeze coming off the river, providing a little cool relief in the heat of the midday sun. Daisy puts in a decent clip, her nose glued to the ground in front of her. I swear there must've been a bloodhound somewhere in her lineage.

Suddenly, maybe a mile or so upriver, she starts pulling me toward the street.

"Where are you going? You ready to go back already?"

I drag back on her leash and keep heading north. Initially she complies but then she suddenly turns around and starts moving along the path back to the house.

Strange, she's not been one to pull hard like this, but for

some reason is in a hurry today. She doesn't let up, not even when I try to slow her down. She just strains against her leash, throwing her entire weight into it, and I'm starting to get an uneasy feeling the closer to home we get.

My truck is still parked behind her car in the driveway to make room for my parents; I haven't had a chance to move it yet. The house looks normal, but my sense something is off only gets stronger when I cross the street. Daisy still does not let up on the leash, in a hurry to get home.

I see it when I walk up the path, a plastic bag hanging off the doorknob.

Daisy is already sniffing it before I get up the steps. Then she takes a few steps back and I hear her softly growl, her eyes on the door. A cold chill crawls up my spine.

Fuck. I didn't lock the door when I left.

Didn't remind Annie to lock it either. I didn't even think of it after the weekend with a houseful. Annie was never alone. Not until now.

I take a careful peek in the bag and immediately close it again, bile surging up my throat. Next I grab the knob, turn it, and swing the door open.

Daisy almost knocks me over as she darts inside, tearing the leash from my hand.

* * *

Annie

"I promise I'll do better staying in touch," I convey to Edward, who had some choice words for me.

He'd watched a Durango PD cruiser, as well as a crime tech van, pull up outside my trailer and had been worried.

He'd apparently gone out there demanding to know what was going on and was intercepted by Keith Blackfoot, who assured him I was all right.

He was still pissed, though.

"You better," he grumbles. "About had another heart attack."

A pissed-off Edward apparently doesn't hold back punches either. Ouch.

"If I have a chance, maybe I'll pop in this week. Hopefully things can go back to normal soon." He harrumphs in response so I add, "Be nice to Hattie, will you?"

"Pain in my ass, that woman is."

"Edward..." I scold him.

"All right, all right, don't get yer panties in a bunch."

Before I have a chance to answer, he's already hung up. He never said anything about my real identity, which I assume means Keith kept that part to himself. I'm thankful for that, because it's something I'd like to address myself, but my neighbor doesn't give me the chance. Old coot.

I already cleared the rest of the week with my manager at the store. To say he wasn't happy would be an understatement. He mentioned Ted had taken my early morning shift and it would be his choice if he wanted to keep it or not. That would be a real bummer, because I like that early shift, but there's nothing I can do about it now.

The only other call to make is to the shelter. More guilt, because I know Margaret is probably shorthanded.

I'm in the kitchen, grabbing a glass of water, when I hear a sound from the front door. Just a slight rustle. Kyle is back already? He's barely been gone ten minutes. But when I hear nothing else, I dismiss it and dial the shelter. Margaret answers right away.

"How are things?"

"Peachy. Critters miss you, though. Feeling any better?"

Yup, there's the guilt.

"Actually, I lied about that. I haven't been ill, but I'm having some personal issues I'm trying to deal with."

"Who do I have to beat up?" she says without hesitation.

"I wish I knew."

"That doesn't sound good."

"It's a little troubling. Remember my car was vandalized? Well, that wasn't an isolated incident. More stuff has happened, someone's been inside my place."

"The fuck?"

Margaret's vehement response startles me, almost making me snicker but I forge on instead.

"Anyway, I'm trying to lay low for a bit—"

"You're coming to stay with me."

"That's kind of you, but—"

"No arguments," she barks.

"Margaret, I'm already staying with Sumo. Remember Blue's partner?"

"The hottie EMT, yeah. Good. Hope you're getting yourself some."

This time I don't hold back my laugh.

"Not gonna answer that, but I am going to need a few more days to sort this out."

"Call the cops is what you oughta be doing."

"They know. They're on it."

It takes me another few minutes to reassure her I'm in good hands, and no, I don't want to borrow her semi-automatic for safety. *Jesus.*

I hear the beep for the washer, put my phone down, and go to switch the loads. Elena had put their sheets and towels in the washer before she left. I put those in the dryer and turn it on, but when I'm stuffing the next load in the washer, something hits me from behind.

"Annie! Annie?"

I swing around just in time to catch Daisy when she jumps up again.

"Hey, girl," I coo at her before calling out to Kyle, "I'm in here!" His face is unnaturally pale when I meet him in the kitchen. "What's wrong? The dog's being funny too."

He holds up his finger, pulling his phone from his pocket and thumbing in a number before putting it to his ear. Then he crooks that finger and motions me closer.

"Tony? Yeah, I need you to come to my place. Someone was here."

What? Here?

Kyle takes a step closer, reaches for my hand and yanks me close. His arm tightens almost painfully around me.

"She's here, she's fine. Right."

The next moment he throws the phone on the counter and wraps his other arm around me too.

"What's going on?"

It's not just the phone call that has my anxiety soaring; it's the tension coming off Kyle in waves.

"Tony is on his way," he rumbles, but says nothing else.

"That doesn't help me." I try moving back from him a little, but he doesn't let go so I tilt my head back. I see a storm brewing in his brown eyes.

"Something was left behind." He swallows hard. "The dog was pulling to get home, almost dragging me along, and when I saw that bag hanging off the door..." He squeezes his eyes shut.

"Kyle, you're scaring me."

His eyes shoot open.

"Swear I'm not gonna let anything happen to you."

"What bag?" I push through the panic welling up.

"Someone hung a plastic bag on the door with a dead bird inside. While...you...were...inside."

He enunciates those last words very carefully through

clenched teeth, and I grab the back of his shirt in my fists, rising up on my toes.

"I'm fine," I assure him, fighting off the shakes that seem to have taken over my body.

"Thank fucking God." Daisy whimpers at our feet and Kyle lets go with one arm, reaching down to scratch her head. "You did good, Daisy-girl. Good dog."

When Tony walks in minutes later we are still in the kitchen, Kyle holding me close.

"You guys okay?"

"Not even close," Kyle answers, and I get the sense he's even more shaken than I am.

"Blackfoot is outside, looking at the evidence. Why don't we sit and you guys tell me what happened?"

While Kyle recounts Daisy's odd behavior and how she led him home, where he found the bag, I put on a pot of coffee. I need something to do with my hands otherwise I might start pulling at my hair.

The possibility my stalker had not only somehow tracked me to Durango, but was able to find me here at Kyle's house in a matter of a few days, has every muscle in me coiled with tension. My fight or flight response fully engaged. Had it been just me—had I kept my distance from people like I'd done for the better part of a year—I would've been gone already.

I lean on the edge of the sink and stare out into the backyard, thinking about these past weeks when I've been less than careful and unwittingly dragged people into this mess. I brought this creep to Kyle's doorstep. Literally. Thank God Bryce wasn't home.

A cold fist closes in my chest and I have to brace myself to stay upright.

Bryce.

"Annie? What is it?"

"Bryce," I squeak, swinging around to find both men looking my way, concerned. "Check on Bryce."

No sooner are the words out of my mouth and Kyle grabs his phone and dials.

"Brick? Bryce in your sight?"

I watch him like a hawk, waiting for his body language to tell me. When he closes his eyes and drops his head back, exhaling hard, the tight fist in my chest releases a little.

"Don't let him out of your sight. We may have some trouble here. I'll call you back." He hangs up and his eyes find mine. "He's fine. Brick will keep him safe up there."

"I shouldn't have stayed here."

"We had this discussion," he says, his face suddenly angry. "We're not having it again."

I don't get a chance to rebut because Keith walks in the kitchen, holding up what looks like a Ziploc bag with a piece of paper smudged with blood.

"What've you got?" Tony asks him.

"A note. Threat," Keith says, looking at me with gentle eyes, before putting the baggie on the kitchen island.

"What does it say?" I ask, even as I approach and stare at the torn piece of paper, smeared with the bird's blood.

No one says anything because we can all read.

How soon you forgot... You are special to ME.

19

Sumo

"What bird was it?"

The three of us turn to Annie.

"What do you mean?" Tony finally asks.

"In the bag; what kind of bird? Was it a finch?"

She appears to be staring in the distance, a vacant look on her face.

"Yeah."

The rumbled response comes from Keith and Annie nods.

"I figured. The other two were finches too. I didn't clue in until now." She whips her head around and looks at me. "He's reminding me what he did to David. Warning me he'll be coming after you." She pokes a hard finger in my chest. "See? I *told* you I shouldn't have stayed."

I open my mouth to disagree, but she is already moving to the stairs.

"She may be right," Tony suggests, grabbing my arm when I step around him to go after her.

"Are you for fucking real?" I snap. "Where is she going to go? You hypocrites wouldn't let your women out of sight and don't try to tell me anything else."

"Calm the fuck down," Tony barks. "I'm saying she may be right about you being in danger."

I shake off his hand and start walking to the stairs.

"I'll take that fucking chance," I fire off over my shoulder before I run up, two steps at a time.

She's shoving the few belongings she brought here in her bag, which I promptly pull out of her hands and toss aside.

"Hey! What are you doing?"

I grab her upper arms and stick my face in hers.

"What the hell are *you* doing? I thought we went over this, Annie? I thought you weren't going to run."

She struggles against my hold, but I'm not letting go. I can't.

"Are you stupid?" Her voice is panicked and pitched high. "He's gonna hurt you if I stay!"

"Calm down. No one's gonna hurt me, Annie." I try to calm my tone, but she's frantic. Tears are starting to roll down her flushed cheeks, and I recognize the wild look of hysteria in her eyes.

"You don't know that!" she screams in my face, now completely out of control. "David said that and he ended up dead! It's happening again."

She plants her face in my chest, sobbing uncontrollably as she sags through her knees. Not much I can do other than wrap my arms around her and hold her tight.

"It'll be okay, *Annie-chan*," I whisper, sitting down on the edge of the mattress and pulling her onto my lap.

Over her head I see Tony peeking around the door. I'm

sure both he and Keith heard her yelling. I give him a small nod to let him know we're good and he backs out of sight. Unfortunately, I'm pretty sure Annie will be mortified after.

Her body quakes with the force of her sobs and I try rocking her, mumbling nonsense. I'm almost at the point where I may have to consider sedating her, when she finally seems to calm a little.

"It was...h-hard when David d-died," she mutters, sniffling, "I don't think I'd s-survive if anything—"

I lightly shake her.

"I'm right here. I believe you, and so do the guys downstairs, but we need to give them a chance to figure this out. In the meantime, we'll do everything we can to stay safe. All of us."

Much calmer now, she nods and climbs off my lap, and I let her go.

"What about Bryce? What if he's in danger?"

Fuck.

"Let's go downstairs and see what options we have. For now, Bryce is safe up at the compound."

She winces when I mention going downstairs.

"I made a scene."

"Come here."

She turns to me, her face a mess from crying so hard, but still so beautiful. I hold out my hand and she grabs it, moving between my legs.

"I'm embarrassed."

"I know, but let's go down anyway. I bet it'll feel better if you take some control instead of waiting for the other shoe to drop."

"Fine," she grumbles without much conviction. "But I have to clean up first."

"Want me to go ahead or want me to wait?"

She leans down and brushes my lips with hers.

"Wait, if you don't mind."

A couple of minutes later she resurfaces, still a little blotchy but looking a lot more composed. I take her hand and together we head downstairs.

"I called Jasper Greene," Keith says, when we walk into the kitchen. He explains for Annie's purpose, "He's local FBI's techie. He's got time this afternoon to pop in and look at some security options."

"Good. I'd planned to look at that when I moved in, but never got around to it."

I'm glad the guys don't seem to pay special attention to Annie and simply continue where we left off.

"Also, I have a crime tech on the way to see if our guy left any prints behind."

Annie slips her hand from mine and walks to the tap, filling a glass with water, and taking a deep drink. Then she turns around.

"How did he find me?"

Her question hangs in the air for a minute before Tony answers.

"It's possible you were followed," he suggests.

She shakes her head. "No, I mean here...to Durango in the first place. How did he find me here?"

"I know we went over this before," Keith responds, "but are you sure there is no way word might have gotten out?"

"Yes, I'm sure. The only person who knew I was settling here was Erin. I didn't discuss it with anyone else. In fact, I didn't discuss leaving with anyone else. I took what I could in cash and not even my accountant would've found that out only after I was long gone."

"Okay, let's try this a different way," Tony suggests. "What do you have here that you had as Annabel Fiore. What did you bring with you? Your phone? Your laptop?"

Annie shakes her head again.

"No. Just some clothes, most of which I've since dropped off at Goodwill because they didn't fit with my life here. I uploaded my files to the cloud, cleared the memory on the laptop I had and trashed it, and I did the same with my phone. I bought this pay-as-you-go phone in Vegas, and the secondhand laptop here in Durango. I only use it to watch movies in bed. I don't go online much."

"Anything else? Jewelry someone gave you, any knickknacks?"

She's thinking, her head slightly bowed, her eyes not focused on anything. Then suddenly she straightens and heads for the living room where her purse is sitting on the couch. She grabs it and returns to the kitchen, dumping it upside down on the island, and starts ruffling through the content.

"What are you thinking?" I ask her.

"I don't know, but maybe there is something. I've had this purse for two years. My agent gave it to me for my birthday."

"Leave it," Keith says, putting a hand over hers. "Let's put it back in the purse and have the tech go over it."

I help her stuff her things back in the bag when I accidentally pick up the plastic baggie with the note, but before I can drop it, Annie grabs my wrist.

"What's that?" she asks, looking closer at the bag I'm holding.

Tony takes it from my hand and flattens it on the counter surface with the message down. A few scribbles are visible on the paper.

"We noticed that. Maybe it's part of a name or a logo, we'll look into it."

"It looks familiar," Annie says. "See this?" She traces her

finger over the curved shape. "It looks like the top of a stylized P."

"It does," Keith agrees. "Can you remember where you may have seen it?"

She's quiet for a moment, focused on the piece of paper before she looks up at him.

"Yeah, it's on the door panel of my neighbor's truck. Parsons Construction."

* * *

Annie

Both detectives and the crime scene tech have left, taking that note, the dead bird, and my purse with them. They'd found a small tracker in the lining.

I shiver, the idea I carried that thing everywhere with me, without knowing whoever is doing this may have known all along where I was, makes me sick. Tony and Keith didn't say much except they'd see if they could trace it. All I can do is wait, which is making me antsy.

Kyle is outside with the FBI tech, who came by to install a few small cameras outside as part of a security system, and I'm standing here in the kitchen, working on a batch of cinnamon rolls. When I'm done with those, I think I'll make some of those Portuguese tarts I introduced Kyle to. I may well be baking into the night, but if I don't do something with my hands I will go nuts.

I snort at myself. I'm pretty sure I'm already well off my rocker; I really lost it earlier. Heck, I scared myself and I'm still shaky.

As soon as I slide the cinnamon buns in the oven and clean my hands, I grab my phone and dial Erin.

"Middle of the afternoon, odd time for you to call me," she answers with. "Are you okay?"

I flop down on the couch and pull my legs up underneath me.

"I had a meltdown."

It's not the first time I call Erin to talk me down—we've been there for each other for years—but the last time I had to call on her was after receiving the news David had died.

"You did? What happened?" I give her the details, up to and including the point where I screamed in Kyle's face. "I totally freaked out on him."

"And how did he react?"

I look out the doors to the deck where the man we're talking about is just peeking in. I wave at him and he gives me a thumbs-up.

"Put me on his lap and held on."

It's quiet for a moment, and then she says, in a thick voice, "I love that for you."

"I do too, but I'm telling you now, I don't think I'll survive if anything happened to him because of me. I'm so scared."

"That's it, I'm calling in—"

"No need, Erin. The troops have already rallied. Durango PD *and* the FBI."

She falls quiet again but I can hear her thinking, so I wait her out.

"That's good, honey," she finally says softly. "Except for that creep making himself known, these are all good things, so what has you so freaked out?"

"I'm scared for him: Sumo...Kyle." She makes an encouraging sound and I know she's seeing right through me and knows that's not the full picture. "And I'm scared because...I don't know what the future looks like."

"Oh, Annie, have a little faith. I know you've lived a

carefully controlled life, and I get you feel like you're free-falling, but trust me when I say it can be a beautiful thing to let go. Trust there is someone who will steady you when you stumble."

That's the crux, isn't it? Here I am, almost forty-five years old, with only an abandoned acting career to my name. The life I've made here is already much more valuable to me than the one I left behind, and I'm afraid of losing that, afraid of losing the people in it.

"I haven't even told him," I confess.

"You've had other things on your mind," she excuses me like a friend would. "Are you eating?"

"Yes."

"Regularly?"

"Yes."

"You'll find the right time, but, Annie, I wouldn't be surprised if he already knows."

"You think?"

She chuckles softly. "Girl, you could've started eating a large pizza for breakfast, lunch, and dinner daily since I last saw you, and you'd still blow away on a stiff wind. You've spent almost a week in the man's house so I'm assuming he's seen you eat, and, honey, he's an EMT."

She makes a good point. David was always pushing me to eat more, but Kyle never does that. He doesn't even question the fact I rarely eat anything of the desserts I make every night.

She's right, he probably already knows.

We end the call with promises to be in touch, when the oven timer goes off. I get up to check the oven just as the door slides open and Kyle sticks his head in.

"Are those cinnamon buns?"

He steps inside, Jasper right behind him, sniffing the air.

"Damn, that smells good."

"I'm just pulling them out of the oven, they'll need to cool off a little before I can ice them."

Kyle is already pulling plates down from the cupboard.

"I don't need icing. You?" he asks the other man, who makes himself comfortable at the island.

"Hell no. Bring it on."

Barely two minutes out of the oven and already two grown men are burning their faces on the hot cinnamon buns.

"Save some for Bryce and his friends."

"Shit," Kyle looks at the kitchen clock. "We should probably head up there."

Ten minutes later, we're heading up to the Arrow's Edge compound, an overnight bag for Bryce and a tray of cinnamon buns on the back seat. Kyle had decided earlier, at Tony's suggestion, to see if his son could stay at the compound for one or two nights. Long enough for Jasper to get the security system installed and for Keith and Tony to track Will Parsons down. My new neighbor is currently at the top of their list, even though I'd never seen the man before he moved in.

The cameras they installed are supposed to be monitored by Jasper, who should be able to see anyone approaching the house, and Keith had promised regular police drive-bys.

I can't even begin to process the difference in the response from law enforcement here, as compared to the apathy I encountered in LA. I guess in part because they all seem to know Kyle, but I also have a feeling, here in Durango, people look after their own. What chokes me up is after only living here for a year, I seem to have been embraced as one of theirs. It gives me a strong sense of belonging I don't think I've felt since leaving home twenty-some years ago.

* * *

"You sit by me."

The black woman introduced to me as Lisa—who seems to rule the roost inside the clubhouse—indicates the chair next to her at the massive dining table. Kyle takes the chair on the other side of me.

I first realized I'd forgotten about my contacts when Brick mumbled, "Well, I'll be damned," as he stared at me, walking into the garage ahead of Kyle. He didn't say anything else, but did invite us into the clubhouse to meet Lisa. She insisted we stay for dinner, and one glance at Bryce's pleading eyes had us accept.

"Gotta say," Lisa says in a low voice, leaning toward me. "Never thought I'd be breaking bread with a celebrity." She catches my eyes darting over to the bar and quickly adds, "Don't worry, only reason these Neanderthals have their eyes on you is because it's been a while since they've seen a new pretty face at the table."

The Neanderthals she's referring to are a handful of rough-looking men at the bar, all focused this way.

"I'm guessing they're not much for daytime TV?"

Her responding laugh has more than just my head turn her way. It turns the rather stern-faced woman warmly vibrant and infinitely beautiful. Brick, the gray-bearded, gruff-looking mechanic definitely notices too. He's sitting across from us, flanked by a couple of the teens I saw with Bryce earlier on one side, and two younger kids I understand to be Lisa's on the other.

Dinner is a lively event here. The kids chatter, especially Kiara, the little girl who doesn't at all seem

impressed or intimidated by all the testosterone repre-
sented, and is so busy talking, she has to be reminded
several times to eat.

The food is the kind that sticks to your ribs and is absolutely delicious, which means I'm struggling to finish
what's in front of me. Lisa—who is a gorgeously rounded
woman—raises an eyebrow when she notices my plate.

"Dinner is incredible, I'm just not a big eater."

"Hmm-hmm," she hums, keeping that eyebrow high.

"She makes killer dessert, though," Bryce announces
loudly, just as Kyle puts a hand on my leg under the table.

"He's right." His fingers give my knee a quick squeeze.

My knights in shining armor.

Lisa doesn't look convinced, but after a few of the kids
clear the table and everyone digs into the cinnamon buns,
she seems to change her mind.

"Dayum," is all she says, but I get the sense coming from
her it's high praise.

"Ready to go?" Kyle asks not much later.

The kids are hanging around on a large sectional at the
back of the cavernous space, watching something on TV.
Brick has joined the other men at the bar, and I just helped
Lisa clean up in the kitchen.

"Sure."

I'm not actually all that sure. As unfamiliar as the clubhouse is, I feel oddly safe here and sense Bryce will be too.

"Hey, kid," Kyle calls out, and I snicker when at least
three heads turn around.

"May wanna be a little more specific," I tease him.

"Bryce, we're leaving," he tries again.

His boy gets up and ambles this way, his teenage
swagger a lot more confident than when I first met him.

"Cool."

"You've got your phone?"

"Yeah."

"And you're okay spending a little time here?"

"Yeah."

"Okay," Kyle says, not getting much more out of the kid. "I'll give you a call in the morning."

"Cool."

"I know you have more words in your vocabulary, kiddo," I jump in. "I heard them myself. You should give them a try, for variation."

He ducks his head to hide his grin. Little smart-ass.

"Give me a hug."

I already have my arms around him and give him a firm squeeze before I let go.

"See ya, Annie."

My face splits into a wide grin.

"You too, brat."

Then he turns to Kyle and holds out his hand, which his father grabs. They do one of those man hugs, which is really more of a shoulder bump, and I swallow the sudden lump in my throat.

"Talk to you tomorrow, Son."

The flash in Bryce's eyes is gone as quickly as it appeared, but I saw it.

"Later, Pop."

The kid casually turns on his heel and saunters back to his buds.

I can barely hear his father's muttered response.

"Well, I'll be damned."

20

Sumo

"I'm going to take a nap."

I tilt my head back and look up at Annie, who is leaning over the back of the couch.

It's been a lazy day and a half with little action, other than Jasper's installation of the alarm system on windows and doors and linking everything to an app on my phone. I can pull up a schematic that shows which locks are engaged and which aren't, and I can pull up the feed from any of the three cameras installed on the outside of the house.

"Kiss me," I tell her, cupping the back of her head when she bends down. When I let her up for air I ask, "Want me to wake you up?"

"Please. Don't let me sleep more than an hour or so, or I won't sleep tonight."

"You know, I've got ways to help you with that, right?"

She doesn't answer me but grins as she heads up the stairs.

I'm not surprised she needs a nap. We were up late and she was already elbow-deep in pastry dough when I walked into the kitchen this morning.

Last night Annie helped me go through the last of the moving boxes I hauled in from the garage. Mostly books and medical journals, but there'd also been a few photo albums my mom brought over years ago. She'd fawned over my preteen pictures. I was a skinny, knobby kid, with teeth too big for my face, but Annie thought I'd looked adorable. Her warm smile had done more to heal the childhood bullying I'd been subjected to than the years of playing class clown, which eventually garnered me some friends in high school.

At the back of one of those had been the architect's sketch I had done for the mountain home I'd hoped of building. I found myself talking about my dream house, the piece of property I'd been eyeing just a few miles up the mountain from here, and the years of saving my hard-earned money, which had received a serious dent after sending over fifty grand for Bryce's medical bills. Something, by the way, I don't regret for a minute.

That got us on the topic of my son, and Annie brought up what he'd said when we left the club the night before. That one word had a bigger impact on me than I would've expected. It's an acknowledgment I don't really deserve, because I've done nothing to earn it.

I flip off the TV I'm no longer watching and get up to let Daisy—who's scratching at the back door—out for a pee. Then I grab my phone, a cold one from the fridge, adding beer to the whiteboard, and follow the dog outside.

The beer is nice and cold on what is a pretty hot day and I down half the bottle. Then I set it on the railing and head down the steps to toss a ball the dog brings me. She needs the exercise, but I'm not going to walk her if it means leaving Annie alone. The last few days we've done her walks together.

Daisy clearly indicates she's had enough when instead of dropping the ball at my feet; she ignores the ball and lies down in the grass. I head to my beer and take a swig when Daisy starts growling, her head up and focus on the house. I'm about to go inside when she suddenly jumps up and sets off around the side of the house, barking furiously.

My phone buzzes in my pocket and I put it to my ear without looking.

"Can you grab your dog before she eats through your gate to get to me?"

"Tony?"

"That's me."

I tuck my phone away and walk around the side of the house to find Daisy with her front legs up against the gate.

"It's okay, girl, it's just Tony."

I grab her collar and pull her back, unlatching the gate.

"She's fierce," he says, holding out his hand for her to sniff and she immediately starts wagging her tail.

"She's been on edge. Last night we took her for a walk and she almost went after a guy jogging along the river."

"Probably picking up on your tension," he suggests, as we walk into the backyard.

"Where's Annie?"

"She just went down for a nap. Why? Did you want her?"

He shakes his head. "No. It's probably not a bad idea I talk to you first."

"Wanna beer while you talk?"

"Little early. I'll take water if you have it."

I go inside and grab a water for him and a fresh beer for me. I don't give a damn about the time.

"So what's up? Got some news for us?"

He cracks the top on the water bottle and takes a sip.

"We're looking for Will Parsons. According to the old man next to Annie's trailer, he hasn't seen the pickup truck in the driveway for a couple of days. He was able to describe Parson's company logo, which matches what Annie detailed, but he'd seen Parson stick them on. Said they were those magnetic decals you can get.

"I talked to the park manager, who was able to give me a phone number but it went straight to voicemail. The manager said last time he saw Parsons, he mentioned something about a mountain property north of Lemon Reservoir he'd be working on. Reception can be tricky up there."

"Convenient," I mumble, putting the bottle to my lips to take a sip.

"Also," Tony says, ignoring me. "Annie's agent is a piece of work."

"Did you talk to him?"

"No, but we finally got those police reports from LA, and received a call from the detective on file shortly after. He wanted to know what we wanted with the reports and when I told him, he was upset. Turns out her agent, Miles Coxwell, had told the detective Annie had a history of mental health problems. He had evidence she'd spent a month in a mental health facility in Arizona the year before. Said she was on Prozac and seeing a psychiatrist regularly. That she was unstable."

A surge of anger on Annie's behalf has me on my feet so abruptly, Daisy—who'd been dozing in front of me—jumps up, suddenly alert.

"That's bullshit."

"Sumo," Tony says in a calming tone. "He was shown documents, confirmed their legitimacy. He said the guy was convincing, so he brushed off Annie's complaints as another Hollywood nutcase creating drama where there was none. He says he hadn't thought about the case until he saw our request for the reports."

"He's wrong." I'm agitated, pacing back and forth; until Daisy's confused whimper has me bend down to scratch her behind the ears. "She's not some mental case."

"You know he's wrong, and I know it, but he went with the word of a reputable Hollywood agent. Look," he adds. "It wouldn't have been the first time a celebrity creates hype to boost their career."

I hear a car door close and an engine start up, as I let my eyes drift to the river and try to process the information. The Annie I know is happy baking pastries for a grocery store. She sits on a concrete floor reading books to traumatized dogs. She's far from an attention-seeker. On the contrary.

"That's not Annie."

"Clearly," he agrees immediately. "Which brings us to Coxwell."

I turn around, leaning against the railing.

"Why?"

"Good question."

"I don't get what he has to gain by derailing that investigation," I think out loud. "Unless he was responsible in the first place."

Tony drains his bottle and stands up, just as my phone starts buzzing in my pocket.

"That's what we're looking to find out."

* * *

Annie

"...evidence she'd spent a month in a mental health facility in Arizona the year before. Said she was on Prozac and seeing a psychiatrist regularly. That she was unstable."

I fight to keep the tears at bay as I jam my keys in the ignition. I'll cry later.

I'd just walked into the kitchen for something to drink when I heard those words. They knocked the wind right out of me.

Unstable.

That label I'd heard one too many times triggered my feet into moving toward the front door. I'd grabbed the plastic bag that now held the contents of my purse, and snuck out the front door.

I'm on automatic pilot, navigating the roads, the fear for my stalker drowned out by the pain of betrayal. Again.

My God, just when I'd started to believe there might be light at the end of my tunnel, I find myself sucked back into the shadows.

Maybe they're right. Maybe I am unbalanced, why else would I find myself turning toward the one place I knew I'd find no judgment?

* * *

Sumo

I pull my phone from my pocket when it starts buzzing for the second time.

In front of me Tony opens the gate and I grab hold of Daisy's collar while I answer.

"Hey, Jasper," I answer, having spotted his name on the screen.

"Everything okay?" Jasper asks.

"Yeah, Ramirez is just leaving, why?"

Tony stops and turns around.

"Because I just watched Annie get in her car by herself and drive off."

"What?"

Worry must be clear on my face because Ramirez takes a step closer, but I brush past him and rush around the corner of the garage.

Her car is missing from the driveway.

"How long?" I snap as Tony joins me, cursing under his breath when he sees the open space.

"Five minutes, maybe a few more. Did something happen? Are you sure you didn't piss her off?"

"I have no fucking clue," I tell him, at a complete loss.

Greene chuckles. "Welcome to the club."

"I've gotta go. I have to find her."

"Let me know."

I tuck my phone in my pocket and rush back into the yard with the dog on my heels. I hear Tony close the gate behind us before he follows me up the steps and inside. The first thing I notice is the City Market shopping bag she stuffed her wallet and things in is gone from the hall table.

"She took her shit," I mutter, before taking the stairs two at a time.

The bedroom looked like it did, the covers slightly rumpled where she must've lain down for her nap, but nothing else looks out of place. Even the bag with her clothes is still at the bottom of my closet. My eyes travel up to the gun safe I keep on the shelf. I'm not in the habit of carrying, but I do keep a gun in my bedroom. My fingers shake when I turn the tumblers on the lock and almost drop the clip when I try to load the weapon.

Tony is on the phone when I join him in the hallway downstairs, the gun feeling unnatural tucked in the back of my jeans.

"Okay, I'll head over there. You keep an eye out," I hear him say before hanging up.

I grab my own keys off the table and open the front door.

"Hang on," Tony calls out. "We're taking my patrol car."

I'm not going to argue. He can drive faster than I can without consequences.

"Where do you think she went?" he asks, sliding behind the wheel as I buckle myself in.

"Fuck, I hope to her trailer."

Tony starts driving at what is probably a decent clip but still not fast enough for me. Up ahead cars are waiting on the other side of the bridge for the light to turn and he's forced to slow down.

"You know," he says, glancing over at me. "It's possible she overheard me talking. Some of what I said would've sounded pretty damning without the proper context."

He's right. If all she heard was him talking about her questionable mental health...

"Fuck!"

I slam my fist on the dashboard, just as sirens sound from behind us. I turn my head to see the engine from Station 3—my own fire station—coming toward us. Tony veers his car toward the curb, like the other cars in front of us, to make room for the fire truck to pass.

I watch them round the traffic into the intersection where they turn right. Heading in the direction we were going. A deep sense of foreboding settles in my bones.

"Go after them."

Tony clearly had the same thought because he's already moving the cruiser around the car in front of us as he flicks on his lights and sirens.

My anxiety spikes when we get stuck in the middle of the intersection on a light change and Ramirez has to do some swift maneuvering to avoid a collision. Up ahead I just see the lights of the fire engine disappear and beyond that a dark plume of smoke curls up from the trees.

"They turned into the park," Tony announces in a flat voice.

The tires squeal as he makes the right turn, gravel flying when we hit the narrow road leading down to the trailers.

The path is blocked by the fire truck, and I vaguely notice my own team jumping down, even as I open my door.

"Sumo, wait!" Tony yells.

My feet are already moving around the truck in front of us, but come to a dead stop when I get a full view of what called them here.

Annie's trailer, fully engulfed in flames.

2 1

Sumo

"Stop!"

I vaguely register Cap's voice as I break into a run up the path. I have only one thought in mind and that is to get Annie out of there.

The heat from the flames shooting out of the busted living room window on the front singe the hair on my arms, but my eyes stay focused on the door at the side of the trailer.

My instincts engage and instead of kicking it in, I touch the knob first. Warm, but not hot. Just as I take a step back to aim my boot at the lock, strong arms band around me, dragging me back.

"What the fuck are you doing, Sumo?" Cap yells in my ear.

I struggle, but I stop when Tony steps into my sight.

"Jesus fucking Christ, man. Her car's not here. Look!"

I turn to find the carport I'm under empty.

* * *

In the past ten minutes since Tony dragged me away and ordered me to stay on this side of the road, I've watched Annie's home and belongings burn to the ground. I know my team did what they could, but other than making sure the fire wouldn't jump to the neighboring trailers by keeping those soaked, there wasn't a whole lot.

Luckily no one appeared to be home at Edward Shelby's place, or at Mrs. Sokoloff's next to him, and the rest of the row works during the day. A small crowd of onlookers gathered beside me and I try to ignore the snippets of gossip that filter my way.

"...only time I saw her was walking that fat little dog..."

"...something fishy. She never talked to anyone..."

I step away from the group; afraid I'll say or do something I'll regret.

Tony joins me.

"Did you try calling her?"

"No answer." I glance over at him. "What did you find out?"

"Fuck all." He runs an agitated hand through his hair. "Middle of the fucking day and no one saw a goddamn thing. Tell me how that's possible?"

"Well, if they approached from the back along the river and waited until Annie's neighbors were gone, no one would've seen anyone. At least not from the road."

"Let's go find her," he says before leading the way to his cruiser. "Where to?" he asks when I get in the passenger seat.

I've been agonizing for the past ten or so minute where else she might have gone. If she has friends outside of her elderly neighbors, she hasn't really mentioned them. The only other place she might...

"The shelter."

"Where?"

"The dog shelter near Walmart."

"Shit," he mutters, putting the cruiser in gear. "Shoulda thought of that."

While we drive I keep trying her phone, but I know if she's there, she'll likely be in the back with the dogs and have her phone in the desk drawer.

When Ramirez turns into the parking lot and I spot her car parked to the side, the knot I've had in my chest releases. I fucking hope she'll talk to me and let me explain, because I'm not looking forward to having to hurt her again with the news her trailer is gone.

"You're not getting out," Tony observes beside me.

"Fucking hate having to tell her she has nothing left but her car and what's at my place. That is, if she'll even talk to me."

"I'm coming in."

He starts getting out of the car but I stop him with a hand on his arm.

"Thanks, but I've got this."

If Annie has another breakdown, I don't want Tony to be there to witness it. Not because I'm afraid of what he'll think, but because I don't want Annie to be embarrassed again.

"Sure?"

"Yeah. Don't hang around for me. I'll give you a call later."

Like the first time I walked in here, no one is at the desk in the front office. I walk straight to the door leading to the kennels and peek through the window.

She's sitting cross-legged on the floor in front of the kennels with the Shepherd Lab mix, who'd taken a shine to Bryce, lying with his head on his legs beside her. She's reading from the book on her lap, one hand distractedly stroking the dog's fur.

"Oh hell to the no," I hear behind me.

I turn to find Margaret holding a carrying tray with two drinks in the one hand as the front door falls shut behind her.

"You are not coming in here making her cry again."

"I have no intention to," I assure her, but realize that may well be a lie when I tell Annie about her trailer. Margaret snorts, clearly not believing me. "I don't know what she told you but—"

"That girl doesn't tell me anything," she grumbles before waving a finger in my face. "But I have no doubt you had something to do with it. *Men.*"

"I think she overheard something that she misinter-preted. It's important I talk to her, Margaret."

She squeezes her watery eyes into slits and tries staring me down, but I don't budge.

Eventually she caves and hands me one of the drinks.

"Oh, fine. But if I see one tear on her."

"Fair warning, there may be tears. I've just come from a fire at her place. There's nothing left, Margaret."

Her face falls and she makes a sympathetic sound. Then she walks up to the small window and lifts up on her toes to see through.

"Well, son of a bitch."

* * *

Annie

As I'd hoped Margaret was here when I walked in, having allowed myself a good cry in the parking lot. She didn't ask any questions, just gave me a hug, accompanied by a muttered string of curses, and told me she'd listen if I was ready to talk.

When I mentioned I just needed some unconditional puppy love, she told me to 'have at it' and she'd be back with some drinks.

Hunter is a good one for judgment-free dog cuddles and all-in for sharing some loving. Out of habit I grab an old copy of *Watership Down* by Richard Adams and sit on the floor with him.

At some point I hear Margaret talking to someone in the front office and put the book down. Hunter whines when I get up, maybe realizing he's about to go back in the kennel. If it were up to me, I'd take him home; a dog this generous with his affection should be surrounded by people who can give it back. Instead he spends most of his time in a kennel while waiting for his owner to get back home.

I should check with Margaret to see what the news is on her.

"I'll be back in a bit," I promise him.

I'm just putting the latch on the gate when the door opens and *he* walks in. Tears instantly burn my eyes and I quickly avert them. I'm determined not to shed one—not in front of him—I'll save them for later.

"What do you want, Sumo?"

I hear his sharp intake of breath at my use of his nickname. It's easier; already detaching myself by using the name everyone calls him.

"*Annie-chan*, why did you run?" His voice is gentle, which makes it only more difficult to hold onto my determination not to show emotion. When I don't answer he prompts. "You don't have to say anything, Annie. I'll do the talking."

"Nothing to talk about." I find my voice and it sounds harsh, even to my own ears.

"I'm gonna say it anyway," he persists. "I know what you heard."

My body involuntarily jerks.

"I also know you didn't stay to hear all of it or you would've known neither Tony nor I agreed with those words quoted from the LAPD police report."

A spark of hope flares in my chest but still I force myself not to look up, even though I want to. I'm afraid all it will take is one look at those warm, brown eyes of his and I'll be utterly vulnerable and stripped raw.

"It was Miles Coxwell who convinced the officer on record that you were mentally unstable."

Now it's my turn to sharply suck air into my lungs and my eyes snap up. Sympathy is stamped all over his face, or is it pity?

"Miles? Why?" The words are out before I can check them, because I'm suddenly reminded of an argument I had with my agent before David died.

"They've been trying to get ahold of him to find out why, but haven't had much success."

"I may know," I share. "For the longest time he convinced me the notes and gifts were probably just an overzealous fan, but when they turned ugly, I told him I would file a report with police. He wasn't happy and strongly advised against it."

"But you did anyway."

Sympathy is replaced by clear appreciation in his eyes, encouraging me to go on.

"I did. I basically told him to fuck off when he suggested I was overreacting."

"Good for you." He takes a step closer and puts his hands loosely on my shoulders. "You did the right thing, but why would he be so set against it? Is there any way he could be responsible for sending them in the first place?"

I'd thought about that. After Keith found that tracker in my purse I'd wondered if it was Miles himself who'd put it there.

"I don't know," I tell him honestly. "I know at the time he was actively shopping me around for a movie role. He was determined to give my career a boost onto the big screen, before I was too old to fit the market."

That had been another difficult conversation, one that had brought home to me how many years I'd already invested in my character's life without having one of my own. I immediately started investing money for the rainy day I realized was probably coming sooner than I thought. Aging can be brutal in that industry.

"It's funny," I continue. "I remember when we were arguing about making a police report, he used that as an argument against it. Claiming I was a hard enough sell for the big screen without adding a police investigation to the mix." I snort at the irony. "I wasn't even interested in movies. Not anymore, that fire had already dulled when I discovered how unpleasant living in the public eye really is."

His hands slide up my shoulders until they brace my neck. He leans in and I automatically grab onto his wrists. A faint scent of smoke comes off his clothes.

"Are you good?"

"Good? No, I'm pissed as hell. At Miles," I quickly clarify when I catch the look on his face. Then I have to ask, "Do you believe me?"

"That you're pissed? Yeah, I would be too. But if you're asking me if I bought into that nonsense about you being mentally unstable." He brushes his nose against mine. "Not for a second."

I close my eyes and take a deep breath in before exhaling. In for a penny, in for a pound.

"Even if it wasn't all a lie? I *was* hospitalized, and I was also on Prozac."

He brushes his thumbs over my cheekbones.

"So has more than half the population at some point or other. You'll tell me about it when you're ready."

Overcome with emotion, I swallow hard and focus on his strong chin. I suddenly feel the need to lay it all out on the table. Make it so there is nothing lurking in the shadows between us. I want him to be the one who sees every part of me: every flaw, every failure, every fault.

"I want to tell you."

He presses a kiss to my forehead before leveling his eyes with mine.

"Fuck, I hate this but, *Annie-chan*, you gotta brace yourself, because first I have something to tell you."

* * *

Sumo

She's killing me.

Those clear blue pools lift up, allowing me to see the hope shimmering under the surface. I hate I have to put hurt and fear there again.

"Brace myself?"

I nod. "When Tony and I were on our way to your place, we were passed by a fire truck." I can feel the muscles in her neck go rigid. "Baby, your trailer was on fire. There's nothing left but part of the frame."

"Edward?"

I close my eyes and rest my forehead to hers. It

shouldn't surprise me, but it does; her first thought is for her elderly neighbor, not herself.

"He wasn't home. No one was on that side of the road. The trailers on either side of yours may have a little water damage but that's all."

She abruptly pulls out of my hold and turns to the door.

"Where are you going?"

"Making sure he and Hattie are okay. They'll be worried."

I just manage to catch the door before it slams shut behind her. She's already grabbing her bag from the desk drawer.

"All made up?" Margaret wants to know.

"My house burned down," Annie announces without even looking at her boss. "I've gotta check on my neighbors."

Margaret's big eyes turn on me.

"*That's* what took you fifteen minutes to tell her? I thought you'd have her up against a kennel by now."

"I'm sorry, we've gotta go," Annie says, seemingly oblivious to what Margaret just said. Or maybe she's just ignoring her.

But Margaret isn't done. She fires her parting shot when I pass her to follow Annie out the door.

"Boy, you need some better material."

22

Annie

"Well, blow me sideways."

We're sitting outside Edward's trailer, watching the fire inspector go through what is left of my trailer. I expected to be more upset than I am, but the longer I look at it, the angrier I get. Kyle had insisted on driving, and I'd taken the opportunity to build up a decent head of steam on the way already.

Hattie noticed my eyes immediately and I just finished filling them in on my identity and how I ended up here. I'm pissed enough I want to draw this creep out from under whatever rock he's hiding, so I'm not hiding anymore.

"Annabel Fiore? Who the hell is that?" Edward asks annoyed.

When we first got here, he mentioned he'd already been on the phone with my landlord and his former neighbor. Something I probably should've done right away. I'll give him a call when we get home and sort out insurance.

"An actress, dipstick," Hattie answers, giving him the pointy side of her elbow. She turns to me. "Mind you, I've only seen your show a few times, but I read the *National Enquirer* religiously and I love awards shows."

She gives me an eyebrow wiggle.

Oh boy. I'm trying to remember some of the stuff that was said about me in the gossip rags over the years. There wasn't much, but I distinctly recall an article about me having an affair with Jason Bateman about ten years ago. A total fabrication, because Jason was happily married with kids, but we happened to be seated side by side at a fundraiser when someone snapped a few pictures and voila, a story was born.

"Don't believe all you read," I warn her. "And no; at no time did I sleep with Jason Bateman."

I also remember how excited Miles had been to see the article and was disappointed when I refused to capitalize on that lie.

"How come I've never seen you in anything?" Edward wants to know, but before I can answer Hattie is on the case.

"Because you only watch John Wayne movies, you old geezer. She wasn't but a blink in her daddy's eye back then."

"Blackfoot," I hear Kyle say beside me, and I look over to see Keith walking this way.

"Folks," he says when he approaches. The man is large and intimidating to look at, but he's been very kind and sensitive with me.

"Hey, Keith."

His eyes come to me.

"How are you holding up?"

"I'm okay," I tell him honestly.

"The fire inspector says he's almost done and then you can go through if you want, although I'm afraid there isn't a lot salvageable."

"I figured. I didn't have much that can't be replaced, though."

There wasn't. A few odds and ends that I bought over the last year, but most of the stuff that has sentimental value is locked safely in a storage unit back in LA. Any pictures I had up—and there weren't very many—I have digital copies of on my Cloud.

Keith nods and then says, scanning our small group, "Can I borrow you for a sec?"

"Sure."

I get up and start following him into the street when I notice Kyle getting up too. I send him a little smile, glad for the support. The detective shoots him a brief look but doesn't hesitate to cut to the chase.

"Preliminary conclusion from the inspector is arson, not that it's a surprise." The thought this might be accidental never even entered my mind. I immediately had assumed it was deliberate. "Unfortunately, despite it being the middle of the day there were no witnesses."

"So he must've approached from the river side," Kyle volunteers.

"Looks like," Keith agrees. "Now, Ramirez is back at the station trying to get a bead on Parsons. I asked around here to see if anyone had seen him recently, but no one has in the past few days. We'll continue to follow that lead."

"What about my agent?" At his raised eyebrow I clarify, "I'm aware of the LA police report."

"I see. Well, he's not an easy person to get ahold of. I left a few messages and am hoping someone in his office will get back to me. Otherwise, we'll have to call in a favor from the LAPD to head over there."

"What about the note and the evidence from the trailer? Any luck there?"

Keith turns to Kyle. "Nothing yet but DNA can take a while, depending on how busy the lab is."

His statement startles me and I'm almost afraid to ask. "DNA?"

I can see the *oh-shit* moment stamped all over the detective's face before he drops his eyes to the tips of his boots.

"We found some biological evidence in your trailer, as well as on the note."

"What biological evidence?" I ask, even though I don't want to hear the answer. I'm afraid I can guess and it has bile surging up my esophagus.

"We found semen on your bedspread and some was dried up on the note left at Sumo's place as well."

Air explodes from my lungs like I've been punched in the gut. Beside me Kyle lets out a string of loud curse words, and I barely register the detective firmly cautioning him. My mind is trying to visualize my bedspread, and I only now realize it must have been missing the last time I was here picking up some clothes. I hadn't even noticed.

It's funny how one piece of information can force you to look at things in a different light. As I'm processing, my eyes drift to the Matrix.

"The car," I mutter.

"What?"

I turn to Kyle and grab his arm, curling my nails into his skin.

"The car. He was in my car."

I experience a full body shiver at the idea I've been driving around with... I can't even bring myself to think it.

Kyle pulls me to his chest, while Keith Blackfoot starts barking orders into his phone.

"What's wrong?" I hear Edward, who walks up to see what the fuss is about.

I tune them out, focusing on Kyle's familiar scent and safe arms. I'm not an idiot, I know I haven't just been stalked, but that son of a bitch actually marked me. He has pulled me into some kind of sick, twisted power game, in a way that scares me more than the dead birds. I almost feel violated in physical sense.

Suddenly I have the strong urge to scrub him from my skin.

"I need a shower."

* * *

Sumo

"Stay."

I freeze in my tracks, turning back to where Annie is tearing off her clothes in my bathroom.

Once the tow truck arrived to take her car to the forensics lab, Blackfoot drove us back home and Annie ran straight upstairs. Worried, I followed close behind until I saw she was turning on the shower.

Apparently she doesn't want me to leave, though.

"Please," she adds, her eyes only briefly on me as she strips naked.

I notice the clear outline of her floating ribs as she reaches up to pull the shirt over her head. Annie is small, although I wouldn't go so far as to call her skinny; she's too muscular for that. Her breasts are no more than a handful and her hips only flare slightly, but somehow she's the sexiest woman I've ever seen.

And I've seen a few in my lifetime in all shapes and sizes. I've never had a particular preference like some men I know—have sampled a wide variety—but I'm definitely hooked on Annie's shape.

If not for the reason she is violently scrubbing her skin with soap, I'd strip down and join her.

"Are you coming?" she asks, sticking her head around the shower door.

It's as if she heard me.

"Are you sure?" I want to know, but I'm already kicking off my shoes and unbuttoning my fly.

She raises an eyebrow and then disappears into the steam, leaving the shower door open. I drop my clothes in the same pile as hers and step inside.

"I've been thinking," she says, sliding her hands up my chest. "I've already let this man take enough from me, lived in fear long enough. I'm done with that."

She hooks her arms around my neck as my hands land on her hips.

"I won't give him another minute. What's more," she adds. "I don't want you to either. There's a security system on the house, the police are out there doing their job, so what do you say we go and pick up your son and bring him home? You can have some quality time before you're back at work next week, and the two of you can teach me how to play *Call of Duty*."

I pull her closer until my cock brushes her belly, and bend my head to touch my nose to hers.

"I like the sound of that."

"I can tell."

She grins up at me and I'm amazed, with the day she's had, there's a teasing twinkle in her eyes. I didn't expect to see this core of steel after the nonstop hits she incurred today, but I'm looking at it.

"You amaze me, you know that?"

Her smile turns lascivious as she rubs her wet body against mine, eliciting a pained groan from my lips.

"Good to know," she whispers. "Even better if you showed me."

She doesn't need to tell me twice.

I slant my mouth over hers and plunge my tongue deep as she hooks one of her legs around the back of mine, her invitation clear. I cup her ass in my hands and lift her up, not hard to do, since she barely weighs anything. Both her legs wrap around my hips as I line up my cock at her entrance.

The feel of her slick skin against mine, and her heat kissing the most sensitive part of me, it takes everything out of me not to surge inside her tight channel. I rip my mouth from hers.

"Condom," I whisper against her lips as her eyes blink open.

"I'm safe. I've had some health issues."

I pull my head back a fraction and read her expression.

"You sure? I get tested regularly."

"Trust me," she whispers and I get lost in her eyes.

I'm barely able to say, "I do," when she rocks her hips, taking the very tip of me inside her.

What little control I had disappears as I press her back to the tiles and plant myself to the root. Her head falls back, mouth open, as I pull out before surging deep again. It's a struggle to stay standing when I lose myself in the punishing rhythm.

"So close..." she mumbles, her fingers clawing against my scalp. "Kyle, I'm so close."

Afraid I'll drop her if I let one hand go, I encourage her to use her own.

"Finger to your clit, baby," I groan, my hips already moving erratically as my balls draw tight to my body.

One of her hands slips between our bodies and I can feel her fingers working furiously where we are joined. The next moment she's bucking in my arms, and my own yell of release drowns out her cries.

When I catch my breath, I pull out and let her slide down my body until she finds her feet, but I don't let go.

"Health issues?" I prompt her. I may have been too eager to inquire before, but I still would like to know.

"Can we dry off first?" she asks, looking uncomfortable.

Five minutes later she takes a seat on the edge of the bed, slipping her feet into a pair of Chucks.

"I have an eating disorder."

I finish buttoning up my jeans and perch on the edge of the dresser. It doesn't come as a surprise.

"Okay."

She seems a little startled by that simple word.

"I've always had a love-hate relationship with food, and with my body, even before I started acting. You know what it's like, it's all about the image." She bends over to tie her laces, although I suspect it's more to hide her face from me. "When I passed thirty, people were telling me I'd better start watching myself because the camera adds extra pounds."

"I've heard that. Always thought it was a myth," I tell her and she lifts her eyes, shaking her head.

"It's true, actually. I did stupid things to my body, took diuretics, laxatives, did cleanses until that was all I was putting into my system. Whenever I wasn't on set, I was trying to burn calories. Treadmill, running, jumping rope, whatever I could. My hair started falling out, my skin was awful. One thing led to another, and to another, until I was so sick I could barely muster the energy to get out of bed. One day, Miles showed up and found me passed out beside the toilet. He called an ambulance."

She shakes her head again, this time at herself.

"Anorexia nervosa."

"Yeah, and it was ugly. The producers of the show gave me the option to either get myself into an inpatient treatment facility, or I was out of a job."

"The hospital stay that son of bitch Coxwell told the cops about?"

"Yup."

"And I'm guessing the Prozac was part of your treatment?"

"Right again," she says with a fake smile, trying to make light of the topic, but I see the uncertainty in her eyes. "Anyway, lots of testing was done during that time and they discovered I was sterile."

"Pituitary gland failure?" There are lots of medical problems that arise from starving yourself and that is one of them. Luckily reversible in most patients.

"They suspect it was preexisting. Especially since over time the outcome remained the same—as did my depression. That's why I was on antidepressants for a few years."

Her agent is even more of a piece of shit than I already considered him to be, and I feel anger stirring my blood.

"Come here."

"Why?"

"*Annie-chan*, come here."

When she's close enough, I pull her between my legs, trapping her in my arms.

"I'm not a violent man," I confess. "I'm supposed to be a healer, but right now if that fucking agent of yours was here, it would take an army to stop me from ripping him apart, limb from limb."

She drops her forehead against my shoulder and leans her weight into me as she chuckles softly.

"My knight in shining armor," she mumbles, humor lacing her voice.

"Damn fucking right I am."

23

Annie

"Behind you!"

I almost jump off the couch when Bryce yells out. I immediately turn around, but it's too late...I already see the gun flash.

It's quiet for a moment as my final life drains out of me, but then the controller is plucked from my hands.

"Afraid you're a lost cause, babe," Kyle says on my other side, grinning.

"I thought I was getting better." Bryce snorts, not too subtly. "Hey," I tell him. "I took that one guy down"

"He probably just collapsed laughing," the kid mumbles under his breath, and Kyle cracks up.

"Fine." I get up and turn my back to the screen, facing father and son. "I see how it is. I hope both of you memorized the taste of those apple turnovers from this morning, because I've decided to take a break from baking. Unless either of you would like to try?"

I grin wide as I walk up the stairs from the basement, leaving the sound of their pitiful lamenting behind me. In the kitchen, I tackle the breakfast dishes I stacked in the sink. There's a dishwasher, but I find hand-washing dishes therapeutic.

It's been a great couple of days, with the three of us mostly putzing around the house, except when taking Daisy for her walks. We do that together as well. The guys have tried to teach me that stupid game, but I think I'll just watch them play, because it's giving me heart palpitations.

We've spent time in the kitchen, the guys watching me bake, and me enjoying a glass of wine while the two of them cook. We've watched a few movies, made a few calls, and spent some time talking. Mostly it was Kyle and I sharing stories for Bryce's benefit—he still hasn't opened up much about his life—but it feels like we've bonded.

What we haven't done is talk about my stalker, and we also haven't seen or heard from the Durango PD. A welcome break, but I don't delude myself into thinking it's anything other than a short reprieve.

Today is Sunday, and it's time we figure out how to go forward from here. Kyle's first shift back starts tomorrow at seven in the morning and I'm going to have to face going back to work at this time is probably not the smartest move. I've given up on wearing my contacts, or my glasses. Who I am is bound to come out sooner than later, given the increasing number of people who know.

It's not like I need the money, which is another thing I should talk to Kyle about, paying my way. I have a feeling we might have some differing ideas on that.

And then of course, Bryce. He's fourteen, so technically he doesn't need a babysitter, but he also can't be expected to look after himself. Not in a strange town, and certainly not with that son of a bitch still out there.

"Were you serious?" Bryce asks, as he grabs a towel to dry. I hadn't even heard him come up.

"About?" I ask innocently.

"Taking a break from baking? Because I wouldn't mind learning. I pick things up pretty quick."

I grin, shooting him a wink.

"Do you know what monkey bread is?"

"My grandma used to make it when I stayed with her."

I glance over at him and notice Kyle has come up and now stands frozen behind his son. As far as I know, this is more than the boy has shared of his life before he came here.

"Wanna help me make some?" I ask to break through the suddenly uneasy look on the kid's face.

"Sure," he says, obviously relieved.

"There's a bag of flour in the pantry and a jar labeled yeast. Grab those for me?"

The moment he disappears I turn to Kyle and mouth, *"Progress."*

Twenty minutes later, Bryce is watching Kyle get his hands dirty to knead the dough. I'm oiling a bowl for it to rise in when one of the phones we left to charge on the counter rings.

"Bryce, you wanna grab that? I think it's mine," Kyle says.

I toss the paper towel I used in the trash and go to wash my hands. Behind me I hear Bryce say, "Hello." When I turn to look at him I see his face has gone pale.

"Kyle," I call out a warning and he turns to his son too.

"Bryce, who is that?" The boy's eyes come up to his father, who is trying to get the sticky dough off his hands. "Annie, take the phone," Kyle orders, and I quickly move toward Bryce, who doesn't move when I pluck it from his ear.

The moment I hear the semi-hysterical voice of the woman on the other side, I hit speakerphone so Kyle can hear.

"...wasn't working for me. But like I said I'm strapped, baby. Got nowhere to go now..." My blood boils listening to her whiny voice. Self-centered bitch. "...Brycie? Momma needs you to look after her, honey, like you used to. Do you think you can get some money off your..."

"Not another fucking word, Chanel," Kyle suddenly barks. "Not a word, and not a goddamn penny. How dare you put that on my son? He's fourteen years old and you put responsibility for your fucked-up choices on his shoulders?"

"You mean *my* son, you've barely known him a couple of weeks!" I hear her screech before Kyle snatches up the phone and takes it off speaker.

I quickly move to Bryce's side, putting an arm around the frozen kid.

"Listen, and listen carefully." Kyle's eyes are on his son as he carefully enunciates his words. "Didn't take more than the first glimpse of his eyes to know with every fiber of my being, I'd fucking move heaven and earth for my son. And if that means protecting him from his mother, so be it. You're a parent, goddammit, you're supposed to be the one looking after *him*, not the other way around."

His eyes, burning with intensity, haven't wavered from Bryce's face, and I feel the boy's body start to shake.

"Try me," he says in a deathly calm voice. "Call me again when you get yourself clean and I'll be willing talk, but you threaten me and you'll find out the lengths to which I'll go for the sake of my child."

Bryce slips out of my hold and runs up the stairs, even as his father ends the call. A door slams upstairs and Kyle makes a move to go after him, but I hold him back.

"First a cool head," I insist. "And let's give him a minute to process. That was a lot for him to take."

He rubs both hands over his head, and I don't have the heart to tell him he's leaving blobs of dough behind.

"She's not to be believed," he growls.

"I know. I feel murderous myself, and I'm not even his parent."

"Fourteen years of that and I wasn't even aware he existed." His voice cracks and I slip my arms around his waist.

"He had a grandmother who made him monkey bread," I offer. "And in the past few minutes you've given him the kind of parent he deserves. It'll be enough."

I feel him shake his head against my hair.

"I don't know."

I squeeze him and tilt my head back.

"I do."

* * *

Sumo

"Let me go up and talk to him."

I take in a deep breath and let her steady presence calm the rage I feel.

"Yeah," I agree. It's probably better to let her offer that same calm assurance to Bryce before I talk to him.

"In the meantime," she continues, her blue eyes holding mine. "You should make some phone calls. Find out what it takes to keep your son here."

"Yeah," I repeat, but this time with a lump in my throat.

She comes up on her toes and I bend my head to meet

her lips. She steps back with a warm smile and then turns to go see about Bryce.

After hearing his mother spew what I'm sure was drug-induced garbage, I'm beyond grateful my son has a good woman who cares about his welfare.

Fuck, I'm in love with her.

I let that sink in for a minute before I turn my attention to my phone. Time to call my captain for some advice.

"Better have a good reason for disrupting my Sunday, Sumo," he answers after the third ring.

"I need a good lawyer."

My announcement is met with prolonged silence before he finally responds.

"Your son," he concludes.

"Got it in one. She's not getting her hands on him again."

I tell him what I know and describe the conversation I had with Chanel just now, feeling bolstered by Cap's sounds of disbelief.

"She did what?"

"She threatened to call the police on me with claims of child molestation if I didn't send her money," I repeat. "Not even the slightest concern about how Bryce was doing, but I bet she was worried about her next fix."

"Got a pen?"

I walk to the whiteboard on the fridge and grab the marker.

"Set."

He gives me a name and a number.

"That's my sister-in-law. She's a goddamn pain in my ass but a killer family lawyer."

"Good. That's exactly what I need. I'll give her a call tomorrow. Thanks, Cap."

"Call her now. The woman doesn't have a life; she'll

probably be at her office anyway. You still coming back to work tomorrow?"

I hesitate, wondering if I perhaps should take another few days to weather this crisis, but decide against it. The sooner we get into some kind of routine, the better it is.

"That's the plan."

"It'll be good to have you back, Sumo."

"Thanks."

I hang up and walk to the stairs to check on my son first, when the sound of subdued voices drifts down. They're talking and I don't want to disturb them. I don't care if he opens up to Annie before he does me, as long as he feels safe enough to talk.

Back in the kitchen I transfer the lawyer's name and number to my phone and dial.

"Mel Morgan."

Cap's sister-in-law sounds curt and to the point.

I introduce myself and mention Cap is my boss.

"You have my condolences," she snaps, and I get the sense there isn't much love lost between the two. I'm not sure how to answer to that so I stay silent. "What can I do for you?"

It takes me almost half an hour to fill her in from the very first phone call last year to the one today.

"The boy's with you?"

"Yeah."

"Good. He settling in?"

"Seems to be. He's making some friends, is doing some kind of summer mechanics' program up at the Arrow's Edge garage and appears to be enjoying it."

"Good. What you have got planned for school come August?"

Fuck. That's only weeks away and I haven't even given it thought.

"Looking into it."

"Mmm," she hums. "We'd better get on that fast. Do you have any documentation?"

"She put him on the plane with a birth certificate and a consent letter. Oh, and I also have the results of a paternity test I insisted on."

"Thank God for that, it'll make the first steps a lot easier. And while you're at it, take him to see a doctor for a full work up."

"Okay."

"Make copies of all the paperwork you have, get it to my office tomorrow, along with a check for my three-thousand-dollar retainer. Or you can give me your credit card now."

She sounds like a ballbuster, which is perfect. I don't need some bleeding heart to hold my hand; I need someone who can get the job done.

I pull my wallet from my pocket and fish out my credit card, reading off the number.

"So what's next?" I want to know.

"As soon as I have the documents I'll file for temporary custody. Any idea where I can find the mother?"

"Last I know she was in Boise, Idaho, but she could've called from anywhere."

"You're a firefighter like my no-good brother-in-law?"

"EMT, but I'm on his crew."

"Good, you got any buddies in the force? I can hire a private investigator, but that's gonna be extra money. See if you know someone who could help find her."

"I'll ask around."

"Right. This the number to reach you?"

"It is."

"Then I'm set for now. You get that stuff to me, I'll get the ball rolling, and I'll be in touch."

She doesn't even say goodbye; she just hangs up.

The impotent rage I felt earlier is mostly just anger—and much easier to check—now that I've taken some progressive steps.

"Kyle?" I hear Annie call down the stairs, and I tuck my phone in my pocket as I make my way over.

"Everything okay?" I ask when I see her at the top of the stairs.

"Yeah. Wanna come up here for a sec?" She leans close when I get to the top. "Be sure when you say yes," she whispers before leading me into Bryce's room.

The sight of my boy with his knees drawn up to his chest, back against the headboard of his bed, and his face wet with tears, has my heart squeeze in my chest.

"You okay, Son?" I ask as I approach, sitting on the edge of the mattress.

He nods. "Are you gonna send me back?"

"Not a chance in hell."

His face registers surprise.

"Then can I stay here?"

I reach out and cup my hand behind his neck, my face inches from his.

"You bet. We still have a lot of things to find out about each other, but I already know I love you."

His lip trembles when he nods, and I have to blink myself.

"Now, what do you say we finish up that monkey bread?"

Immediately a watery grin breaks through and he climbs off the bed and darts out the door. I look over at Annie, who's waving a hand in front of her eyes, blinking away tears.

"That was perfect," she says, putting her hand in mine.

We're halfway down the stairs when my phone rings again. This time it's Tony.

"Can I call you back?" I ask, but his answer is not what I expected.

"We've got him. We arrested Will Parsons."

24

Annie

I feel like a child behind the wheel of Kyle's truck.

He was on his way out the door early this morning when we realized the cops still have my car. I ended up dropping him off at the station so I'd have wheels to drive Bryce to Arrow's Edge, which is where we're heading now.

Knowing Will Parsons is in custody gives me peace of mind, and I may actually stop by the bakery when I get back to town. At the very least to hand in my notice and check in with the bakery crew. I already told Margaret I'd be by this afternoon.

The kid has been mostly quiet this morning and I don't want to push him. After the emotional turn of events yesterday, an afternoon with his buddies may just be what the doctor ordered.

It had been heartbreaking to find him sobbing into his pillow, and I know he was mortified for me to see him that way. I wasn't sure where to start so I told him how my parents had been older, already in their forties when I came along as a surprise. I share how I inherited Mom's love for baking—something she did plenty of—and one of the first things she taught me was how to make monkey bread.

The monkey bread got him talking about his grandmother, where he apparently spent a large portion of his life before her health forced her to move into a long-term care facility. He still didn't share a whole lot about his mother, only that for a long time she wasn't a steady presence in his life.

When his grandma died and his mom moved them to Boise, he mentioned she never enrolled him in school. She'd often disappear, leaving him alone in their one-bedroom apartment, sometimes days at a time. He told me he'd pick up odd jobs cleaning people's yards, doing groceries for a few elderly neighbors, or washing cars, just so there'd be some food in the fridge.

Last month there'd been an eviction notice on their small apartment, which is when his mom told him he'd have to go stay with the father he didn't know he had. He broke down and cried he didn't want to go back; he felt safe here and wanted to go to school just like other kids his age.

It broke my heart.

Then last night over dinner, we talked about logistics with Kyle going back to work. I mentioned I was thinking about handing in my notice at the bakery. Kyle looked at me oddly but didn't say much, and I didn't want to ask with Bryce sitting right there. That's why I also didn't address the money issue. I'll wait for tomorrow when he's rested up from his shift. Yesterday was tense enough.

He did share he'd been in touch with a lawyer and asked if I could drop off papers for him, which I plan to do when I get back to town. Then pop into the bakery, do a few hours at the shelter, and head back up the mountain to pick Bryce up. I'm thinking maybe I'll take him out for dinner somewhere after.

"Do you need me to pick you up anything?" I ask him. "I've gotta make a few stops in town after I drop you anyway."

"I don't really need anything, but maybe…no, never mind."

I glance over and when he looks back I slowly raise an eyebrow, making him grin.

"Let's try that again, shall we? Anything you need from town?" I tease him.

"Maybe sometime this week could we leave a little early and stop at the library? I wanna see if I can get some books on cars."

"For sure. I wouldn't mind looking around either. I need to find something to do with my time other than baking."

"Not on my account," he protests, making me chuckle.

"You and your father are peas in a pod."

It's quiet as I turn into the dirt driveway up to the compound. Then he says, "You think we're alike?"

I slip through the open gate and pull up in front of the garage, putting the truck in park before I turn toward him.

"Yeah, you are."

"He says he wants me to stay."

"I know."

He glances up at me with eyes that match his father's.

"I'd like that."

"I know that too." I smile at him and he shows me a lopsided grin. "How about we grab a burger in town after I pick you up this afternoon?"

"Cool," he mutters, and unclips his seat belt.

"You're a good kid, Bryce." I reach over to ruffle his hair, but he ducks away from my hand.

"Yeah, whatever."

But his smile is big when he gets out of the truck.

* * *

"I have a delivery for Mel Morgan?"

The girl sitting at the desk in the front office looks up from her computer, taking me in head to toe and back up.

"You look familiar."

I smile at her. "Yeah, I get that a lot."

She hits a button on her phone.

"Mel, I've got...what's your name?"

"I'm dropping something off for Kyle Matsumoto."

"I'll be right out"

Two seconds later I hear a door open and soft footfalls coming down the hall.

Kyle's lawyer is unexpected; from the long silver gray hair falling in waves around a classically beautiful face, to the black tank over cropped cargo pants. A gorgeous, colorful tattoo peeks out the neck of her shirt and seems to extend down her rounded left arm. Her feet are bare.

She looks completely out of place in the sleek industrial design office.

"Who are you?"

Her abrupt question startles me.

"Annie Flowers, I'm a friend of Kyle Matsumoto."

From the corner of my eye I see the girl lean her elbows on her desk, unapologetically nosy.

"You share his bed?"

I glance over at the girl again, before turning back to the lawyer who still hasn't introduced herself.

"I don't see how that's—" I start but she cuts me off.

219

"Right. That tells me enough. Linds, hold my calls," she orders the girl before she points a finger at me. "You, come with me."

She turns on her heel and pads back down the hall and I have no choice but follow along, clutching Kyle papers in my hand.

"Well, don't just stand there," she grumbles when I stop just inside her office.

I take it to be an invitation to sit, so I sink down in one of the two stylish leather chairs facing her desk. This woman can't be hurting, judging from the high-quality design of her office, and yet she doesn't dress the part. Interesting.

"So, Annie Flowers, who are you and what are you to my client? And before you get your knickers in a knot, I'm trying to get custody for my client and won't have that railroaded by a relationship I was not made aware of."

She's right, I was about to tell her where to get off but I get why she needs to know. Although, I'm guessing she's not known for her tact, but I should tell her. I should tell her everything.

For the next hour I do exactly that, and by the time I leave her office I almost like the woman.

Unfortunately I never make it to the bakery. It'll have to wait for another day.

Sumo

"Hey, buddy. What's your name?"

The kid blinks his eyes a few times.

"J-Jake."

"Hi, Jake, we'll take good care of you. Just a few questions, okay? How many fingers am I holding up?"

He blinks again, his gaze darting everywhere looking panicked.

"Jake? How many fingers?" I wiggle them in his face.

"Three."

"Good. Do you know what day it is?"

The kid has a good gash somewhere on the back of his head; he's lost quite a bit of blood. He doesn't answer and looks like he's going into shock. I want to get a collar on him before I move him to look at his head, but I need Blue for that.

I look up to see her jogging over with the bag and backboard.

We got a call about a skateboarding accident in a park near the high school. It has a designated concrete skate area, which is surrounded by a chain-link fence, so we couldn't get the rig any closer. We'll have to carry him out, but I'm guessing he's no more than eighty or eighty-five pounds. Maybe twelve years old.

"Hey, Jake?" I help Blue slide the brace around his neck.

"Yeah?" He looks at me like he's never seen me before.

"How old are you?"

"I'm...I'm..." he mumbles, and then stops talking as we carefully roll him on his side, Blue holding his head stable while I check the back of his head.

I'm not saying Billy Bapcock isn't a good medic, but there's nothing like the silent communication Blue and I have developed over years of working together. It's effortless.

The back of Jake's skull has a large depression that really worries me, and I quickly cover the area with thick padding before wrapping a quick bandage around his head. We roll him onto the backboard and strap him down. His eyes are still open but he doesn't make a sound.

"IV?"

I shake my head. "Let's get him loaded first. I wanna get out of here quick."

She nods and bends down to pick up the board by his feet when Ben Conley, a patrol officer who's been talking to possible witnesses, walks up.

"No one knows where he lives. Does he have a phone on him?"

"Give me a hand loading him and I'll find out," I tell him. "Blue, grab the gear?"

In minutes we have Jake loaded and Blue is working on getting a line in. I hand the phone I fished from the kid's pocket to Conley.

"Tell his parents he's awake and was talking," I tell the officer.

That's something I wouldn't usually do, but for the first time in my life I have a clearer understanding of the shock awaiting his parents. I hope I never have to experience a call like that.

"Line's in," Blue confirms, and I close the back doors.

"You good?" I climb in behind the wheel and call over my shoulder.

"Let's go."

I hear the urgency in her voice and I flip on the lights and siren.

* * *

"Are you okay?" Blue asks.

We're on our way back to the station after dropping a very seriously injured Jake off. It took us a while to get the back of the rig clean—head wounds tend to bleed a bit—

and the whole time I was thinking what I would do if anything ever happened to Bryce.

"Fine."

"Please, that's such a chick thing to say. You've barely said a word since we got the call."

I glance over at her and see her face shows strain too.

First day back on the job for both of us, and it occurs to me my partner is a new parent too.

"Was it hard leaving Esme behind?"

"Yeah," she confirms, her eyes drifting out the window. "I was eager to get back to feeling useful. Thought I'd be happy to get back in the swing of things, but…"

"I hear you. First serious call of the day and it being a kid doesn't help."

"No."

I snort. "Stupid. A few weeks ago I wouldn't have blinked. Now I'm a father, the call suddenly bothers me."

"Scary, isn't it?" I feel her eyes on me.

"Fucking terrifying," I have to agree.

"He's okay, though, right? When you're working?"

"Yeah, Annie's there. She says she's handing in her notice at the bakery."

"Oh no! I'm gonna miss her pastries."

"I'm sure she'll be happy keeping you supplied. She does us. At least for now."

I think of Annie barefoot in my kitchen, wearing her baggy jeans and a tank, her hair sticking out every which way, and those blue eyes shining when I walk in.

Fuck. I didn't want to ask in front of Bryce—or maybe I was just afraid to hear the answer—but when she mentioned giving up her job at the bakery, I realized maybe this was inevitable.

She's a TV star who was happy enough leading a simple life when she had no other choice, but with Parsons caught, I'm sure it won't be long before she'll be looking to go home. Giving her notice at the bakery is the first step in that direction.

"For now? I thought she moved in with you?"

"She's staying with me, yeah. She's got nothing left to move. I'm sure she'll be heading back to LA at some point."

"Did she tell you that?"

I turn into the fire station and turn the rig around so I can back into the open bay.

"Why wouldn't she? Her life is there, why would she want to give that up?"

I open my door when Blue punches my arm hard.

"Are you an idiot?"

She yells so loud, Chief Aimes, who is inside his office, turns his head to see what's going on.

"Don't wanna talk about it," I tell her, getting out of the rig. She does the same on the other side and catches up with me before I can hit the stairs.

"You *are* an idiot," she hisses, pulling me around by my arm. "God, men are so fucking frustrating. Why don't you try talking instead of always drawing the wrong fucking conclusions?"

"Everything okay here?" The chief comes walking out of his office.

"No. Sumo's being a stubborn ass. He's about to let the best thing—okay, maybe second best thing because Bryce is first—that's happened to him walk out the door without a fight."

"Trouble in paradise? Already?"

Hog, one of the guys on my crew, is at the top of the stairs, a big grin on his face.

Clearly there are no boundaries in this firehouse or secrets in this town. Everybody's up in my fucking business.

"Fuck off, Hog. Mind your own business."

His grin only gets bigger when Cheddar steps up beside him, a matching one on his face as he clearly has something to contribute as well. Assholes.

"Can I just say, Sumo; it's a beautiful thing to witness Karma biting you in the ass."

25

Annie

"Hey, Tony."

We just walked in the door when my phone started ringing.

I spent the afternoon at the shelter, where I discovered Hunter's owner sadly passed away. Somehow I think the dog knew because he wasn't his exuberant self, and refused to come out of his kennel, so I ended up sitting in front of his pen reading, and occasionally reaching in to scratch his head.

I watch as Bryce gives Daisy a good rubdown and wonder if I could convince Kyle to consider adopting another one.

"Your car is clean."

It takes me a second to understand what he's talking about.

"It is? No...yuck?"

His warm chuckle fills my ear.

"No yuck," he promises. "You can pick it up whenever."

"Maybe later tomorrow? Kyle's working."

"I know," he says a smile in his voice. "So is Blue."

"Duh. Of course. Is there anything else new?"

I notice a hesitation before he answers. "We finally managed to get ahold of your agent this morning. No offense, but he's a piece of work."

"Believe me, I know," I agree. Or at least I'm learning he's more of a snake than I already suspected.

"Swears he didn't put anything in your purse. He suggested there were others on the set, with access to your dressing room, who could've easily slipped something inside. We're going to have local law enforcement follow up with him, but if what he says is true, he's been in LA the whole time."

"He's right about other people having access," I comment. For my sake I hope Miles was telling the truth, the thought my own agent was and is involved makes me sick. "Makeup, wardrobe, catering, production staff; there were always some who needed access."

"I'm guessing the production company would have that information?"

"I would think so."

"You do realize the more people we talk to, the higher the chances this'll hit the press at some point?"

"Trust me," I assure him with a forced chuckle. "I'm well aware. So be it. I want this over."

"All right then. We're still looking into a few things, but for your peace of mind; Mr. Parsons is still a guest of the DPD. Should we find out more or anything changes, I'll be in touch."

"Thanks, I appreciate that." I'm about to end the call when I have a thought. "Hey, Tony?"

"What's up?"

"You wouldn't be in the market for another rescue, would you? Hunter is a—"

"Don't even, Annie," he warns me. "I have my hands full refusing my wife. Why don't you take a rescue?"

"Yeah, but I'm staying with Kyle, so I kinda have to check with him."

This time he laughs heartily.

"That's perfect; you ask Sumo and make sure to tell him I think he should say yes."

"I'll do that, and we'll be by sometime probably in the afternoon."

"Whenever is fine."

"Sounds good."

I end the call and walk into the kitchen where Bryce is already feeding the dog. He's such a good kid, it's hard to believe with the kind of upbringing he's had so far, but I attribute it to good genes from the Matsumoto side and a positive presence in his maternal grandmother.

"Did you have enough to eat?" I ask him. As I've become accustomed to, at dinner he scarfed down his burger and finished both his and my fries, his appetite endless.

"For now," he answers and I grin.

"How about we take the dog for a walk and when we get back, we can make some popcorn and watch a movie?"

"Cool," is his standard response.

We end up watching *The Goonies*, one of my favorites and a great distraction from reality. I discovered Bryce had never seen it before. He ate most of the giant bowl of popcorn we shared and just went up to bed.

I grab a glass of wine, my phone, and settle back on the couch to make a phone call I'd rather avoid, but if I want to get ahead of the fallout, I need to do this.

It rings four times and I'm getting ready to leave a message when he suddenly answers.

"Who's this?" His bark is typical. He's never been the most pleasant of people.

"Miles, it's Annabel."

"Well, well, well. Where the fuck have you been? Durango? I need you to get your ass back here..."

He continues to ramble on without listening, which is also typical of him. His dogged determination is a good thing when he's working on my behalf, but not so much right now. I catch snippets of what he says, but when he starts talking about this perfect comeback part in what is supposed to be a great new project he's sure he can secure me, I cut him off.

"I'm done, Miles. I was tired of it years ago. I'm calling to let you know I want to make arrangements to ship whatever is in storage here."

He laughs like I said something funny, but I'm dead serious.

"You can't mean that. I can have you back on top in no time."

Now it's my turn to laugh.

"Newsflash, Miles. I was never *on top* of anything, and I'm fine with that. I had a good run, but I'm done. Done with this industry, done with this stalker, and frankly I'm done with you. I just wanted to give you a heads-up I'm moving on to bigger and better things."

"In Durango, Colorado?" he scoffs.

"Miles," I try for a soothing tone, "I want to dissolve our professional relationship as amicably and equitably as possible, but if that isn't possible I can have my lawyer set the necessary steps in motion."

I don't tell him the lawyer I'm referring to isn't really mine, and specializes in family law. I'd love to see ball-buster Mel Morgan go a few rounds with Miles. I'm pretty sure she'd rip him to shreds.

He concedes reluctantly after that, asking to give him some time so he can make arrangements.

"That's not a problem," I agree. "Just let me know when—"

I don't get to finish my sentence because he's already hung up.

Still, I feel a lot lighter when I bring my glass to the kitchen and let the dog out back for a quick pee. Then I make sure the house is locked up and the alarm set for the night, and I head up to bed.

* * *

"Morning."

Kyle walks in; looking a little the worse for wear, as I'm sliding some cheese biscuits in the oven.

"Hey, honey." I smile and walk up to him, slipping my arms around his neck. "How was your first shift back?"

He bends his head and his lips meet mine for a brief kiss.

"It was okay. Bryce is still in bed?"

"Yeah. He crashed after watching *The Goonies* with me."

That earns me a grin, thank God, I was starting to worry. Still, he looks worn and he didn't exactly answer my question.

"There's fresh coffee if you like. Biscuits will take ten minutes, and how about I whip up some bacon and eggs to go with that?" I suggest.

"Sure."

I try my luck again when we're sitting at the island eating breakfast.

"Did something happen, Kyle?"

He runs a hand over his face and sighs deeply.

"My first patient today was an eleven-year-old boy who was near comatose by the time we got him to the hospital."

"What happened?" I ask softly.

"Skateboarding accident. He wasn't wearing a helmet."

I sharply suck air in through my teeth.

"Oh, no. I can't imagine how tough that must be."

I reach out to touch him but he abruptly gets up and takes the dishes to the sink. I try not to let it sting.

"I'm beat. Gonna grab some sleep. I'll make sure I'm up to take Bryce up the mountain."

"No need. I'll take him, you sleep."

He doesn't argue, just nods, walks right past me, and heads up the stairs.

Clearly not a good time for a heart-to-heart, I'll have to save it until later.

* * *

Sumo

I haven't moved since I heard her come back a few minutes ago.

It had been so tempting to let her comfort me earlier, but if I allowed myself to get used to that, it would only be harder when she eventually goes back to California. I do feel guilty not waiting up so I could see Bryce before he leaves, but I'll see him later this afternoon and tonight.

I turn my head and look at my alarm. Eleven thirty. If I want to get a good night's rest in tonight, I'd better get up. I swing my legs out of bed and grab my phone off the charger on the nightstand. First I need to know.

"Mercy emergency."

I recognize the voice.

"Melanie, it's Sumo. Looking for an update on Jake, the young kid with head trauma we brought in yesterday. Skateboarding incident."

"Hang on," she says, and I hear the clicking of fingers on a keyboard. "Depressed skull fracture of the occipital bone. The brain was swelling so they took him into surgery overnight to relieve the pressure. He's in the ICU."

"Thanks."

"No problem. Always tough with kids, isn't it?"

"Yeah."

"Be prepared, it never really gets easier once you have kids of your own," she says before ending the call, proving that the Durango grapevine is alive and well.

I grab a quick shower; pull on a pair of board shorts and a shirt, and head downstairs, my heart heavy.

The first things I notice are two large stacks of books on the coffee table. I'm just about to check them out when Annie walks in from the kitchen.

"What's all this?" I ask her, indicating the odd collection of car manuals and romance books.

"Oh, I took Bryce to the library before I dropped him off." I look up and see the smile on her face. "We both got library cards. I'd forgotten how nice it is to have my hands on an actual book."

I stare at her. She got a library card. Not exactly what you'd expect from someone who's ready to pack her bags.

"Kyle? Is that okay? I hope I didn't overstep taking him, but he seemed so—"

"No." I clear my throat. "I'm...glad you took him."

"Okay."

She seems uncertain at my reaction and I'm not so sure what to think myself at this point.

"We need to talk." She blinks those blue eyes, looking

like I just slapped her. "Please," I add, reaching for her hand and pulling her down on the couch.

"I wanted to talk to you too," she admits. "I talked to my agent last night and I think we need to figure out where we're at. I'm grateful you let me stay here, but—"

"Whatever you want," I snap, dropping her hand.

Fuck. I knew it. The entire remainder of my shift Blue tried to convince me I was wrong, but this sounds like the start of a brush off.

"What is wrong with you?" she suddenly flies off the handle. "You've been weird for a couple of days now—moody—and I don't know why. I feel like I'm walking on eggshells. If I did something wrong, I wish you'd just say it. Are you tired of having me around? Then tell me." She jumps up and starts pacing as she rants. "Jesus, it's a good thing I didn't bring home Hunter yesterday. What a mistake that could have been."

"Another dog? And what happens when you leave?"

She stops in her tracks and stares at me slack-mouthed.

"When I leave?" She grabs handfuls of her hair and growls. "You know you could've just told me I've outstayed my welcome, and I wouldn't have gone through the trouble of getting my agent to send all my stuff here."

Wait. What?

I get to my feet and hold my hands up.

"Hold on. What did you talk to your agent about?"

She rolls her eyes and lets out a harsh breath. "I have some things that have sentimental value in storage I asked him to send here. He's not happy, but he knows I'm not coming back."

"You're not?"

She looks stunned as she drops back on the couch, looking at me like I've gone mad. Maybe I have.

"Kyle," she says, and it sounds like she's mustering up all

the patience she can find. "Why don't we take this from the top, because right now I feel like we're speaking different languages."

I hate to admit it, but I get the sneaky suspicion Blue may have had a point. I sit down on the coffee table across from her.

"A couple of days ago you mentioned handing in your notice at the bakery, right after we found out Parsons was in custody. I assumed you were getting ready to head back."

"Are you nuts? What were you thinking?"

I guess she didn't have a lot of patience left because her eyes are shooting angry darts at me.

"I was thinking how much it was gonna suck to watch the woman I'm in love with walk out that door," I confess, laying it all on the table, but Annie can't hear for the steam coming out of her ears.

"Why didn't you ask? I wanted to hand in my notice because I don't need the money." She's agitated, talking with her hands. "I took that job because it allowed me to do what I enjoy, but I figured I could just as easily bake here, for you guys. I don't need the bakery for that. I'm at a loss how you translated that into me leaving..." All of a sudden her face goes slack and her wide eyes come to me. "You're in love with me?"

I grin and shake my head as I lower it.

"You're gonna make me repeat it, aren't you?"

"Well, yeah. I wanna make sure I heard it correctly. Unless, of course, you didn't mean it."

When I lift my head I see mischief in her eyes.

"Now you're challenging me," I accuse her, and she shrugs her shoulders with a grin.

"Hey, if you—"

I don't let her finish the words as I hook my hand

behind her neck, pull her close, and cover her mouth with mine in a claiming kiss.

"I'm in love with you, *Annie-chan*."

I watch as she licks her still kiss-swollen lips before I lift my gaze to her eyes. I can see the truth in their depths but I still want to hear the words.

Instead she asks, "What does that mean?"

"That means I want you to stay—here—with Bryce and me. It means I want to walk into the kitchen, and still be able to smell whatever it was you baked last. It means I'm flying blind and I can't make any guarantees I won't fuck up along the way—according to Blue it's a given, because...testosterone—but I'm asking you to give me a chance."

She slides a hand along my jaw and brushes her thumb over my cheekbone.

"I'll stay, and I'll bake, and I'll give you that chance, but I want to pay my own way."

I can feel my jaw clench. The disparity between what I bring in and however much she has amassed in her career feels like a giant divide and I'm not quite sure how to bridge it, but I want to try.

"It's important to me that I provide my family with the safety and security of a home," I start, and feel immediate relief when her eyes soften, encouraging me to go on. "I'll probably want to pay if we go out for dinner as well, but I'm willing to negotiate on that," I concede. "Everything else is fair game I guess."

"So I can give gifts?"

I can tell from the smirk on her face this is probably a trick question, but that doesn't stop me from telling her, "I guess."

"Excellent." She leans forward and presses her lips to mine. "And for the record, I think I was in love with you the first time you sat down on the concrete floor at the shelter and started reading to the dogs."

"Yeah?"

"Mhmmm," she hums, getting to her feet and pulling me up. "Let's go."

"Where are we going?"

"Picking up a gift for Daisy," she says with a chuckle.

I knew it.

26

Sumo

"This is so cool."

Annie twists in her seat to look at Bryce sitting next to Hunter in the back seat. In the mirror I can see both are grinning. I never believed a dog could actually smile until I met Hunter; he is absolutely the happiest dog I've ever seen.

"Dee is gonna go through the roof," he adds, and I can't hold back the snort.

We'd gone straight to Arrow's Edge—after officially adopting Hunter—to pick up my son, whose face broke into a huge smile when he spotted the dog in the back seat.

I'm not an idiot, I know full well I've been conned, but I'll be honest; I couldn't care less. Even Margaret's cackle and whispered, _"Sucker,"_ when we walked out of the shelter with Hunter couldn't kill my happy buzz.

I may have to eat some crow to let Blue know she was right; it absolutely pays to talk about shit instead of stewing on it. The proof is sitting in the seat beside me, happily gabbing with my son in the back while I drive us home.

"Oh, Kyle?" I glance over at Annie. "Do you think we could stop at the City Market? I never made it in there yesterday, and I want to let my boss know I won't be back."

"Are you sure about that?"

"Yeah. I was hiding. I'm done with that. I'd like to stay on at the shelter, though, but I need some time to get my life sorted, you know? I'd rather get that done before I think about what else I might wanna do with my life."

"You mean aside from keeping us supplied with pastries?"

"Hell, yeah," Bryce pipes up from the back seat, making me chuckle.

"Is that all I am to you guys? Your personal baker?" she asks with mock indignation.

"Nah, you're nice to have around, right, Son?" I give her knee a squeeze.

"She's all right," he says in his typical understated way, but I can hear the smile in his voice.

So can Annie, who rolls her eyes, but then spends the rest of the drive to the grocery store softly smiling out the window.

"Bud, you okay staying in the truck with the dog? I'm just gonna go in with Annie and grab a couple of things."

We're halfway to the store when I hear him shout behind me.

"Yo, Pop? Can you grab me some more Diet Coke?"

I raise a thumb in the air and when I drop my hand Annie grabs onto it, her fingers sliding between mine. Fucking perfect.

It doesn't take me long to gather up the makings for Pad Thai, a favorite at the station, but tonight I'm cooking it for my family. I go in search of Annie, who is standing at the bakery counter talking to a young woman I've seen before.

"Almost ready?"

She looks up at me when I step up beside her and drape my arm over her shoulders.

"Yeah, sure." Then she addresses the girl. "Well, when you see him, can you tell him I enjoyed working with him? I'm staying in town so I'll pop by again."

"I will." The girl looks a little starstruck and I'm guessing Annie just 'came out' to her. "I still can't believe I didn't see it."

"You're not the only one," I tell her with a wink, before gently steering Annie to the checkout.

I'm loading groceries on the counter when I hear Annie softly swear behind me. When I turn she pulls a magazine from the rack—one of those gossip rags they keep at the cash register—looking at it closely. I peek over her shoulder and mutter an expletive of my own.

On the front cover, in the top right corner, is a close-up of the old Annie wearing a baseball cap. It's a candid shot of her smiling at something. Her blue eyes popping off the page. The caption reads:

What happened to Annabel?

"Sixty-three ninety-five, please."

I pluck the magazine from her hands and drop it on the counter.

"Can you add this?"

"Sure. That makes it sixty-six ninety-four, please."

I feel Annie slipping past me as I settle with the cashier, and she's already heading to the doors with one of the bags. I grab the rest and rush to catch up with her.

"Fucking Miles," she mutters when I fall in step beside her.

"You think he's behind that?"

She stops and flashes me a pair of angry eyes. "I know it. Rags stopped talking about me about eight months ago. Gossip only sells while it's hot, and the truth is, I wasn't all that hot to begin with. Never made the front page until now, so I'll leave you to link the dots."

A car honks and I realize we're in the middle of the parking lot. I nudge Annie to keep walking, but she stops again when we get close to the truck.

"Where's Bryce?"

I look up and see the back door of my truck open a bit. No Bryce or Hunter. Immediately my eyes scan the parking lot, even as a jolt of fear steals the breath from my lungs. I rush over and pull the door all the way open, looking inside to make sure it's empty.

"Bryce!" I hear Annie yell, still standing in the same spot, looking around her.

I drop the bags in the back of the truck and pull out my phone.

"Ramirez."

"Tell me you still have Parsons," I snap.

"I was about to call you with some news on that."

"Did you let him go?"

"Let him go? No way, the DA just formally charged him. I was going to stop by with some evidence I'd like—"

"*Fuck.*"

"What the hell is going on?" Tony wants to know.

"It's Bryce, he's—"

I don't get to finish my sentence because suddenly Annie calls out. "There he is!"

I follow the direction she's pointing, where I can see my son come jogging around the dumpster beside the grocery store, Hunter running alongside, his tongue lolling out of his mouth. I bend over, bracing myself with my hands on my knees, when I hear a muffled, *"Sumo, fuck! Talk to me."*

I bring the phone I held pressed against my knee up to my ear.

"It's all good. False alarm," I manage, the residual fear still coursing through my blood, making me breathless. I don't take my eyes off my son until Annie intercepts him, giving him a piece of her mind. "Couldn't find Bryce for a minute, but he's here. It's all good."

"Jesus, man, you scared the crap out of me," Tony grumbles.

"Tell me about it."

"Look, are you gonna be home soon? I've got some stuff I want to go over with Annie."

Bryce looks at me with guilt in his eyes and slowly comes toward me.

"Give us half an hour, okay?"

"Yeah, sure. See you then."

I tuck my phone in my pocket when Bryce stops right in front of me.

"Fucking hell, kid," I swear at my son. Probably not the best example of parenting, but I can't seem to come up with anything else right at this time.

"I'm sorry. I wasn't thinking. It's just Hunter was whining and I though he needed to pee."

I pluck the leash from his hand and get the dog in the back seat before turning back to Bryce. He looks worried and I force myself to calm down.

I may have overreacted.

No, I know I overreacted, but hindsight is twenty-twenty and in my defense, shit has been a little chaotic lately.

"Come here," I tell him, even as I notice Annie rescuing

the groceries I'd dumped in the back seat from a very excited Hunter.

Bryce takes a tentative step closer, but I tag him behind the neck and yank him to my chest.

"Scared the crap out of me, Bryce. Feel my heart pounding? That's fear because I didn't know where you were." I feel the boy's hands fist in my shirt by my sides. "I panicked. That's on me, but I'm kinda learning on the job here, so help me out a little and don't disappear without telling anyone."

I release him and he takes a step back.

"But you were inside…"

"Yeah, and you've got a phone. Coulda called us to let us know." He drops his head dejectedly and I put a hand on his shoulder. "Hey, we both kinda messed this one up. Next time we'll both do better, yeah?"

"Yeah."

I press a kiss to the top of his head—something I'm pretty sure is illegal to do to a teenager—and nudge him toward the truck.

Half an hour later, Bryce is in the basement playing a game, both dogs probably by his side. Their reunion had been heartwarming, and after ten minutes running around the yard, they'd come inside, Daisy leading her buddy to the water bowl.

Annie went upstairs to gather up dirty sheets to wash, and I'm making a start cutting vegetables for dinner, when the doorbell rings.

* * *

Annie

. . .

I have my arms full when I make my way down the stairs. The low rumble of men's voices reaches me from the kitchen and I head in that direction.

Both Keith and Tony are sitting at the kitchen island and Kyle just pulls his head from the fridge, holding a beer.

"Want one?" He holds up the bottle to the guys.

"No thanks."

"Not while I'm on the clock."

Then he turns to me. "You, Annie?"

"I'll pass. Hey, guys," I greet the others. "Let me get this started."

I dive into the laundry room, stuff the sheets in the washer, and get the machine going. Back in the kitchen I sidle up to Kyle, who immediately throws his arm over my shoulder, when I notice a big envelope on the counter in front of the detectives. My car keys are on top.

"Shit, I totally forgot about the car."

Tony grins. "No worries, looks like you had a busy afternoon." He scratches Hunter, who'd come up to check out the new visitors. "Clearly you got your way." He smirks at Kyle.

"Wait a minute, how many dogs do you have again?" Kyle fires back. "Oh, and cats?"

"Whatever," Tony dismisses him before turning back to me. "Anyway, since we were coming here anyway, we brought your car."

That leaves me curious about the envelope.

"Thanks for that. So...Kyle said you charged him? Parsons?"

"The DA did, yeah. He feels there's sufficient evidence we pulled from his trailer," Keith volunteers. "A few things we'd like to go over with you, though."

I shrug. "Sure. What is it?"

Keith picks up the envelope and slides the contents on

the counter. A bunch of snapshots from what I can see, and what looks like a pair of panties in a Ziploc bag.

"Ewww," escapes me, and then I look closer. "Wait a minute…I recognize those." I grab the bag to take a better look and immediately drop it when I notice a few areas marked with a circle. "Double ewww." I shiver and Kyle pulls me tighter to his side. "Is that…?"

"Afraid so."

"We pulled these pictures and the panties from the drawer in Parsons' nightstand. All of them together."

"Good thing he's locked up," Kyle announces in a growly voice while I sift through the snapshots.

Some were taken of me walking Blossom—I feel vindicated knowing someone actually was watching me—a few of Kyle and I kissing in front of my trailer, and one of me putting out the garbage behind the bakery.

"You haven't seen these pictures before, Annie?" Keith asks.

"No. Shit, I shouldn't have touched them, should I?" I pull my hand back.

"These are copies," Tony takes over. "We have this evidence, a shirt of his with soot stains on the front, and also an empty gas can with his fingerprints on it we found in the tree line behind your property. He claims he knows nothing about the pictures or the underwear, and says his gas can was stolen from the back of his pickup two weeks ago. Claims he has no idea how the shirt got dirty."

"Of course he'd say that," Kyle states.

"And then there's the…yuck he left behind," I bring up.

"Yes, we should get the results on that any day now. Lab's been backlogged."

Keith slides the items back in the envelope.

"The DA didn't want to risk letting him walk so he

decided we had enough to charge him," he says, but I can't help notice a hesitation.

"You're not sure?" I ask.

"I wouldn't say that. I just like things tied up neatly and we still have a few loose ends. The DNA obviously, but there's also the tracker we found in your purse, we haven't found anything to show Parsons was in LA, and the fact those pictures in his nightstand don't appear to have a single fingerprint on them."

"Doesn't mean he wasn't there," Tony jumps in. "It just means we haven't found evidence to that effect yet. And as for the pictures, maybe he used gloves handling them, who knows?"

"Guy is safely behind bars," Keith says, getting up. "Not to worry, it's just a matter of fitting the last few pieces in place."

Tony rounds the island and pulls me in for a hug.

"Breathe easy, honey."

"I will, right after I sic a lawyer on my agent's ass."

"Why? What did he do?"

I untangle myself and walk up to the fridge, pulling the gossip rag off the top where Kyle had tossed it. Tony takes it from my hand.

"Shit. He didn't waste any time, we just talked to him yesterday."

"I don't think he could've pulled these kinds of strings overnight, but you've been trying to get ahold of him all weekend, I suspect he put this game in play as soon as he got your first message. I wouldn't put it past him. Just his way to try and force me back into the spotlight."

"Doesn't sound like you wanna be there," Keith suggests.

"Not particularly."

The large handsome man grins and slaps Kyle on the back.

"Lucked out there, my friend."

Kyle looks at me with his warm eyes.

"Don't I know it."

* * *

The phone calls started early this morning.

Kyle just left; it was barely quarter to seven when it rang for the first time. The *National Enquirer* was first on the trigger. The woman caught me off guard when she asked for Annie Flowers, but I hung up as soon as the reporter identified herself. I've basically been answering with "No comment" ever since.

This last one was creative, claiming to be UPS with a delivery for Ms. Flowers, and had been given this phone number. Could I please confirm the address.

I toss the phone on the counter by the sink.

"You know, you could just turn off your phone," Bryce says through a mouthful of the waffles I managed to bake him between calls. As usual he slept in, so this is more brunch than breakfast, but I don't care. Kyle and I talked last night and he's going to try and make an appointment with the local high school to get the boy enrolled.

"Are you being a smart-ass?" He grins, his mouth still full. "Ewww, I don't wanna see your regurgitated food," I scold him.

He shrugs, unimpressed, and shovels his last forkful in his mouth.

I reach for the phone and turn the sound off.

"There, better?"

He nods, covers his mouth with his hand and mumbles, "Much."

I return my attention to the dishes when he walks up beside me and slides his dirty plate in the sink. Then I feel his arm go around me, giving me a hug.

"Thanks, Annie."

Overwhelmed, I quickly aim a kiss at his cheek. He immediately lets me go as I grin down in the soapy dishwater.

"Welcome, Bryce."

My phone starts buzzing on the counter and he casually walks over and cancels the call.

"It's already almost ten thirty."

"Yeah, that's what happens when you get out of bed at ten. Time flies."

"But we're dropping in the engine this morning, I don't want to be late."

"Let me just finish this, and we can take the dogs for a shorter walk now and a longer one this afternoon."

"How about I take them quickly while you finish up?" he suggests, already calling the dogs.

"Fine. Make sure you hold on to them good."

"Annie?" I turn around and look at him standing there with a mischievous grin on his face. Damn, the kid is just like his dad. "You may be older, but I'm bigger."

He heads toward the front door, but I can hear his chuckle, and I have to blink furiously at the tears.

I quickly finish the dishes and tidy the kitchen before he comes back. I'm about to shove my bare feet in my Chucks when I hear a knock at the door. Probably forgot his key.

But when I pull open the door it's not Bryce.

"Hey, what are you doing here?"

27

Sumo

We hit the ground running this morning.

I'd barely tucked my bag in my locker when a call came in for a three-vehicle crash at the intersection of Maine and Junction. One person was pinned inside one of the cars, so the engine pulled out in front of us.

The driver of a black SUV had blown through a red light, broadsided a silver Toyota, crumpling the driver's side pinning the driver inside. The Toyota then careened into a third car waiting for the red light on the opposite side of the intersection.

The scene was chaotic. With traffic backed up on Main to 32nd, cars had to get up on the sidewalk to let us through. Blue was able to get in the back of the silver car to check on and stabilize the driver, while I did a quick check of the other victims. It took us almost an hour to safely extract the young woman and load her in the back of the rig.

On the way back from Mercy, after dropping the patient off, we were called to a fall in the Walmart parking lot. That one was mostly scrapes and bruises, but because the old man indicated he was on blood thinners, we convinced him to let us take him to the hospital to get properly assessed.

Another forty-five minutes later and we're finally heading back to the station, after Blue makes me stop at Durango Joes Coffee. We're about to turn onto 32nd when the radio crackles again.

"You've gotta be fucking kidding me," I mutter under my breath as Blue answers the call.

"...*Vehicle versus pedestrian on River Bend...*"

Jesus, that's right around the corner from me.

"...*caller says to use caution, two large dogs on scene...*"

I don't hear anything else.

With sirens blaring I turn left onto River Bend.

"Easy, Sumo. We can't know for sure," Blue offers, but my gaze is focused on a small group of people standing on the side.

In the middle of the road is a prone figure, two dogs I recognize standing guard.

I hit the brakes, slam the gear in park, jump out, and start running. I can hear Daisy's low growl at a distance and when I get closer she bares her teeth. Behind her is the prone body of my son. Panic hits me hard, but I force it down.

"Daisy-girl, it's me. Dee? You're gonna have to let me get at Bryce. You did good, Daisy, protecting him. Good girl, Dee."

I have no idea what I'm rambling but Hunter has come over to me, his tail low but wagging. Daisy starts to whimper, looking behind her at Bryce and then back at me.

"I've got him, Daisy, I've got him."

I can't wait any longer and take a step closer when I hear Blue call behind me.

"Wait for—"

"That's my fucking son," I yell back, even as I reach out my hand to the nervous dog. "Good girl, Daisy. You're a good girl."

She smells me and immediately goes down on her belly on the ground.

"Good girl," I mumble, stepping around her and sinking down on my knees beside my son.

His left leg is bent at an awkward angle and I don't need X-rays to know it's broken. There is no blood under his head, but I'm afraid to touch him. Afraid of what I'll discover. Instead I put a hand on his chest and feel it rise and fall. I want to cry with relief.

"Can someone give me an idea what happened here?" I yell out at the people on the side of the road.

"Saw a van tearing out of here," one of them calls back. "Figure he must've hit the kid."

I keep an eye on Daisy as Blue approaches with the gurney and our bag on top. Behind her I can see our engine pull in beside the ambulance and Cheddar jumping down.

"I've got him, Sumo, you get those dogs secured," Blue says, but I can't bring myself to get up, even as Blue takes over with steady hands. "Sumo! Get those dogs out of here before we have more patients!"

I notice Daisy started growling again, freezing Cheddar in his tracks. I take one last look at my son's still face and get up, grabbing the dogs' leashes dragging on the ground.

As I approach the house I notice the front door open and for the first time I wonder where Annie is. Her car is in the driveway, but where is she?

"Annie?"

I run through the house, look in the laundry room, the garage, out in the backyard. When I return to the living room I see her phone on the floor, the screen cracked.

"Annie!"

I run upstairs, fling open doors even though I already know I won't find her.

"Sumo!" Tony is at the bottom of the stairs as I come down.

"She's not here. Her phone..."

"I saw. I'm on it. But they're loading up your son. You need to get your ass in the ambulance, brother."

"But Annie..."

He grabs my shoulders and shakes me—*hard*.

"Right fucking now. Keith and I are on Annie. Go." He gives me a shove in the direction of the door and I keep going, feeling utterly helpless.

I ignore the additional cruisers starting to fill the street and focus on the back of the rig where Cheddar is closing the doors. I break into a run.

"Hold up!"

Cheddar turns his head and sees me coming.

"Get in the back, brother. I'll drive."

Blue is inside, slipping an IV needle in his forearm. His face is pale and his eyes are still closed. I hesitate only for a moment before I shake the paralysis off and climb inside, taking a seat on the other side of the gurney.

"What've we got?"

"You've seen his leg. Nothing exposed but the bone is displaced. It'll need to be set. He's got some abrasions along his left side."

"His head?"

"No depressions, no cuts, but quite to goose egg on the back of his skull." I feel her eyes on me and tear mine away from his face. "He'll be okay, Sumo. His heart is steady and strong, as is his breathing."

"Okay."

I sound dubious even to my own ears, and it's not that I don't appreciate what she's saying, but the reality is he could have internal bleeding which is not always immediately obvious.

"Oh, before I forget, I found his phone when I cut off his pants."

She leans over the gurney to hand it to me. She's about to sit back down, when we hear in a faint voice, "Is it broken?"

I slide on my knees beside the gurney, grab his hand and press my forehead to the back of it.

"Hey, buddy," Blue says. "You've got a broken leg, yeah."

"No, my phone."

"That looks to be in one piece," she assures him.

"Dad?"

I have to swallow hard before I lift my head.

"Right here, kiddo."

"He took Annie. Dad, I tried to stop the van. I took a picture with my phone." I watch his eyes fill with tears. "Look at the picture," he insists.

I pull up his picture library. The last picture he took was of a delivery van.

"It was from the grocery store."

I look at Bryce. "Grocery store?"

"Had the City Market logo on the side."

Jesus. Someone she worked with?

"He had her over his shoulder and threw her in the back."

I can hear Blue talking to someone, but I'm too focused on my son.

"The guy from the bakery. It was him."

* * *

Annie

Thirty minutes earlier.

"I heard you quit."

Something about the way he stands—his feet spread, arms down and slightly away from his body—gives off tension. Like a coiled spring, waiting to be released.

"I did. My life is taking a new direction."

I'm not sure why I'm telling him this but he's making me a little uneasy, especially when he softly chuckles.

"I'm aware."

There's a world of understanding in those two words hitting me all at once, and suddenly I see the threat under the charming, handsome veneer. This man is nothing like the Ted I thought I knew.

Luckily I never let go of the door but the moment I move to close it he springs forward, shoving me back so hard I land on my ass on the floor. He slams the door shut behind him and looms over me.

"Ted, what are you doing?"

"I tried to warn you, Annabel," he mumbles, pulling a roll of duct tape from his pocket.

I'm terrified. Bryce could walk in any minute. I try to crab-walk away from him but my back hits the wall. His long strides easily bridge the distance before I have a chance to move. He suddenly reaches down and starts pulling me up by a fistful of my hair. I desperately grab on to his wrist, the pain in my scalp bringing tears to my eyes.

FREYA BARKER

My legs wobble underneath me as he lowers his face to mine.

"Please," I plead, trying to distract him while I find my footing. Then I sharply pull up my leg, aiming for his balls, but he's quick and I ineffectively land my knee to his thigh.

The next moment his body pins me to the wall. Revulsion ripples through me when I feel the hard outline of his erection against my stomach. When he lowers his head, I try to turn away but I can't avoid his hot, stale breath hitting my face.

"Help! Someone!" I manage to scream before he slams my head into the wall.

"Shut up," he hisses, drops of spittle hitting my face. "Scream again and we'll wait for the boy. Maybe leave his body as a present for his father."

Oh, God, please no. I press my lips together to indicate I'll be silent.

He said wait for the boy, I assume that means he intends to take me. I know they say you should never let yourself be taken to a different location, but if it means leading him away from the people I love, I'm not going to fight him.

Not yet, anyway, because I have no intention of making things easy for him once we're away from the house.

He brings the roll of tape up and tears off a strip with his teeth before slapping it on my mouth.

"Good girl," he mumbles, his lips brushing my cheek and I almost gag. "I knew you'd eventually see it my way. It'll be so good, you'll see."

He keeps up his muttering as he flips me around, taping my wrists together, and I try hard not to listen to his deranged words but it proves impossible.

"I knew it the first time you smiled at me. Do you remember?"

254

I'm pretty sure I'd never seen him until he started working at the bakery, December of last year. I must've somehow conveyed that because he looks up from where he's taping my ankles.

"You will soon enough."

For the first time in my life, I wish I were three times my size when he all too easily throws me over his shoulder. He hesitates for a moment on the front step. Hanging upside down I still recognize the store's delivery van at the curb, the back doors open and engine running.

I bounce against his back as he jogs toward the street, unable to do much to stop the movement with my hands taped behind my back. I'm tossed unceremoniously into a large plastic bin in the back of the van, and without my hands to break the fall; I land hard on my hip.

"Hey!" I hear a familiar voice yell outside, a fraction of a second before I hear the doors slam.

Then another door slams and the van starts moving, sliding the bin around the back. I feel the vehicle veer right and hear a sickening thud before it straightens out and speeds off.

"I brought you a sandwich," he starts talking over the noise of the engine, as if we're having a casual conversation.

Yet all I can think of is the sound of the van hitting something. I silently apologize to Daisy or Hunter, hoping it was one of them and not Bryce, whose voice I heard calling out.

"You were sitting at your dressing table, turned your head and smiled at me. I knew right then you were meant for me."

Dressing table? He's talking about my room on the set. Was he part of the catering crew? I try to remember as hard as I can, but I can't place him there. I'm embarrassed to admit over the years support crew would come and go, and I'd long stopped paying much attention.

"I sent you notes, gifts, waiting for the right time to claim you. I'd even made sure I knew where you were at all times." He's talking about the tracker. He must've planted it in my purse at some point. "So I knew when you started seeing *him*." His voice gets harder as the bin slides and hits the side of the van hard when he takes a sharp curve. "I warned you then too, but you didn't listen. Why wouldn't you listen?

"I did the right thing. Gave you some space, patiently waiting and watching. Then I noticed that guy across the road watching you too. He even looked like the other one. It was easy to get into his place, leave some things behind, set the fire. I had to make a statement, send a message."

It's eerie, almost like he's talking to himself, as if I'm not even here.

I'm wedged in my tight confinement, unable to properly test the tape at my wrists, when I feel the van slow down. It makes another sharp turn and then stops.

"I'll be right back," I hear him say. "Picking up a surprise for you; don't move."

He follows it up with a strange giggle that has every hair on my body stand on end. As soon as the door slams shut, I know if I don't do something now I may not get another chance.

Since my ability to move is limited, I use my weight to rock the bin from side to side until the momentum tips it over. With my arms no longer wedged, I'm now able to pull at my restraints, finding I don't have a lot of movement. One side of the van has shallow metal shelving, with L-shaped poles screwed into the floor and ceiling.

I manage to sit up, slide my back to a pole, and frantically feel around with my fingers for a rough edge. I find it where a crossbar is attached with a simple screw instead of a bolt. Separating my wrists as far as the tape will allow, I rub it against the tapered back of the screw.

In what feels like an eternity but in effect is probably only a minute or two, I feel the tape ripping, and with a little added force I'm able to get my hands free. With the use of my fingers, the tape around my ankles is not that hard to remove.

There's nothing like a handle or something to open the back doors, so I dive between the seats to the front, peeking out the side window. It looks like we're parked at the back of the Walmart store. I don't see anything other than the trees bordering the back of the parking lot and two containers about ten feet from a loading door.

With no one in sight, I try the door, which opens easily. Ignoring the pain in my hip, I lower myself from the cab. I freeze for a moment, unable to decide whether to try and make it to the front of the store where I can find help, or run the opposite way and hide in the trees.

Then I realize I have a third option.

28

Sumo

It's tearing me apart.

"Sumo, he wants to talk to you."

Blue hands me the phone, and I try to throw Bryce a reassuring smile to alleviate the worry in his eyes as I put it to my ear.

"City Market van?" Tony barks.

"That's what he said. Guy from the bakery." I close my eyes and try to picture the man I've seen less than a handful of times. "Dirty blond, light eyes. Maybe six one… or two. Average. *Fuck*, I can't think."

"You're doing fine. Name?"

Shit, I'm positive she mentioned it before. I remember the girl, Jenny, but I can't think of…

"Ken, I'm pretty sure… No, it's Ted. Yeah, Ted; I'm sure of it."

I hear Tony relay the information before he's back on the line.

"Keith is already pulling up to the City Market. We'll get him."

The line goes dead and I look over at Bryce, who winces when we hit a bump.

"He's in pain," I tell Blue, handing her back her phone.

"Already gave him something. Give it a minute to work."

"Coming up on Mercy," Cheddar calls from the front.

"Dad, you should go find her."

I take his hand and kiss it.

"I'm not going anywhere, kid."

"What about Annie?"

Fuck, ripping my heart right down the middle. I want to go out there and find her so badly, but I know my place is here.

"Cops will find her, Son."

"Are you sure?"

Hell, no, I'm not sure. Whoever has her has been able to fly under the radar for a couple of years already. *Christ*, he's been right under our noses the whole time.

Still, I lie to my child.

"I'm positive."

* * *

Annie

The smell is overwhelming.

When I flung myself over the edge of the dumpster, I landed in a pile of rotting produce, but I'm afraid to move. I'm not sure how long it's been, but it feels like an hour has passed. Maybe it would've been a better idea to make a break for it after all, but I'd been too afraid I'd run right into him. The bins seemed a better way to go, hoping he'd go look for me behind the parking lot in the wooded area first. I would've waited for him to disappear into the trees and then made a run for the front of the store. Now I wonder if that was a smart move.

I hear footsteps approaching and I tilt my head slightly to better hear. The containers block the view of the van to anyone approaching, since they're closer to the corner of the building. I realize too late I never shut the passenger side doors. He'll be able to see it as soon as he starts passing the bins. He'll know right away I'd escaped.

"No! You fucking bitch," I hear him yell as the footsteps suddenly run past.

I'm afraid to breathe but my heart is beating so hard, I wouldn't be surprised if he'd be able to hear. Another volley of curses and then I hear the van door slam.

A few steps, and then silence. I press my hand against my chest to try and muffle the sound of my heart beating out of my chest, swallowing the whimper that wants to escape.

More steps, these sound like they're coming closer, until suddenly I can hear running. The sound is moving away. When I can no longer hear them, I carefully straighten up, peeking over the edge of the bin.

He's pacing back and forth on the far side of the lot, peering into the brush.

It's now or never.

I find a handhold, lift a foot on a metal crossbar, and hoist myself over the edge without looking back. I land hard, catching my forward momentum with my hands. I ignore the sharp sting in my palms and despite the pain on my left side; I force my legs to move. The moment I clear the back of the second bin, I can hear him yelling behind me, but I'm already moving.

My legs are pumping and my eyes are laser focused on the corner of the building, coming closer with every step. Blood is roaring in my ears so I sense more than hear him closing in behind me. He yells again for me to stop, this time a lot closer and I force myself to run faster.

The instant I turn the corner, I run full speed into what feels like a solid wall if not for a distinct 'harrumph.'

Next thing I know a pair of arms band around me, pressing me with my back to the wall.

"Keep moving along the wall," the voice whispers before I'm abruptly released.

Only then do I notice two police cruisers blocking the alley.

* * *

Sumo

I'm going nuts, pacing back and forth outside the doors of the surgical wing.

The good news is Bryce has a concussion but no extensive head or brain injury.

Unfortunately, they took him straight to surgery to realign the bones in his lower leg and plates fixed to keep them in place. He won't be able to put any weight on it for at least eight weeks, so he'll have to get used to crutches to get around.

Good thing Blue was there, taking notes, because I barely heard anything the surgeon said when he was briefing us beforehand. She wouldn't leave my side until I asked her to get us some coffee, needing a few minutes to myself.

I sink down in a chair and lean forward, my head in my

hands. It's been almost two hours since we got here, and I still haven't heard anything from Tony. I'm going crazy with worry for Annie, worry for Bryce. It hurts my head and my heart.

Well over two hours since that creep took Annie and God knows what he's done to her in that time. I feel sick to my stomach. I don't know what I'd do if anything happens to either of them.

The doors at the other end of the hall swing open and I jump to my feet. Tony walks through, pushing a wheel-chair holding Annie. I barely notice Blue following behind.

"She's okay, we've got the guy in custody," Tony says, but my eyes are for Annie only.

Unable to speak, I drop down to my knees in front of her, putting my face in her lap. Immediately her hands come up and stroke my hair.

"I'm okay, honey," she whispers, as Tony and Blue keep walking, leaving us sitting in the middle of the hallway.

"Are you hurt? Let me look at you."

I lift my head and reach for her face. There is some redness around her mouth and I carefully touch it with the pad of my finger.

"He taped my mouth, that's all. My hip is a little bruised so Tony insisted on the chair," she babbles nervously, while I let my hands run over her face and body, needing to check for myself. "I smell, because I was hiding in a pile of rotting vegetables." Suddenly she starts crying.

"Hey." I pull her forward in my arms and she buries her face in my neck. "It's okay, you're all right."

"I'm blathering on because I'm too scared to ask how Bryce is," she sobs.

I set her back by the shoulders and cup her face in my hands.

"He's in surgery. They're fixing his leg. It may take some time but he should recover just fine."

"Are you sure? I heard it, when the van hit..."

"Shhh. He'll be fine."

I quickly press my mouth against hers, tasting the salt of her tears on her lips. When I pull back I brush my thumbs under her eyes.

"No more—"

"Sumo?" Blue calls out.

I turn around to see the surgeon come through the doors.

* * *

Annie

"Thank you."

Blue grins at me. "No problem. We often steal scrubs from the hospital. We get puked on regularly and I don't like walking around in a dirty uniform."

"I bet."

Blue just wheeled me into a washroom after the nurse came to get Kyle. Bryce is still in recovery, but starting to wake up and apparently got a bit agitated when he didn't see his father. Blue offered to help me get cleaned up a bit. I guess I was starting to stink up the waiting room.

"Here, I nicked you a towel as well. Unfortunately the only soap is the antibacterial stuff from the dispenser."

She helps me on my feet and I wince when I put weight on my left side. I really did a number on that hip.

"Sure you don't want that checked out?" she asks, helping me out of my jeans while I pull off my shirt. "Yikes, you'll wanna ice that as soon as you can." I look down to see a nice big bruise forming. "Let me find a bag for these," she rolls up the dirty clothes, "and an icepack for your hip. You gonna be okay?"

"I'll be fine."

Ten minutes later I'm washed up—I even stuck my head under the tap—am wearing clean scrubs, and have an icepack wedged against my hip when Blue wheels me into the elevator. Apparently Kyle came looking for me because they were moving Bryce to a regular room on the second floor.

Kyle is waiting when we get out of the elevator, looking exhausted but smiling when he sees me. He leans over and kisses me sweetly.

"Feeling better?"

"Much."

"I can't get him to rest, he keeps asking for you. Wants to make sure you're really okay."

"I'm gonna leave you guys to it, find Tony, and see if he can give me a quick ride to the station," Blue announces. "Cheddar took the rig."

I watch as Kyle wraps his partner in a hug, mumbling, "Thanks," in his partner's ear before letting her go. With a wink for me she steps back in the elevator.

Bryce looks small in the hospital bed. His eyes are open when Kyle rolls me up to the bed.

"Are you hurt?" he asks, and I promptly start tearing up again. Seriously, such a good kid.

"I'm fine, just a bruise. I'm more worried about you."

"I'm sorry. I tried to stop him."

Damn kid is breaking my heart.

"Are you kidding right now?" I grab his hand in mine. "Detective Ramirez told me what you did. I would've been in big trouble without you telling them how to find me. You saved my bacon, Bryce. I'll never forget that."

He manages a wobbly smile.

"Cool."

Then he asks me how I got away, and I give both of them the whole story. I watch Kyle—who took a seat on the other side of the bed—as he wrings his hands in his lap. I can tell he's struggling with something but that'll have to wait until later.

Later comes sooner than I thought when after I make Bryce laugh with my dumpster story, he promptly falls asleep. A nurse comes in to check on him and gently informs us maybe it's time to let him rest.

Kyle leaves Bryce's phone on the nightstand where he can reach it, and jots down his phone number for the nurse, who promises to call if Bryce wakes up and needs us. Then he bends over the bed and kisses his son's head before wheeling me out of the room.

To my surprise, a tall police officer meets us in the lobby downstairs.

"Was about to bring your keys up to you. Ramirez told us to drop your truck off," he says to Kyle before looking down at me. "It's parked a few rows over. Let me quickly pull it up for you."

"Thanks, Jay." Kyle claps him on the shoulder.

I'm surprised to find it's getting dark outside. I've lost all sense of time.

In minutes we're on our way home, and the tension I felt coming off Kyle earlier seems to have returned.

"What's wrong?" I finally ask him when he pulls up to the house after a silent drive home.

He puts the truck in park and turns the engine off before turning to me, his head hanging low as he looks at me from under his eyebrows.

"Killed me, *Annie-chan.*" His voice is so low I can barely hear him.

I reach over and put a hand on his arm. "I'm fine, honey. I promise. Bryce is gonna be fine too."

He shakes his head.

"I was so torn, look for you or go with Bryce. If something had happened to you I—"

I put my hands on his cheeks and force him to look at me.

"Enough. I would've been pissed if you'd left that boy to come looking for me. You understand me? Of course you went with your son, that's not even a question." I plant a hard kiss on his lips. "Now let's go inside, those dogs have been cooped up long enough by themselves. We'll be lucky if we don't find any surprises they left for us," I tell him firmly, before letting him go and opening my door.

I hear him getting out the other side and wait for him to help me down. Instead he lifts me in his arms and starts walking to the door. There he sets me carefully on my feet so he can unlock it, but before he opens the door he turns to me.

"I love you, Annie Flowers."

29

Annie

My hip still bothers me a little when I climb out of my car.

A barren plot of dirt is all that's left of what was my little haven. The burned-out remnants removed at some point this past week.

I hear a muffled woof walking up the path to Edward's place, as the door opens and the little chubby pug jumps down the step and waddles up to me.

"Hey, Blossom-girl." Her body wiggles, turning figure eights around my ankles.

"I see you haven't forgotten about us," Edward grumbles by the front door, and I grin up at him.

"How could I, with that sunny disposition?"

I hear Hattie laugh uproariously from right behind him.

We brought Bryce home from the hospital yesterday afternoon. Kyle was able to take the rest of the week off to hang out with his boy, who is mostly confined to the couch in the living room. This morning I left them playing the game system Kyle temporarily moved upstairs, and they were so absorbed in the game, I'm pretty sure they won't miss me.

I hand the tray of butter tarts I baked last night—his favorites—to Edward and am rewarded with the barest twitch of his mouth.

"Guess you're gonna want coffee," he mutters before yelling over his shoulder, "Hattie, get Annie some coffee, will ya?"

"I swear, you holler at me one more time, all you'll get is my frying pan over your head, you old cantankerous coot!" comes from inside.

I see things haven't changed much here.

What used to be a single chair by the side of his door has grown into a small table with two chairs and a third folded up, leaning against the trailer. Edward slides the tray on the table before taking a seat and—assuming the second one is Hattie's—I grab the folded chair. My old neighbor doesn't say anything but he nods his approval.

"How are you feeling?" I ask him.

He shrugs. "Half the time I can't tell for the pain that woman puts me through."

"I heard that!" Hattie says, stepping out of the trailer with a tray holding coffee accoutrements, and I watch Edward hide a grin from her. I make room on the table for the coffee and catch her hissing at him, "I'm thinking I'll sleep back in my own trailer tonight."

Yowza. Edward looks over and shamelessly winks at me.

These two. I'm learning their constant bickering is more of a love language to them. It makes me happy to think of them together. Especially since I'm here to break the news I won't be coming back, not even after the new trailer is delivered.

I also intend to give them my new phone number, the one to the new phone I bought yesterday after it became clear the gossip rags weren't ready to let me off the hook just yet.

"I'm moving in with Kyle."

"Good for you," Hattie is the first to respond. "If I could get my hands on a hunk like that I wouldn't think twice either."

I snicker when I witness the dirty look Edward throws her.

"Don't let the door hit you in the ass," he grumbles.

"Oh, keep your socks on. I'm here, ain't I?" she fires back.

"He good to you?"

Edward's question surprises me.

"The best," I respond honestly.

"You don't think it's fast?"

"Normally I'd probably agree, but given the circumstances it makes sense."

I proceed to tell them about the events of the past few days and I notice Edward's nostrils flaring.

"Shoulda called," he finally complains.

"Instead of calling and worrying you, I thought I'd come tell you in person so you could see for yourself I'm fine."

He harrumphs and grabs another butter tart off the tray.

"Last one," Hattie decrees, earning her a glare she completely ignores. "And the boy? How is he?"

"He'll be laid up for a bit but he's home, and he's young and healthy, so he should bounce back."

"What about that one," Edward asks, lifting his chin at the trailer across the street. The one where Parsons lives, but his truck is not in the driveway.

Guilt rushes over me. I've hardly even thought of the man in the past few days, assuming police would've let him go, but now that I'm looking at his trailer, I realize I owe him an apology. After what Ted told me in that van, the only thing Will Parsons ever did was have an interest in me. I'm the one who pointed him out to the police.

"He was as much a victim as I was," I confess as I turn back to Edward, not liking the idea I'd been so wrong about the man.

"Speak of the devil," Hattie announces, looking over my shoulder where I hear the crunch of wheels on the gravel.

"That him?" I ask, getting to my feet.

"Looks like."

"Right. I'd better have a word before I get myself home."

I walk around the small table and give Hattie a hug. Then I move on to Edward, who eyes me warily as I bend down to kiss his cheek.

"In a few weeks, when Bryce feels a little better, we'll have to have you over for a cookout."

"I like cream puffs," Hattie calls after me.

"So noted," I toss back, as I make my way down the path.

Will Parsons stands next to his truck, watching me approach with an unreadable expression on his face.

"I'm sorry," I start when I'm still ten feet away. I watch his body give a little jerk and his face register surprise. I'm not sure what he was expecting but an apology wasn't it.

I stop a few feet away. He smooths out his expression, leans against his truck, and crosses his arms over his chest, making himself look relaxed but still guarded. I take a deep breath in.

"I moved here to escape a stalker," I explain. "And it was quiet for the better part of a year when things started happening again." He raises an eyebrow, and I swallow before forging on. "Around the time you came up to me in the Laundromat." The eyebrow drops again, but he stays quiet. Dammit, he's not making this easy. "Started paying me attention, and I was suspicious. I was also wrong, and I'm so sorry."

He then unfolds his arms and stands up straight, even at this distance making me feel like he's towering over me.

"I see. Gonna make a man think twice before he decides to show a pretty woman interest. And just to say; you're even prettier without the glasses, shows the color of your eyes." I feel an embarrassed blush warm my cheeks and look down at the toes of his work boots. He was just being nice and I repaid him by accusing him. His deep chuckle draws my attention to his smiling face. "Hand to heart, Annie, all I was interested in was gettin' to know you better."

"I know that now," I answer meekly, feeling about a foot tall, if that.

"Right. Then you should also know I don't blame you. I blame the asshole who pinned that shit on me. I just wish we coulda met under different circumstances." He holds out his hand.

"I can't tell you enough how sorry I am," I mutter again, shaking his hand.

He holds on a little longer than comfortable.

"It's all good, Annie." With a last little squeeze he releases my hand.

"I should be on my way."

He tips an imaginary hat and with an awkward little wave I turn toward my car. Now that I know he's not a creepy stalker, he actually seems like a really nice guy. It's on my lips to invite him over for the cookout too, but realize just in time that might be insensitive.

Still, as I climb behind the wheel of my Matrix to head

home, my heart is much lighter.

* * *

Sumo

"I'm hungry."

Bryce fell asleep on the couch not long after Annie left to visit her old neighbors.

I've been restless ever since. Rationally I know the guy's in jail and may well be extradited to California where he could face charges for the murder of David Finch, but my gut would prefer to have Annie within reach.

I look over at my son, who is rubbing the sleep from his eyes.

"I can do hungry. What do you feel like?"

"Grilled cheese," he says without thinking. "And can you put tomatoes on again?"

I duck in the fridge, giving myself a mental pat on the back. Last week he'd almost gagged when I told him I put slices of tomato sprinkled with oregano between the cheese slices before I grilled it. I got him to try and he wolfed them down, but didn't say a word.

"What'd I tell ya? Just like pizza, right?" I taunt him.

"Whatever," he mumbles, unwilling to concede.

I recognize myself at that age. I was a smart-ass, too cool for my boots, and my parents didn't know anything worth knowing. Bryce is tame in comparison. I'm lucky.

I'm about to start putting the sandwiches together when the front door opens.

"Hey, babe," I call out. "Just making us grilled cheese, want one?"

"Sure, doll!" comes back in a horrendous falsetto.

I swing around to find Blue, Annie, and fucking Tony standing by the couch, all of them grinning, Bryce included. I ignore them and zoom in on Esme, looking on from the car seat dangling from Tony's hand.

"Hey, baby-girl," I coo, earning her curious gaze as I abandon the grilled cheese under construction.

Disregarding the adults, I kneel down in front of her and deftly unclip her from the harness, plucking her from her seat. She immediately cuddles her body to my chest as I round the couch and sit down beside my son.

"Next time leave your annoying parents at home, okay, peanut?" Her response is a kick of her legs as her hand grabs hold of my bottom lip, attempting to detach it from my face. "I need to introduce you to someone." I sound like a drunken sailor, with my mouth still in her death grip and I careful pry her little fingers back.

"Bryce, meet Esme—Esme, this is your new best friend, Bryce."

Without warning I lift the baby from my shoulder and hand her to Bryce, who looks like she's a venomous snake.

"She won't bite," I assure him.

"Just don't get your fingers close to her mouth," Blue's dry warning drifts over my shoulder and I bite down a grin.

"I'll hurt her," he mutters, a panicked look on his face as he reluctantly holds out his hands.

"Nah," Tony pipes up. "She's pretty bendy. You can just put her on your lap if you like." To me he says, "Now what's this about grilled cheese?"

"Fine," I grumble, getting to my feet and walking over to Annie, dropping a kiss to her lips. "You girls too?"

"Is my name Blue?" My partner is a smart-ass.

"I'll give you a hand," Annie says smiling.

"Everything okay with Edward?" I ask when she steps

up to the counter beside me and starts slicing tomatoes.

"He's fine. Hattie's seeing to it." She wiggles her eyebrows.

"Oh." I pretend an exaggerated shiver and Annie snickers. "Didn't need that visual."

She bumps her shoulder into my arm.

"Don't worry, I'll replace it with something better later."

We haven't done much more than cuddle and sleep these past few days, so at her suggestive tone my cock jumps to attention.

"Now you're just being cruel," I mutter under my breath. "We've got company."

I turn around and see Blue sitting beside Bryce on the couch, talking quietly. Then my glance slides to Tony, who is just taking a seat at the island.

"If you want a drink, grab it yourself," I tell him, and he gets back up to dive into the fridge, coming up with a Diet Coke. "No beer?"

"I've gotta go back in this afternoon. Better stick to this." He sits back down. "We just took Esme to her checkup. She's perfect."

"Of course she is," I agree. I can't help it, I adore that little human, despite the huge pain in my ass her parents can be.

"I actually wanted to stop by to give you guys an update. The DA dropped all the charges against Parsons and he was released last night."

"I know," Annie says, handing me the next sandwich to drop in the pan. "I talked to him."

"You talked to him? You didn't tell me that." My tone is a little sharper than I intended, but the thought of her alone with that guy doesn't sit well with me.

She turns her face to me, one eyebrow arched up. "Not like I've exactly had a chance," she snips back. "I saw him just as I was leaving Edward and Hattie and went to apologize." She rolls her eyes dramatically when I growl. "In full view of both Edward and Hattie the entire time—calm your tits."

Tony bursts out laughing and Blue calls from the couch. "What's funny?"

"Annie just told Sumo to calm his tits," he happily volunteers.

"Awww," my partner mocks. "Just like a real couple."

I'm annoyed with the two until I hear Bryce snicker as well. I nudge Annie with my elbow.

"Next time, leave them outside. If they wanna come and harass me, they'll have to call for a damn appointment."

"So noted," she mumbles back, but she's grinning too.

"Keep an eye on these," I point at the two pans I have going. "I'll grab us some drinks."

I get orders from everyone but Tony, and we collectively agree to eat in the living room so Bryce doesn't have to move. The dogs are put outside. Esme who apparently has taken a shine to both Bryce and his controller—which she's currently trying to stuff in her mouth—is put back in her car seat, and the rest of us dive into the stack of grilled cheese sandwiches I set in the middle of the coffee table.

Tony is finished first and continues his update.

"Ted Murphy was officially charged this morning after we got a report from the LAPD. Murphy worked for Stars Catering in Long Beach for four years before he handed in his notice almost a year ago."

"They catered the show for years," Annie volunteers, and I watch with some satisfaction as she plucks another sandwich off the plate.

"We also searched his apartment. It's not too far from the trailer park, over the flower shop on East 39th."

"Within walking distance," I point out.

"Sorry, Annie, but it was pretty clear the man was obsessed with you. I won't go into detail—"

"Please don't," she tells him.

"Right. Anyway, all the evidence from the apartment and the Walmart parking lot, along with your testimony, is more than enough to make sure he stays locked up. Then of course there's the death of David Finch in LA which had been ruled an accident, but the LAPD now wants to have another look at."

"He didn't tell me in so many words, but he implied he was responsible for that."

"Let's hope there's enough evidence left to corroborate that, but regardless, he's got a shitload of charges against him here that'll earn him a good many years behind bars."

A few minutes later Tony and Blue get up to leave, Esme protesting loudly when Blue plucks the controller from her hands and gives it back to Bryce.

"One thing I meant to ask," Annie addresses Tony. "Did he tell you why he stopped in at Walmart? He said it was a surprise, and it's been bugging me."

Tony glances over at me, a warning in his eyes, before he answers.

"He dropped a bag containing, among other things, a length of chain and padlocks."

"That son of a bitch," I grind out when I feel Annie stepping up beside me, slipping her arm around my waist.

"Among other things?" she asks, leaning close.

"Yeah, he also had some medical supplies, a lab coat, and a...uh... white lace lingerie."

You don't need a lot of imagination to put those pieces together and I'm trying to hold on to my cool for my son's sake, but at fourteen he's already much too smart.

"Ewww," he blurts out, a grimace on his face. "That's gross."

30

Annie

Three weeks later.

"Hey, Annie."

Mel's assistant—and as I've come to find out, her daughter—smiles when I walk into the office. I was here last week to see if Mel would help me deal with Miles Coxwell. The man has been relentless, talking to the gossip rags, connecting my name to the arrest of Ted Murphy, something the cops had tried hard to avoid. As a result, there have been paparazzi around town, and it's only a matter of time before they land on our doorstep.

Mel called me in to talk about a strategy for dealing with them.

"How are you, Lindsey?"

"I'm good. Heading off on vacation on Monday so I'll be even better."

"Oh yeah? Where are you off to?"

"South of France with a couple of friends. One of the girls is getting married," she says with a big grin when Mel comes walking down the hallway. Barefoot again.

"That's what kids do these days," Mel says, shaking her head. "Instead of getting a few drinks, or hitting up a strip club for a bachelorette party, they turn it into a damn European vacation for a week. Most ridiculous thing I've ever heard. The money spent on weddings is already outrageous. No wonder the divorce rate was up again last year."

"Oh, quit your complaining," her daughter fires back. "That divorce rate keeps you in business."

I'm having a hard time not bursting out laughing at these two. I wait for Mel to fire back but instead she tilts her head, shrugs her shoulders, and says, "Yeah, you're probably right."

She invites me back with a grand gesture, and I'm still chuckling when I take a seat in front of her desk.

"Miles Coxwell is the dried slime at the bottom of a bucket of eels."

"That may be the most apt description of him I've heard," I tell her with a grin. She shoots me a rare one back. The woman is striking when she wears her resting bitch face but when she smiles, damn, she's gorgeous. "I gather you've had contact?"

"Yes, and for the record, I could've happily lived out the rest of my life without that pleasant experience. He's a scumbag, but a smart scumbag. He clued in pretty fast I wasn't messing around when I told him I'd not only drag his ass in court with a civil suit that would make his ears ring, but I'd call my buddy in the Los Angeles DA's office and make sure he'd get nailed with a felony charge for providing false information leading to a homicide. He didn't like the sound of that."

"You have a buddy in the DA's office?" She never mentioned that in our discussion last week.

"Well...not right now, but I make friends easily," she deadpans, and I start laughing again. "Anyway, he agreed to have your things shipped to my office—I don't trust him with your address—and will refrain from speaking to any press about you.

"He's aware if at any time he fails to adhere to those directives, I will follow through on the civil suit and will pursue felony charges against him. Linds is working on the written agreement we will shoot off to his lawyer. I'll need you to sign it before you leave."

"I don't know how to thank you."

"No thanks needed. I live for taking assholes with underdeveloped genitals down. It was my complete and utter pleasure. Now, about Bryce. I've tried calling Kyle but I guess he's working?"

"Yes, his shift doesn't end 'til seven tomorrow morning."

"Okay." She shoves an envelope across the desk. "This is the emergency temporary custody order the judge signed off on this morning."

"Thank you so much for pushing this through." I take the envelope and stuff it in my purse.

Kyle had run into a snag trying to enroll Bryce in the local high school. The school secretary made it clear the limited paperwork he had for his son wouldn't be enough. We were missing health and immunization records, previous academic records, and most important of all—since Kyle's name was left off Bryce's birth certificate and he only has the lab test to prove paternity—proof of guardianship or custody.

Bryce will have to do an academic equivalence exam because he missed at least one year of school while in Boise with his mother, but I'm pretty sure he'll be able to pass that. His eidetic memory will come in helpful; he's been cramming in preparation every night these past two weeks. Even though he's already missed the first days of school, he's determined to make it into ninth grade like his buddies up at Arrow's Edge.

Hopefully with this order he can join them next week.

Twenty minutes later I walk out of Mel's office, my John Hancock on the agreement with Miles, which I hope will be the last time I need to hear or see his name. I wish I could say I've left that life behind, but the reality is there will always be someone who recognizes me.

Kyle and I talked about it, and instead of trying to duck and dodge the media indefinitely, I'll be doing one interview with a reputable publication. It'll probably result in a bit of a stir for a little while, but after that the press will hopefully forget about me.

The dogs almost take me down when I walk in the door, bags of groceries in my hands. They're always like this when we come home, acting like we've been gone for weeks instead of an hour, and constantly battling for attention.

"Hey, bud."

I can just see Bryce's hair stick up over the back of the couch. The kid's going to need a haircut before he starts school.

We started leaving him alone at home for short periods of time. I'd been a little uneasy at first, but Kyle reminded me Bryce is fourteen and was used to being left alone much longer than that before he came here. He said it would be good to show him we trust him.

"Hey, Annie."

"What are you up to?" I ask, as I head straight for the kitchen, dropping my load on the counter.

Bryce follows me into the kitchen, managing his crutches as if he's done nothing else his whole life.

"I was reading..." Since that first time to the library we've been back three times already. He goes through books like hot cakes, another thing I've come to love about this kid; his quiet yet voracious curiosity. "...but now I'm hungry."

I chuckle as he dives into the bags. We have a hard time keeping the fridge stocked against his appetite.

"Instead of just digging around for something to eat, why don't you unpack them so I can put some of that away first?"

Everything is tidied away a few minutes later, and Bryce sits at the island, scarfing down one of the pizza buns I brought home for him, when the doorbell rings.

"You finish, I'll get it," I tell Bryce when he starts to get up.

I've never seen the woman standing on the doorstep, but I know instinctively who she is.

"Who are you?" she has the gall to snap at me, trying to look over my shoulder into the house.

I step outside, forcing her back as I pull the door almost shut before Bryce hears, not quite latching it.

"Look," I tell the gaunt-looking, slightly disheveled woman in front of me. "You rang my doorbell, so why don't you tell me who *you* are first?"

I get a defiant look and an arrogant tilt of her chin.

"I'm here to pick up my son."

"Ah, Chanel, is it? Well, I'm afraid you'll have to contact Bryce's father first. Kyle is at work, so he may be difficult to reach, but I can tell him you stopped by."

I can see the steam gathering. I'm guessing this isn't how she imagined this would go.

"Is Bryce in there?" She tries to crowd me out of the way and when I don't budge, she yells over my shoulder, "Bryce!"

"You need to leave now." I square my shoulders and try to make myself look bigger than my lean five foot four.

"Like hell I will. I'm not leaving my son with you, bitch," she spits. "You have no right to keep him." She leans in my face. "If you don't move, I'll fucking move you myself. Bryce! Get your ass out here!"

She hauls back and I'm not quite fast enough to duck my head out of the way. Her fist hits the side of my face just as the door behind me is yanked open.

"Get out of here." Bryce's voice is soft, but the low growl from the dogs makes it sound menacing as he pulls me inside and behind him.

"Baby…" her face softens for her son.

"No," he barks. "You don't get to do this anymore. I already called Dad and he's calling the police. You need to leave."

"But…"

I watch as her face crumples and I actually feel sorry for her when he slams the door in her face. His cheeks are flushed and his eyes shiny. His mother is still yelling on the doorstep.

"I'm so sorry, honey."

He gives his head a shake. "Are you okay? Did she hurt you?"

He reaches for my face but I don't give him a chance and wrap my arms around him, one of his loosely curves around my back.

"You're a good kid, Bryce," I mumble in his shirt.

"I caught Dad at the firehouse. He's on his way."

"Seriously good," I emphasize.

We stand like that for a few minutes until we hear the squeal of tires outside and then a car door slam.

"Dad's here."

* * *

Sumo

I was about to start dinner for the crew when my phone rings.

"Dad, Mom's here, she's outside yelling at Annie. Should I call 911?"

Fucking hell. I knew things had been too easy.

"I'll call. Stay put, Bryce, I'm on my way."

"Trouble?" Cap, who's helping me prep, wants to know.

"His mother's at my fucking door, facing off with Annie."

"Go. I'll call it in."

When I pull into my driveway, I see a woman I barely recognize banging on the closed door.

"Hey!" I yell out as I jog up the path. "What the fuck do you think you're doing?"

She swings around and I'm shocked at the destruction years of drug use has left on her once-pretty face. Her pupils are no more than pinpoints, her eyelids heavy and drooping. If I had my guess she's pumped full of heroin. Jesus.

"I'm picking up my son. That bitch tells me I can't have him."

In self-preservation I shove my hands in my pockets, or else I might be tempted to use them on her.

"The woman you're talking about is my soon-to-be

wife, and she lives here, but what the fuck are *you* doing here, Chanel? I thought I made it clear to you last time not to bother contacting me until you got your ass clean, and I can tell from a distance you're doped up on something. Heroin, am I right?"

She tries to avoid my eyes as her bottom lip starts to wobble.

"I need help. I have nothing." Her pitiful whimper should have an effect on me, but it doesn't. I feel nothing but contempt.

"Wrong. You had everything and you squandered it. For what, Chanel? A quick fix?"

Behind me I hear a vehicle pull up to the curb. A quick glance shows Jay VanDyken getting out.

"You don't understand," she whines, but when she catches sight of Jay's cruiser her tears magically disappear and her mouths draws in a thin line. "You have no right to him," she hisses at me.

"Everything okay here?" Jay asks, coming up the path.

"He's taken my son!" she yells, pointing a dramatic finger in my direction.

"Is that a fact?" Is VanDyken's dry response, just as the door opens and Annie walks out, an envelope in hand.

"It's not, actually. This is an order granting Kyle custody of his son," Annie states calmly, holding up the envelope.

I get a glimpse of a red mark on the side of her face.

"Babe, what happened to your cheek?"

"It's not a big deal," she says, but I notice Chanel quickly avert her eyes.

I walk up to Annie and lift her chin. There's swelling that is already starting to push on the corner of her eye.

"Right. Did you ask her to leave?" I ask Annie gently, and she gives me a barely-there nod. Tucking her under my arm I turn to Jay. "I want to file a complaint for trespassing and assault."

"You can't do that!" Chanel screams when Jay steps up to her, getting out his handcuffs. I expect Annie to protest, but she's looking at the other woman with pity in her eyes.

"Chanel, swear to God, you brought this on yourself. For Bryce's sake, please, get your shit sorted," I tell her before steering Annie inside.

"Sumo?" Jay calls out, as I'm about to close the door on the mess outside.

"Yeah?"

"Take some pictures of her face, will you? Someone will be by later to get your statements."

I give him a thumbs-up; shut the door, and turn to find Bryce two feet away, tears in his eyes. Oh fuck. I just had his mother arrested.

"Bryce, I had no choice."

"I know," he mumbles, walking straight into my arms.

I hold him tight, glancing over his shoulder at Annie. The soft smile she sends me melts any lingering anger away like snow for the sun.

Reluctantly I let Bryce go.

"She didn't even recognize her," he points out.

"What?"

He turns his tear-streaked face to me. "Mom, she didn't even recognize Annie. She watched that show for as long as I can remember. She was messed up, wasn't she?"

"Yeah, Son. She was."

It kills me to see the hurt in his face, but he's already seen too much for me to lie to him about that.

"What's gonna happen to her?"

Fuck. I didn't know this parenting shit would be this hard.

"She'll probably be assigned a defense lawyer and will likely be seeing a judge in the next day or two."

"And then she'll go to jail?"

The defeat in his voice kills me, and I don't know what to say. But Annie does.

"I have an idea," she says, telling me with her eyes to hear her out. "What if your dad and I talk to the judge? Maybe we can suggest that if he sends her to a drug treatment center for as long as it takes for her to get clean, we'd be willing to drop the charges?"

"You can do that?" I can hear the hope in his voice.

"We can try."

"Dad?"

It still hits me in the gut hearing that, ever since I graduated from Pop to Dad.

If it were up to me the bitch could rot, but for my son's sake I can live with Annie's suggestion.

"Yeah, we'll try."

31

Annie

Two months later.

"Sweet Jesus, Kyle..."

It's five thirty in the morning and I woke up a few minutes ago with Kyle's mouth between my legs.

He has to be at work at seven and I have to get Bryce up for school, but in these early morning hours all I can think of is the magic of his tongue toying with my clit.

My hands hold onto his head as I rock my core against his mouth. Almost there.

"Please, honey..."

He slides two fingers into my pussy, curving them to hit the perfect spot that sends a charge straight down to my toes. Then he sucks hard on my clit while humming deep in his throat, and I burst apart.

Before I even draw my first breath, Kyle is braced on

one arm, looming over me. His dark eyes burn with lust as he uses his other hand to brush the crown of his cock along my slick, tender folds. My body still spasming in the aftermath of that orgasm, he drives inside me, planting himself to the root.

"Fuck, *Annie-chan*, you couldn't be more perfect."

* * *

"Bryce! Get your ass out of bed or I'm sending up the dogs!"

I'm yelling up from the bottom of the stairs when Kyle walks up behind me, kissing the spot at the base of my neck that always gives me shivers.

"I've gotta run, babe. You sure you're gonna be okay?"

"Go. I'll be fine. I'll grab a bucket of water if the dogs don't work."

I feel his body vibrate with a chuckle at my back.

"Give me your mouth."

I twist my neck and do as he asks, my nipples instantly pebbling at the hunger still in his kiss after that early morning delight he woke me up with. He pulls back, kisses the tip of my nose, and heads out the door.

Still no movement upstairs.

This isn't new. Our boy is definitely not a fan of mornings and every day is a challenge to get him out of bed.

"Okay, guys," I tell the dogs, who've been obediently waiting for their cue. "Your turn. Where's the boy, go get the boy!"

The two rather large bodies race up the stairs. I wince when I hear the door slam into the wall when they barge into his bedroom. Bryce's disgruntled sounds filter down the stairs and I walk back to the kitchen, knowing the dogs won't let up until he's out.

Twenty minutes later, he gets into the passenger's side of my new Volvo XC40. I still have the Matrix; it's up at the Arrow's Edge compound where Brick and the boys are helping Bryce rebuild the engine after it conked on me last month. I told him if he could make it run he could keep it. He'll be fifteen in two months and will be able to get his learner's permit. It scares the crap out of me.

His leg healed well, they just want to take out the stabilizing plates they put in because the doc says he's still growing. That'll be done next Friday, his fall break, that way he doesn't have to miss school.

"Have everything?" I ask when he buckles in. For all his smarts, the kid would forget his head if it wasn't screwed on.

"Yeah," he grunts, still not quite awake.

"I was gonna make tacos for dinner."

"Cool," he says with a smidge more enthusiasm.

The rest of the drive to school is silent as it is most mornings, but I don't care; my favorite part of the day is coming up. I stop outside the front door and Bryce is already out of his seat belt.

"Have a good day, honey."

His lanky body leans over the center console as he reaches over to kiss my cheek.

"Later, Annie."

He throws me that grin I'm sure will have most of the schoolgirls melting and jumps out on the curb. I sit for a minute to watch him saunter all cool and casual to the front door. From there he flips me a peace sign before darting inside.

I drive to my appointment up the mountain with a smile on my face.

Autumn is already waiting for me with the contractor.

She and I finally connected at Erin's urging, and I was

kicking myself I hadn't done so earlier. I've only known her for two months, but we've bonded quickly over our similar histories with stalkers. That, and she's hilariously forthright and unapologetic. Other than Erin, she's the only one I've told about my plans, mainly because I discovered this beautiful piece of land is smack dab beside her and Keith's.

I'd been doing a little snooping and found which one was Kyle's real estate agent. I contacted him, told him what I was looking for and was beside myself to find out the same property he'd set his sights on last year was still on the market.

God's country. I can see why he loves this so much. From the road, the property slants up in the front, but when you get to the top, the view of the valley below is breathtaking. Very similar to the view from Autumn and Keith's back deck.

"Annie, this is Jed Mason," Autumn introduces us. "Jed, meet Annie Flowers."

"Good to meet you, Annie."

"Likewise."

"Gorgeous piece of land you've got yourself."

"Thank you. Autumn tells me you live up here too?"

"About a mile and a half up the main road," he confirms. "So did you bring the drawings?"

"Oh, hang on, let me grab them."

I jog back to the Volvo and open the back door. I'd hidden them under my seat. I'm not ready to spring my surprise just yet. Ideally I'd like ground to be broken before I tell Kyle, that way he won't have to wait too long for the finished product.

"You say these were done with this property in mind?"

"As far as I know, yes."

"Okay, let's take a walk."

An hour later Autumn and I watch as Jed drives off, taking the drawings with him so he can prepare me a quote.

"I can't believe you're doing this."

A sudden wave of nausea overwhelms me and I bend over, holding onto my knees. Autumn places a hand on my back.

"I can't either," I admit. "It seemed like such a good idea when I bought the land, but now it feels like I'm stealing his dream."

"Nonsense. You're giving him his dream, but I'm thinking maybe instead of waiting, you should tell him now. Think about it, maybe he'd planned on doing some of the work himself. It's a guy thing. Keith built most of our house with his own hands and it's a matter of pride for him. Guys like to be in on the construction part. Once it comes to decorating, he'll probably be happy to leave it in your capable hands."

Shit. I didn't think about that. I thought I was being so clever, using his own words against him when he refused my money but would allow gifts. Goes to show how limited my experience is with relationships.

"Don't look so dejected." Autumn nudges me with a chuckle. "I'm sure you'll find a creative way to tell him."

That thought haunted me all the way home.

* * *

Sumo

I'm pissed.

I thought these bloodsuckers were done, but apparently not.

291

The first two weeks after Annie's interview was published, the odd reporter would show up outside our house, looking for a sound bite. I'm not sure how they found out where we lived, but I guess word travels. After that things had died down, until Hog tossed one of those gossip rags at me while we were having breakfast at the diner this morning.

On the front page was a small inset picture with the caption,

A real-life hero for Annabel

It was a picture of me doing CPR on an elderly woman my team had just pulled out of a burning apartment just up the road from the station about two weeks ago.

I never noticed anyone taking pictures. I'm pissed because that woman didn't make it and now her family had to potentially be confronted with that image in the checkout lane at the grocery store.

"To what do I owe the pleasure?" Mel says when she answers.

"Have you seen *The Star*?" I snap.

"Not in the habit to read the gossip columns, so why don't you tell me why?"

I explain the situation to her.

"Is that even legal?" I want to know.

"You do know I'm a family lawyer, right?" When I don't answer, she sighs dramatically before she adds. "But I suppose I can find out, although my guess is there's little you can do about it now. It's already out there. My advice is to let it die down. The likelihood is, every now and then when Hollywood has a slow week; someone may come up with the idea to check in on old Annabel Fiore. You're gonna have to live with it."

"I don't like that answer."

"Tough. You're gonna have to live with it. This stuff comes with the package. Unless..." I growl at her implication and she starts laughing. "That's what I thought. Suck it up, buttercup. You've got a good thing going."

"Fine. I assume you'll be sending me a bill for your time?"

"Ha! You better believe it."

The next moment I have dead air.

I'm still annoyed when I get home.

"What's wrong?" Annie asks, meeting me at the door.

"Tired," I lie, trying to pass her but she plants herself squarely in front of me.

"What's wrong?" she repeats, looking worried. "Bad call?"

I immediately feel guilty. So what if some moron gets his kicks from taking snapshots. I get to come home to a house smelling of vanilla and sugar, and a beautiful woman I can't imagine life without.

Shaking off any residual irritation, I take her face in my hands and kiss her deeply.

"I love you."

"So does that mean you're not tired?" she says with a hopeful smile, and my mind immediately dives in the gutter.

"Nah. Bryce is at school, right?"

I grin at her and start backing her up to the stairs.

"Yes, but wait." She plants both hands on my chest. "Let's save that for later."

"Later?"

"Yeah, I want you to come with me." She looks a little nervous.

"Where are we going?"

"You'll see." She puts her coat on, grabs my hand, and pulls me to the door. "We're taking the Volvo."

"Fine, but only if I get to drive."

She hasn't let me drive her new toy yet. She narrows her eyes at me when I hold out my hand.

"That's blackmail."

"Oh, I know."

She tries to wear me down with her stare until she finally concedes, "Fine," and drops the keys in my hand. I make my way over to the driver's side and open the door. "But don't touch the settings, I've just—"

I already have the seat a mile back and the steering wheel tilted up.

"I'll put it back for you," I promise, grinning at her.

"Famous last words."

She directs me up Florida Road. This is familiar territory for me, not only because Keith lives up here, but this area is also where I'd been looking last year.

"Are we going to Keith and Autumn's?" I ask, when she tells me to turn right onto the dead-end road their house is on.

"No, just keep going."

Up ahead I see the familiar real estate sign, except it has a smaller SOLD sign across the front. That last little balloon of hope I'd been holding onto deflates. Fuck.

"What are we doing here?" That didn't exactly come out too friendly and Annie looks like I slapped her. "I'm sorry, that came out wrong."

She forces a smile, making me feel like an even bigger asshole.

"I have a basket in the back, would you mind grabbing that for me?"

"A little cold for a picnic, isn't it?"

"It's not bad."

I get the basket, as she grabs a quilt from the back, and follow her up the incline to the top. There I set it down and walk up to the edge. This view is what I'd hoped to look at from my living room window.

"This is the land, isn't it?" she asks behind me. "The property you had your eye on?"

"It was."

I'm not quite sure why she'd bring me up here if she knew this was the property. Seems a little insensitive, which is unusual for her.

"Would you like to open the basket?"

Puzzled, I turn around to find her standing beside it, her hands clasped in front of her.

"What's going on?"

"I wanted to come up here to give you your early birthday present."

"My birthday isn't until December."

"That's why it's an early present," she fires back, rolling her eyes. "Open it."

The first thing I see is an envelope and I pull it out.

"This?"

"That first, yes."

I scan the papers I pull out but when I read the names at the top I sink to my butt on the cold ground. I'm a little light-headed.

"It's the title to this property."

"It is."

"How did you know?"

"I may have snooped a little," she admits with a little smile, as she sits down next to me. "Keep going." She points at the basket.

I pull the drawings out next, but attached to it is one of those certificates they give out to kids in school, complete with balloons and animals. I look up at her with an eyebrow raised.

"Hush," she snickers. "It's all I could find."

You gave me a home; I'm just returning the favor.
Happy birthday to the man who gave me new dreams.

Part of me is pissed she pulled a fast one on me, part of me wants to bawl at the gesture, but what I end up doing is tackling her to the blanket she tossed on the ground.

Bracing myself on my elbows, I look down in her beautiful blue eyes and brush a strand of hair from her forehead.

"You've been plotting behind my back."

She smiles with only a hint of guilt.

"I have."

"Don't know whether to spank you or kiss you."

Her smile deepens as she winds her arms around my neck.

"Why don't we save the spanking for later?"

I growl as I slam my mouth down on her smiling one.

Much later, after we—well, mostly me—brushed off the custard tarts she made me, and most of the bottle of champagne she had hidden in the bottom of the basket, we sit quietly enjoying the view. I have my back braced against a tree trunk, Annie sitting between my cocked knees, her back against my front.

"Jed says if he can get the permits through quickly, he'll be able to break ground before the weather gets too cold."

"I may have a few connections at City Hall," I tell her.

She tilts her head back and smiles at me.

"Next summer the three of us will be sitting here, on our deck, taking in this view."

I bend down and kiss her softly.

"On top of the world, *Annie-chan*."

THE END

* * *

Keep reading for an excerpt of "EDGE OF TOMORROW," third book in my new Arrow's Edge MC series featuring Brick Paver and Lisa Rawlings.

EDGE OF TOMORROW
Arrow's Edge MC series #3
Coming to you September 21st, 2020

Lisa

"Don't forget your lunch!"

Ezrah—who bailed out of the car the moment the wheels stopped turning—grinds to a halt halfway to the front door of the school and comes running back. I lean over to hand him his lunch bag through the passenger window.

"Best not be getting another call from the principal's office today, boy," I warn him.

All I get is a grunt in response. Dear Lord, but that child tests my patience.

Ever since we found a home in Durango two years ago my grandson has gone from a timid, beaten down little boy to this mouthy child with an attitude that won't fit through the door. He never fails to find an argument, it doesn't matter who's across from him. Yesterday he went head to head with his teacher during history class. Argued with her when she claimed slavery was abolished in the US since 1865. Ezrah disagreed. Loudly.

My grandson was not wrong, given that up until two years ago we lived in service to a family of white supremacists, but calling his teacher bat-shit crazy wasn't the right way to convey the message. I ended up having to pick him up from the principal's office, and back at home had Trunk sit him down for a good talk.

Ezrah looks up to Trunk, our resident child psychologist and a black man. My poor grandchildren haven't really known any father figures—anyone to take guidance from —until we came here. Of course, in an MC testosterone runs rampant, and although all good, decent men, they're not known for their tact. My grandson emulates what he sees.

I watch him run to the door and slips inside.

"Nana, is Ezrah in trouble?"

I turn around in my seat and look at my baby, my Kiara.

"Not if he behaves. Now, let's get you off to school."

Kiara just started Grade One this past August, but not at the same school as Ezrah. I did that on purpose, because the boy is so protective of his sister, she wouldn't get a chance to forge friendships of her own, which is important. She's surrounded by boys at home, she needs some space to develop her own person.

I park at her school, not ready to let her walk in by

herself. She's my baby, I practically raised her from birth, after their momma disappeared.

I was sixteen when my daughter Sunny was born, and head over heels for her father, a twenty-year old neighborhood punk named James Weston. She'd been an easy child and our life in the tight, one-bedroom apartment on the wrong side of town had felt like a dream come true. Until James was killed in a drive-by shooting that riddled our small apartment with bullets when Sunny was only three months old.

Life wasn't so idyllic after that, but I managed—even without a high school diploma—to keep us afloat. Despite my determination to give my daughter a better life than mine, she fell in with the wrong crowd. She got pregnant at nineteen, had Ezrah at twenty, and by the time she disappeared at just twenty-four, she had two kids and no clue who their fathers were. She was found dead of an overdose two months later.

I'd been only forty at the time and left with a four-year old and an infant to raise.

"Have a good day in school, baby," I tell Kiara when she turns at the door and tries to fit her small arms around my waist.

"Bye, Nana."

She lifts her face for a kiss and I pull the door open for her, scooting her inside before returning to my car. It's starting to rain again.

Normally I do groceries with the help of one of the club's prospects to help me haul groceries, but with this impending thunderstorm I don't want to go out more than is necessary. I'm only two blocks from the grocery store so I decide to get them now before the weather gets worse.

By the time I pile my second grocery cart high I can see conditions haven't improved outside. The skies are dark and I can see the wind has picked up. Once I cash out, one of the baggers is kind enough to wheel the second cart to my car, despite the steady rain coming down. I slip him a few dollars for his help before loading up my little Toyota to the brim with bags.

I'm a drowned rat when I get behind the wheel, sitting in a puddle. The hair I get up an hour early every morning to subdue into smooth waves springs out in rebellious little curls I'll have to live with the rest of the day. Curls now, untamed frizz when it dries. Lovely.

A burst of lightning followed almost immediately by a loud crack of thunder rattles me when I turn up Junction Creek Road. The rain is now coming down in sheets and my windshield wipers work hard to give me at least a glimpse at the road ahead. At some point halfway up the mountain a river of rainwater is coming down the road and—afraid my little car will start hydroplaning—I quickly pull off onto the shoulder. Better to wait it out.

I've sat there for a few minutes when my phone starts ringing in my purse. It's the garage.

"Hi."

"Where the hell are you?" Brick barks and instantly my hackles go up.

"Good morning to you too."

Brick joined the Arrow's Edge MC around the same time I started working for them. He runs the garage up at the compound. A rugged, rough around the edges, but at times kind man who seems to have infinite patience for the boys, but none for me. Sometimes I think he's doing some kind of penance, looking out for me, because he certainly doesn't seem happy about it.

Not that I ever asked for anything, he just seems to feel the need to jump in and rescue me. I can't lie, there've been times I would've been up shit's creek without a paddle if not for him stepping in. Like when Ezrah busted open his head and I ended up in the hospital with him without insurance. Brick walked in, handed over his credit card and told me to put a sock in it when I objected.

I think he sees me as some kind of charity case.

"You left two hours ago, it normally takes you half an hour tops to run the kids to school, and the weather is shit. For all I know you're in a goddamn ditch somewhere," he grumbles.

I roll my eyes but realize he can't see that.

"I pulled off to the side to wait out the storm. The road is a bit of a mess."

"Where?"

"Halfway up Junction. I think the rain is getting a little lighter, I'll try again in a few minutes."

"I'm on my way."

"I'm fine," I snap, but the next thing I know the line is dead.

See? It's like he doesn't even hear me. I'm not some wilting flower. I've seen and been subjected to more shit in my life than many ever will, but still he acts like I can't take care of myself.

The fact I've developed a thing for the man over the past two years doesn't exactly help.

He still pisses me off.

* * *

Brick

Damn stubborn woman.

She nips at my hand every goddamn time I reach one out.

So pigheadedly independent.

"Shilah, need you to come with me."

The young prospect, or cub as they're called in this club, wipes his hands on a rag and jogs after me to the truck.

"Where are we going?"

"Picking up Lisa, she's stuck on the mountain in this weather. You're gonna drive her car home."

I crank the heat in the cab of the truck and drive out of the gates.

"There."

Shilah points at Lisa's piece of shit car barely visible through the windscreen. I drive past, hit up the first driveway I come across and turn back up the mountain. I pull up beside her car and tell Shilah to get out.

"Get her in here. Pull her the hell out if you need to," I grumble, even though I know he'd never do that.

I watch as he opens her driver's side door and gestures at the truck. I can't see her reaction, but I can guess. The moment she gets out her angry dark eyes meet mine, but she climbs into the truck. I try not to notice the way her clothes look drenched and plastered to her body as she buckles in, her generous mouth pressed into a tight line.

"You hair looks nice."

Don't ask me what makes me say that. The only excuse I have is that I'm trying hard not to check out the hard nipples visible even through the sweater she's wearing so I focused on her hair. I think this is the first time I've seen it natural and I like it.

"Save it. The hair's a mess and you know it," she snaps, keeping her head averted as she looks out the side window.

I figure it's better just to keep my mouth shut until I let Shilah pull her car out in front of me and I see the back of her car packed with grocery bags.

"Groceries? Why would you go—"

She holds a hand to my face, effectively silencing me.

"Just don't, Brick." Her voice sounds tired, weary, and instead of tearing a strip off her for going to the store without help, I shut my mouth and put the truck in gear.

Back at the compound Shilah is already unloading the groceries as I pull up right outside the clubhouse so she can get out without getting wet. The moment she unclips the seat belt I reach over and touch her arm.

"I'll go pick up the kids this afternoon."

She turns to me, a little smile on her lips but she keeps her eyes down.

"Thanks, Brick, but I'm sure the storm will have blown over by then."

"For crap's sake, woman, would you let someone lend a hand from time to time? You're plum worn out 'cuz you're too stubborn to accept any help."

So much for my good intentions.

"I'm fine. I do fine by myself."

"I ain't debating that, and if it was just me I wouldn't argue at all—I know you can barely stand to be around me —but plenty of other folks have offered and you turn us all down. Don't know if you noticed but being family is a huge part of being part of an MC. We have each other's backs."

"Good for you," she spits, getting out of the truck before turning to face me. "I'm not part of any MC, I'm just the cook."

With that she throws the door shut and stomps into the clubhouse. I curse under my breath and put the truck in gear, pulling it up to the garage.

That afternoon I watch her climb into her wreck of a car and head back down the mountain to pick her kids up from school.

She probably already has something going for dinner, which she cooks for anywhere from six to nine kids and between six and a dozen adults. It all depends what is going on, and who is pulling up a chair at any given meal. Club events, holidays, cookouts, there are even more mouths to feed. On top of that she cleans, does laundry, and has her own place behind the clubhouse to maintain. Sure, she gets help from the kids, but sometimes I wonder if that's not more of a headache than it's worth.

Seven days a week and as far as I know she's barely had a single day off since she came here. From what little I know she's been looking after others her entire life. That's gotta change. I'm going to have to have a word with Ouray.

With Shilah finishing up the brake job we were working on, I head inside to catch Ouray before Lisa gets back.

I find him in his office.

"Got a minute?"

He drops his pen and leans back in his chair.

"Sure. Sit."

I take a seat across from him but then don't know where to start.

"It's about Lisa." Ouray folds his arms over his chest and waits me out. Typical Ouray. "She's tired. She needs a break."

"Did she tell you that?"

"No, and that's the problem. I can see it in her, Chief, she's worn but she'd never ask anything for herself."

He leans forward, his forearms on the desk, hands folded.

"What would you like me to do? Think I haven't offered her time off? Most she was ever willing to take was a weekend and she ended up back in the kitchen by Sunday afternoon. I can hardly force her to take time."

Trunk walks in, stops, and looks from Ouray to me and back.

"Am I interrupting?"

"No," Ouray says, just as I tell Trunk, "Yes."

The asshole grins wide and pulls up a chair. Last thing I need is our resident psychologist to sit in on a conversation I'm already regretting.

"Brick here is worried about Lisa."

Trunk turns to me, his eyebrow raised.

"Shee-it. About fucking time, brother."

"Jesus," I grumble, standing up. "The woman could use some time off, that's all. You idiots wanna make more outta that, do it on your own damn time."

I turn for the door and almost run into the subject of conversation, and she's not happy.

"Lisa..." But she's already moving down the hall.

I want to go after her but Trunk grabs my arm.

"Brother, word to the wise," he shares. "Glad as fuck to see you're pulling your head outta your ass, but that woman is an uphill battle. Think Mount Everest."

I pull out of his hold.

"Thanks, fucking Ann Landers, but I'm just worried she's gonna keel over on the job one day. Then were'd we be?"

I walk out of there, but not fast enough to miss Ouray's comment.

"Goddamn it, we're heading for another round of drama around here."

Jesus, these guys are worse than a fucking quilting bee.

I find Lisa busy in the kitchen. Ezrah and Kiara are sitting at the table having a snack.

"I'm busy, Brick," she says, her back to me. I lean my hip against the counter beside her.

"You're not superwoman, Lisa."

"I know that," she hisses, glaring at me, but her eyes are shiny.

Fuck, is she gonna cry?

Deciding whether to grab the tissues, or run for the nearest exit, my phone rings. The perfect distraction; I don't even bother checking before I answer.

"Yeah."

There's a heavy silence, and then a painfully familiar voice.

"Dad?"

Want more?

EDGE OF TOMORROW will be available on Amazon and in KU

on September 21st, 2020.

ABOUT THE AUTHOR

USA Today bestselling author Freya Barker loves writing about ordinary people with extraordinary stories.

Driven to make her books about 'real' people; she creates characters who are perhaps less than perfect, each struggling to find their own slice of happy, but just as deserving of romance, thrills and chills in their lives.

Recipient of the ReadFREE.ly 2019 Best Book We've Read All Year Award for "Covering Ollie, the 2015 RomCon "Reader's Choice" Award for Best First Book, "Slim To None", and Finalist for the 2017 Kindle Book Award with "From Dust", Freya continues to add to her rapidly growing collection of published novels as she spins story after story with an endless supply of bruised and dented characters, vying for attention!

Freya
Website
Facebook Page
Reader Group
Twitter
BookBub
Instagram
Or sign up for my newsletter:
https://www.subscribepage.com/Freya_Newsletter

ALSO BY FREYA BARKER

PICTURE PERFECT (coming soon!)

NORTHERN LIGHTS COLLECTION:

A CHANGE IN TIDE

A CHANGE OF VIEW

A CHANGE OF PACE

ROCK POINT SERIES:

KEEPING 6

CABIN 12

HWY 550

10-CODE

PASS SERIES

HIT & RUN

LIFE & LIMB

ARROW'S EDGE MC SERIES

EDGE OF REASON

EDGE OF DARKNESS

OTHER

WHEN HOPE ENDS: LIFE BEGINS

VICTIM OF CIRCUMSTANCE

There are many more books in this fan fiction world than listed here, for an up-to-date list go to www.AcesPress.com

You can also visit our Amazon page at:
http://www.amazon.com/author/operationalpha

Special Forces: Operation Alpha World
Christie Adams: Charity's Heart
Denise Agnew: Dangerous to Hold
Shauna Allen: Awakening Aubrey
Brynne Asher: Blackburn
Linzi Baxter: Unlocking Dreams
Jennifer Becker: Hiding Catherine
Alice Bello: Shadowing Milly
Heather Blair: Rescue Me
Anna Blakely: Rescuing Gracelynn
Julia Bright: Saving Lorelei
Cara Carnes: Protecting Mari
Kendra Mei Chailyn: Beast
Melissa Kay Clarke: Rescuing Annabeth
Samantha A. Cole: Handling Haven
Sue Coletta: Hacked
Melissa Combs: Gallant
Anne Conley: Redemption for Misty
KaLyn Cooper: Rescuing Melina
Liz Crowe: Marking Mariah
Sarah Curtis: Securing the Odds
Jordan Dane: Redemption for Avery
Tarina Deaton: Found in the Lost
Aspen Drake, Intense
KL Donn: Unraveling Love
Riley Edwards: Protecting Olivia
PJ Fiala: Defending Sophie

Nicole Flockton: Protecting Maria
Michele Gwynn: Rescuing Emma
Casey Hagen: Shielding Nebraska
Desiree Holt: Protecting Maddie
Kathy Ivan: Saving Sarah
Kris Jacen, Be With Me
Jesse Jacobson: Protecting Honor
Silver James: Rescue Moon
Becca Jameson: Saving Sofia
Kate Kinsley: Protecting Ava
Heather Long: Securing Arizona
Gennita Low: No Protection
Kirsten Lynn: Joining Forces for Jesse
Margaret Madigan: Bang for the Buck
Kimberly McGath: The Predecessor
Rachel McNeely: The SEAL's Surprise Baby
KD Michaels: Saving Laura
Lynn Michaels, Rescuing Kyle
Wren Michaels: The Fox & The Hound
Kat Mizera: Protecting Bobbi
Keira Montclair, Wolf and the Wild Scots
Mary B Moore: Force Protection
LeTeisha Newton: Protecting Butterfly
Angela Nicole: Protecting the Donna
MJ Nightingale: Protecting Beauty
Sarah O'Rourke: Saving Liberty
Victoria Paige: Reclaiming Izabel
Anne L. Parks: Mason
Debra Parmley: Protecting Pippa
Lainey Reese: Protecting New York
TL Reeve and Michele Ryan: Extracting Mateo
Elena M. Reyes: Keeping Ava
Angela Rush: Charlotte
Rose Smith: Saving Satin

Jenika Snow: Protecting Lily
Lynne St. James: SEAL's Spitfire
Dee Stewart: Conner
Harley Stone: Rescuing Mercy
Jen Talty: Burning Desire
Reina Torres, Rescuing Hi'ilani
Savvi V: Loving Lex
Megan Vernon: Protecting Us
Rachel Young: Because of Marissa

Delta Team Three Series
Lori Ryan: Nori's Delta
Becca Jameson: Destiny's Delta
Lynne St James, Gwen's Delta
Elle James: Ivy's Delta
Riley Edwards, Hope's Delta

Police and Fire: Operation Alpha World
Freya Barker: Burning for Autumn
B.P. Beth: Scott
Jane Blythe: Salvaging Marigold
Julia Bright, Justice for Amber
Anna Brooks, Guarding Georgia
KaLyn Cooper: Justice for Gwen
Aspen Drake: Sheltering Emma
Deanndra Hall: Shelter for Sharla
Barb Han: Kace
EM Hayes: Gambling for Ashleigh
CM Steele: Guarding Hope
Reina Torres: Justice for Sloane
Aubree Valentine, Justice for Danielle
Maddie Wade: Finding English
Stacey Wilk: Stage Fright
Laine Vess: Justice for Lauren

Tarpley VFD Series

Silver James, Fighting for Elena
Deanndra Hall, Fighting for Carly
Haven Rose, Fighting for Calliope
MJ Nightingale, Fighting for Jemma
TL Reeve, Fighting for Brittney
Nicole Flockton, Fighting for Nadia

As you know, this book included at least one character from
Susan Stoker's books. To check out more, see below.

SEAL of Protection: Legacy Series
Securing Caite
Securing Brenae (novella)
Securing Sidney
Securing Piper
Securing Zoey
Securing Avery
Securing Kalee (Sept 2020)
Securing Jane (Feb 2021)

SEAL Team Hawaii Series
Finding Elodie (Apr 2021)
Finding Lexie (Aug 2021)
Finding Kenna (Oct 2021)
Finding Monica (TBA)
Finding Carly (TBA)
Finding Ashlyn (TBA)

Delta Team Two Series
Shielding Gillian
Shielding Kinley
Shielding Aspen (Oct 2020)
Shielding Riley (Jan 2021)
Shielding Devyn (May 2021)
Shielding Ember (Sep 2021)
Shielding Sierra (TBA)

Delta Force Heroes Series
Rescuing Rayne (FREE!)
Rescuing Aimee (novella)

Rescuing Emily
Rescuing Harley
Marrying Emily (novella)
Rescuing Kassie
Rescuing Bryn
Rescuing Casey
Rescuing Sadie (novella)
Rescuing Wendy
Rescuing Mary
Rescuing Macie (Novella)

Badge of Honor: Texas Heroes Series

Justice for Mackenzie (FREE!)
Justice for Mickie
Justice for Corrie
Justice for Laine (novella)
Shelter for Elizabeth
Justice for Boone
Shelter for Adeline
Shelter for Sophie
Justice for Erin
Justice for Milena
Shelter for Blythe
Justice for Hope
Shelter for Quinn
Shelter for Koren
Shelter for Penelope

SEAL of Protection Series

Protecting Caroline (FREE!)
Protecting Alabama
Protecting Fiona
Marrying Caroline (novella)
Protecting Summer

Protecting Cheyenne
Protecting Jessyka
Protecting Julie (novella)
Protecting Melody
Protecting the Future
Protecting Kiera (novella)
Protecting Alabama's Kids (novella)
Protecting Dakota

New York Times, USA Today and *Wall Street Journal*
Bestselling Author Susan Stoker has a heart as big as the
state of Tennessee where she lives, but this all American
girl has also spent the last fourteen years living in
Missouri, California, Colorado, Indiana, and Texas. She's
married to a retired Army man who now gets to follow *her*
around the country.

www.stokeraces.com
www.AcesPress.com
susan@stokeraces.com

Made in the USA
Coppell, TX
18 April 2021